Andi felt a little embarrassed

by the mess they'd encountered in the room.

She was grateful that Rayne was there, investigating the dark, dank basement with her. His large presence protected her and the light touch of his hand on her back soothed her.

She flicked the flashlight over stacks of boxes, furniture and racks crammed with clothes. In a dark corner, metal rattled, startling her. She backed up and bumped into Rayne. "My goodness, I'm jumpy," she said, her hand at her throat. "Sorry."

"Nothing to be sorry about," Rayne returned.

She swept the beam across the room...and both she and Rayne froze.

The light had touched something that gleamed... something alive...

Eyes!

Simon Says

SHERYL LYNN

SILHOUETTE

Intrigue

*First published in Great Britain in 1994
by Silhouette Books, Eton House, 18-24 Paradise Road,
Richmond, Surrey TW9 1SR*

© Jaye W. Manus 1994

Silhouette, Silhouette Intrigue and Colophon are
Trade Marks of Harlequin Enterprises B.V.

ISBN 0 373 59358 9

55-9407

Made and printed in Great Britain

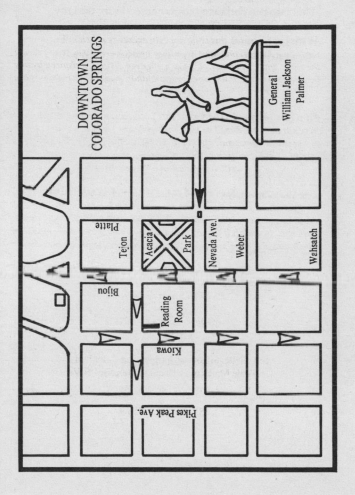

DOWNTOWN
COLORADO SPRINGS

General
William Jackson
Palmer

Platte

Tejon

Acacia
Park

Nevada Ave.

Weber

Wahsatch

Bijou

Reading
Room

Kiowa

Pikes Peak Ave.

This book is dedicated to my hero, Tom; and my partner in crime, Betty Duran; and my friends Barbara Samuel and Nancy Starts who have seen me at my craziest and like me anyway; and with special thanks to Pesha Rubinstein.

Chapter One

Andi Blair had weathered some bad times in her life. Finding a dead man in her backyard rated right up there as one of the worst.

When Detective Paul Sevilla arrived, he asked Andi if she lived here. Yes. How long? All her life. Did she live alone? Yes. Could she identify the body? Absolutely not. Where had she been prior to arriving home? At work. Had she ever seen the deceased before today? Never. Any prior signs of problems or disturbances? Of course not.

This was Mulberry Street! A quiet neighborhood tucked at the base of a hill near downtown Colorado Springs, boasting Victorian-era houses shaded by old trees, and neighbors who mowed their lawns on Saturday and picked up trash out of the street. Bad things did not happen here. Harboring a faint hope this was a mistake, Andi peeked past the detective.

The dead man still reclined at the base of a hundred-year-old oak tree.

Andi closed her eyes, seeing herself park her car and walk through the back gate, spot him with his greasy black hair parted in the middle and scruffy clothes, and reach to shake his shoulder... and seeing the knife hilt sticking out of his chest and his filmy eyes staring back at her.

She shook off the creepiness crawling under her skin.

Police officers and technicians seemed oblivious to the corpse. They plucked debris from the shrubbery and the ground, took pictures of everything enclosed by the weather-bleached fence, sketched in notebooks and laid out grid works made of string. They stepped over the dead man, walked around him, and a few of them laughed.

She turned her back on the yard. A golden orb spider had built her spoked web between a rose trellis and a back porch post. With one skinny black leg extended to touch the web, the spider hid in the shade of a rose leaf. Andi wished she could hide, too.

"Ma'am?"

Andi faced a policeman. He wore a Colorado Springs Police Department uniform and his name tag said Morris. His flaxen hair shone under the lowering sun. Sweat beaded on his ruddy face. "No one will mind if you go inside," he said.

Detective Sevilla now spoke to a technician. The two men examined the rough trunk of the oak tree.

She drew a shuddery breath. "Are you sure it's okay? Can't they cover him or take him someplace?"

"Soon, ma'am. Do you know who he is?" He followed her inside.

"I've never seen him before." She leaned on the kitchen sink and looked out the window. Mr. Dipwell, her neighbor, peered over the fence between their properties, watching a technician take a photograph from directly above the dead man's face.

"This is a nice house." Morris lifted his gaze to the coved ceiling. "Victorian, right? I like these old neighborhoods. The new subdivisions don't have much character."

"Thank you. Can I offer you something to drink? Ice tea?"

He craned his neck to see out the open back door. "No thanks. So you live here alone? Attractive lady like you must have a boyfriend."

Officer Morris was good-looking, but this didn't feel like the time or place for him to flirt with her. She forced herself away from the window and crossed her arms over her chest. "What happens next?"

"That's up to Sevilla. He's in charge. But I wouldn't worry too much." He wandered to the wide doorway separating the kitchen from the living room and peered around the wall into the dining room.

Worry about what? That strangers were going to make a habit of dying in her yard?

A man snapped, "Morris!"

The policeman went rigid, his pale eyes guarded. Detective Sevilla stomped inside. "Get back to your post. I don't want any reporters or gawkers in that alley."

"Sure, Sarge." Morris edged past his superior.

Through the window Andi watched Sevilla catch the officer's shoulder. Morris wore the face of a teenager caught smoking behind the school. Guilt tweaked Andi. She hadn't meant to get him in trouble.

A technician carrying a plastic bag containing a baseball cap caught her attention. She hurried out the back door. Reaching for the bag, she cried, "Excuse me!"

The technician shot her a startled look and jerked the bag to the side.

"Where did you get that hat?" It was black, emblazoned with a purple Rockies logo.

Sevilla touched Andi's elbow. "Does it belong to you, Miss Blair?"

The hats were a hot item in Colorado Springs. For all she knew, this one belonged to the dead man. Except, in her heart, she suspected it was the very same Rockies cap she'd given a month ago to her best friend, Mr. Simon.

"IF THAT'S WHAT you think best, sir," Rayne Coplin said through his teeth. "I'll send my bill." He hung up the telephone and stared blankly across the office. Three in a row, he thought. "He's not going to press charges."

His partner looked up with an indulgent smile. "Perhaps there are extenuating circumstances."

Rayne threw a paper clip, but it fell short of Ford's desk. He stalked to a counter and poured a cup of coffee. "What is wrong with those people?" he asked, wincing at the coffee's overbrewed bitterness. For the past month he'd been working his tail off to collect evidence against larcenous employees. In each case his client, the business owner, declined prosecution at the last minute and handled the matter in-house.

Translation, the thief lost his job, but so what?

Rayne held a simple philosophy. There were good guys and bad guys. Good guys who went soft and let the bad guys get away with it were suckers. Didn't they realize crooks never felt remorse?

Ford hooked his hands behind his neck. He grinned. Rayne growled at him but it made no difference. An earthquake could level the Rocky Mountains to rubble, but Ford would keep on smiling.

"I've had it with in-house security, man," Rayne said. "Give me a nice workman's comp, a missing person—a domestic!"

Ford laughed. Rayne heard what he'd said and managed a grin. He and Ford despised domestic cases—spying on cheating spouses was a lousy way to earn a buck.

"I'm putting a new clause in our contract." Rayne swigged the bitter coffee. "They have to press charges or I double my fee. No more of this bleeding heart crap and—"

"It's your clothes," Ford said.

Rayne stopped short. "Huh?"

Ford slid his thumbs under his lapels. "Jeans and boots fit well into the mountain mystique, but as a professional private investigator, perhaps you might consider a change of image. Such as pure cashmere, hand dyed and woven in Scotland."

Busy trying to figure out the meaning of this turn of conversation, it took Rayne a few seconds to register Ford's eye gestures. His partner indicated the door.

Rayne turned around.

A woman stood with one hand on the doorknob. "Are you open?"

Ford rose and smoothed his jacket with a neat tug. "Hayes and Coplin Investigations at your service, madam. Please, do come in."

Andi Blair hesitated. Hiring a private eye seemed like something a fur-swathed blonde who spoke in a mysterious accent might do. Scenes from *The Maltese Falcon* kept flitting through her mind.

Except, instead of a seedy room with overflowing garbage cans stinking of cigars and booze, sunshine streamed through the windows of this office on the second floor of a downtown brownstone. Desks, with a computer, telephone and stacks of baskets for papers on each, sat on either side of the room. A bank of file cabinets lined one wall. The office looked clean, even cheerful.

The two men didn't fit her idea of private eyes, either. The older man, his snowy hair impeccably barbered, wore an expensive suit perfectly tailored for his slim frame. He had the air of a court diplomat.

The younger man made her a little nervous. Over six feet tall, he had the carriage and muscular jaw of a man in superb physical condition. Dark hair fell in boyish disarray over his brow, but his hard eyes weren't boyish in the least. He seemed angry.

"Please," the older man said.

She shifted her grip on her purse. "I guess I should have called, but it's only a few blocks from where I work. I'm not interrupting anything?"

The younger man's eyes softened with his smile. The smile made him so good-looking, for a moment Andi forgot the purpose of her visit. She dealt with the public at the bookstore and saw many handsome men, but they never made her mouth go dry.

"Ford Hayes, at your service." The older man extended his hand. She shook hands introducing herself. Then he introduced her to his partner, Rayne Coplin, who didn't offer his hand and greeted her curtly. Ford then invited her to sit on a low, gray tweed couch and offered coffee or tea. She asked for tea.

She said, "I'm not sure if I need a private eye."

Ford sat on the couch. Rayne sat on the edge of a desk with his arms folded across his broad chest and his long legs stretched out, one boot crossed over the other.

"Explain your problem, Miss Blair," Ford said. "Then we shall decide together if you require our services."

His courtly speech amused and relaxed her. "You're ever so much nicer than the police."

Rayne's smile faded. Ford's remained the same.

"They aren't mean or anything. But they always seem to have better things to do than talk to me. Except for Officer Morris."

The men exchanged a glance. Ford asked, "John Morris?"

"Do you know him?"

"I spent twenty-six years on the Colorado Springs police force. We are acquainted. Might I inquire as to how you know him and does it pertain to your being here at the moment?"

"Sort of. He arrived first when I called about the body."

"Body." Ford leaned back on the couch. "Are you embroiled in legal difficulties, Miss Blair?"

"Me? No. But it happened in my yard."

"The body was in your yard."

Rayne leaned forward. "Last Monday. I read about it in the paper. Keller Poe was stabbed. That was your yard?"

"Stabbed" made her wince. "And trust me, the newspapers aren't saying the half of it. It's been awful." She grimaced. "First the police, then the reporters, and now the neighborhood is full of strangers looking over my fence. I never realized there were so many morbid people lurking about."

"Miss Blair," Ford said, "I must disabuse you of any notion that I or my associate can interfere in the investigation of a homicide."

It took a few seconds for Andi to figure out what he meant. "Oh no, that's not why I'm here. It's Mr. Simon. He's missing."

"Does his being missing have to do with the demise of Keller Poe?"

"At first I thought so, but the police don't think he has anything to do with it. He's just missing and I'm worried about him."

Rayne Coplin fascinated her. Despite dark hair and suntanned skin, his eyes were blue, strikingly pale under thick black eyebrows. She ventured a smile and he seemed to find his buff-colored boots of great interest.

"Please begin at the beginning," Ford urged.

"I don't know where the beginning is. I haven't seen him since Sunday. He's pretty regular, so this isn't like him." Saying the words aloud loosened her grip on the fear she'd been trying to contain all week; it clawed stealthily through her throat and lodged in her chest. No matter how she tried to justify any number of innocent reasons for Mr. Simon's disappearance, she knew something was wrong.

"Are the police looking for Mr. Simon?"

"Officer Morris says they aren't. He says the cap isn't evidence."

"Cap?" Ford cocked his head.

"Mr. Simon's Rockies cap. I gave it to him. The police found it in my yard, but since Mr. Simon mows the lawn and stuff, then he could have lost it some other time. Or maybe it belongs to the dead man or it blew into the yard. You can buy them anywhere. Officer Morris said filing a missing person report with the police won't do much good, but that maybe you could help."

Ford looked skeptical.

"He didn't mention you specifically. I looked in the phone book. Since your office is so close... *Can* you help me?"

"Perhaps." Ford indicated Rayne with a graceful sweep of his hand. "My associate will take the particulars and see if this is within our realm of expertise. If so, we will gladly do what we can to be of assistance. Rayne?"

Rayne pushed away from the desk. "Right." He invited her to bring her tea to his desk and pulled up a chair for her.

He opened a desk drawer and brought out a printed form. When he leaned over, Andi caught a whiff of his smoky-sunshine scent. "Let's start with your relationship with Mr. Simon."

She liked the controlled tone of his voice. All business, but sexy. "We're friends."

"Romantically friends?"

She laughed. "Good heavens, no! He's quite elderly. We're just very good friends."

He wrote on the form. "And the last time you saw him was on Sunday."

"A week ago Sunday. We had dinner. Curried chicken and rice. I made him brownies to take home with him. I'm sure he didn't have anything to do with the body in my yard. It seems like everybody has one of those Rockies caps."

"It's only been a week, Miss Blair."

A tiny tremor gripped her chin and she lifted it, forcing away the as yet unwarranted fears. She gave herself a shake and drew back her shoulders. Be calm, be cool. "It's too long for him. This isn't like him."

He glanced at a window. "We've been having a lot of rain. You say he's elderly. Maybe he doesn't feel like getting out and about. You've checked his house?"

She pulled in her chin. "I don't know where he lives. Maybe I'm worrying needlessly, but I can't help feeling something is wrong. This past winter when it was snowing or the wind was blowing hard, he'd call to tell me he couldn't make it. And when I was sick right before Christmas, even though the weather was awful, he came by every day to make sure I was all right."

"Have you looked for him?"

She shrugged, loath to tell him about the hours she'd cruised the streets and all the people she'd questioned. "I tried, but I don't know where to look. Officer Morris checked the hospitals for me." She took a quick sip of tea. "He says Mr. Simon isn't dead."

"That was good of him."

"He knows how upset I was about the dead man, so he's checked on me a few times and we've talked. But I hate to keep bothering him." She sighed. "Even with that man."

Rayne looked up. "What man?"

"The one following me."

"You didn't mention that."

She raised her fingers to her mouth. "I shouldn't have. Never mind. It just seems that every time I turn around, he's...there. I'm sorry, I have a bad habit of thinking aloud. This has been an awful week."

"I understand."

Did he? She didn't. For the first time in her life she felt afraid. "First the body, then Mr. Simon. It's as if everything has been turned upside down. I hear noises and imagine someone is in my house. I keep losing things and now I'm imagining someone is following me. I go around with chronic goose bumps." She tried to gauge his reaction, but his expression told her nothing.

"Do you live alone?"

"Over on Mulberry Street. West of the freeway."

His lips twitched as if he fought a smile. "It sounds as if you've been through a lot."

"It's like I stubbed my toe and now I'm overly concerned about stubbing it again. I keep waiting for bad things to happen. I don't mean to sound crazy, but I can't even make myself walk through my back gate. If I can just find Mr. Simon everything will be okay."

He put down the pencil. "Before we begin, I need to make two things perfectly clear."

Andi hated stipulations. She leaned back on the chair and tightened her grip on her purse.

"First, finding a missing person can be expensive. Sometimes it takes a few phone calls. Sometimes it can run into thousands of dollars."

"Okay."

His cheek muscles tightened and his eyes narrowed. "I've seen it go as high as twenty thousand."

"I have plenty of money. Honest."

He flicked a skeptical glance over her purple tank top and patchwork skirt. "Second, Mr. Simon has a right to privacy. When I find him, I will tell him you're concerned. Contacting you is up to him."

She fingered the base of her throat and her bangle bracelets clinked on her wrist. "You won't tell me where he is?"

"Only with his permission. That's how I work."

"I see." She looked at his computer and the baskets piled with papers. A busy desk, but not a dirty desk. He wore a chambray shirt with the sleeves rolled up to reveal forearms corded with hard muscle—all business, no vanity. He exuded confidence. She sensed he was good at what he did. She drew a deep breath and pulled back her shoulders. "I need to know if he's okay. That's all I want."

"I need his full name and Social Security number." He held the pencil at ready.

She sat up higher to see the form on which he prepared to write. It had spaces for names, addresses, friends, relatives, physical description and identifying numbers. Part of her was impressed by the efficiency; mostly she was embarrassed.

She huffed and sat straighter. "Mr. Simon."

"First name?"

"I don't know. I'm sorry."

"How long have you known him?"

"About a year." She loosed a discomfited laugh. "The people I work with call him the Invisible Man. He's shy."

Rayne used the pencil to scratch above his ear. "How about his age?"

"Around seventy or so."

"And you don't know where he lives." He clicked his tongue and raked his fingers through his thick hair. Mouth twisted in a wry smile, he put pencil to paper. "Let's see what you do know."

Frustration squeezed Andi. How could she hold Mr. Simon so dear to her heart and know so little about him? She knew what he looked like, what he wore and what he liked to eat and read. Beyond that the man was a cipher. Hindsight made her realize that in the year she'd known her friend, he'd learned a lot about her but he'd been very careful about not allowing her to learn much about him.

If her ignorance frustrated the private eye, he did not show it. He filled out the form. "You're sure the police aren't looking for him. Not even as a witness?"

"Officer Morris says they aren't."

"He checked the hospitals for you."

She nodded.

"You said you think someone was in your home and a man is following you."

Embarrassed, she laughed. "I'm sorry I mentioned it."

He faced the computer. He asked for her name, address and phone number and typed quickly.

He printed out two copies of a finished contract. Andi read it with interest. Mr. Simon was the "claimant/subject" and she was the "client." What interested her most was the block at the top called Service Requested. It listed such intriguing items as Skip Trace, Asset Search and Personal Security. He had X-ed Missing Person. She signed and dated the contracts, then wrote a check for a retainer.

When she handed him the check, his fingers brushed hers and a little jolt shook her. Way back in her mind, she thought, *Wow, a real-life, sexy private eye.*

"Anything else?" She hoped. He was the one nice thing to happen to her this week.

"Let me do some checking. I'll get back to you."

She rose and smoothed her skirt. Aware of him watching, she glanced at him. He dropped his gaze to the desk and shuffled papers. "Thank you very much, Mr. Coplin. Mr. Hayes."

Rayne handed her a business card. "If you think of anything or if he shows up, give me a call. Night or day."

"Thank you."

Ford said, "Miss Blair . . ."

She turned to him.

"Should you suspect a person is indeed following you, whether or not it is only nerves, do call. There is no need to take undue chances."

Relief softened the woman's pewter-colored eyes. Annoyance at the police pricked Rayne. In this day and age, when so many men turned mean against women, he couldn't believe a cop passed off her reports as "nerves."

After she'd left, Rayne sat on the edge of Ford's desk. He crossed his arms. "Missing persons are your speciality. Why did you stick her with me?"

"You need a change of pace."

"Right."

Ford flipped a hand. "No need for you to grow stale. I smell a mystery and that is exactly what you need to get your juices flowing again."

"Mystery, huh." Rayne swung his head side to side.

"A beautiful blonde and a hard-boiled private eye. There are interesting possibilities here." Ford winked.

Rayne threw back his head and laughed.

"I thought her most attractive. Why do you laugh?"

"She's cute, I guess—if you like the type."

"Type?"

"No stockings." He held his hands a foot from each side of his head. "All that hair and the turquoise jewelry. The Rocky Mountain High type. Probably eats tofu."

Ford rested his chin on his fist. "Methinks the lad doth protest too much."

Rayne wisely shut up and returned to his desk. Beautiful blonde, indeed. Her looks, despite a glorious smile, didn't matter—he never fooled around with clients. That was his number one rule.

"Do you think the old man's disappearance has anything to do with the stiff?" Rayne asked.

"Ah, Keller Poe. The world shall miss him. His ambition was exceeded only by his ineptitude."

Rayne made a knowing sound. "You busted him."

"When I worked robbery. He plagued jewelry stores, fancying himself a smash-and-grab artist. He had mastered the smashing and grabbing part, but his artistry was sadly lacking. He never quite got it through his head that security cameras were created for the likes of him."

"A jewel thief and an old guy who mows lawns. Can't see a connection."

"One of those unfortunate coincidences." Ford pointed at Rayne's telephone. "His advanced age is your first clue. I suggest you begin by checking hospitals and mortuaries."

"She said Morris checked for her."

An expression as close to nasty as Ford ever got creased his face. "Exactly."

Rayne got the message. "Right."

Chapter Two

Sharon leaned against the bookstore service counter and said, "Deb tells me you hired a private eye."

Avoiding her boss's eye, Andi fiddled with a dump display.

"I thought you had a doctor's appointment."

"I didn't say doctor. I said appointment. Sorry." She should have been straight with Sharon, but the woman tended to worry and fuss. "He's good-looking and very nice."

Sharon tapped her fingers on the counter. "Oh, really?"

"Dark hair, wears it short." She held her hands apart. "Big shoulders, tall. Nice hands, nice voice. Very good-looking." She wondered if Rayne Coplin was married. No wedding ring, but not all men wore one.

"Is he as nice-looking as your policeman friend?"

Andi picked up on Sharon's dangerous tone. She swallowed hard. Officer John Morris's prowling around the store with his keys and handcuffs rattling, and his habit of snapping and unsnapping his holster, made customers nervous.

"I've asked John not to come by anymore." She wished he'd take the hint.

Sharon straightened items on the service counter. She'd owned and operated the Reading Room bookstore for more than twenty years. Always serious, sometimes stern, she treated her employees like wayward daughters. Her disapproval came through loud and clear.

"You'll probably never meet Mr. Coplin," Andi assured her. "And even if you did, you'd see he's not sleazy at all. He doesn't look like a private eye."

"I'm worried about you," Sharon said.

"Me? Why?"

Sharon nudged her eyeglasses higher on her nose. "I'm not sure how to say this without hurting your feelings."

"You won't."

"Your mother was an invalid for how long?"

Uncertainty about where this was leading subdued Andi. "About four years."

"And you cared for her full-time. Saw to her every need until the day she died, right?"

"She was my mother."

"Then you met Mr. Simon. You're always feeding him and giving him rides. You take care of him." Sharon's eyes narrowed. "It's not healthy. It's nice you have such a good friendship, but hiring a private eye?"

Andi turned to the magazine rack. She shifted magazines into proper order.

"Lately you've been distracted. It's hurting your job performance. You lied to me yesterday. You've never done that before. It's not like you to be so—" Her face reddened and she blurted, "Irresponsible!"

Shame washed through Andi. She was scatterbrained occasionally, silly sometimes, but irresponsible? That hurt. "You don't understand how much he means to me. I'm worried about him." She risked a glance at her boss. "Sorry I fibbed."

"You're the worst liar in the world." Sharon loosed a heavy breath. "You're too nice, too trusting."

"You think he takes advantage of me? If anything, it's the other way around. You ought to see what he's done for my yard. He replaced my back porch steps. He changes the oil in my car."

Sharon threw up her hands. "Okay, okay. I'm sorry I said anything. But you remember one thing, young lady. At work, you're on my time. If you need time off, tell me the whole truth."

Andi murmured, "Yes, ma'am."

That evening as she walked up the stone path to the porch, her neighbor called a greeting. Andi waved at Mr. Dipwell.

He dragged a garden hose to the fence. They'd been neighbors since Andi was six years old, and she adored him and his wife. She felt a little sorry, though, for Mrs. Dipwell these days. After more than forty years of working for the utility company, Mr. Dipwell had retired. He was bored and needed something to fill his hours. He meant well, but Andi's sympathies lay with Mrs. Dipwell. Especially now that he considered Andi his latest hobby.

Every morning when she left for work, he watched with an eagle eye until she got in her car. Every evening he waited for her. She'd seen him marching down the alley with a rake slung over his shoulder, peering over fences and rattling the padlock on her garage door.

He called, "Any problems, Andi?"

"Everything is fine."

He shook a finger at her. "It'll stay that way, too, or my name isn't Horace Dipwell! I'll stay right here until you turn on the lights."

"Thank you."

Sylvia Dipwell yelled, "Horace! Leave that poor girl be! Crazy old man."

The couple began arguing and Andi slipped inside her house. Tossing her purse on the couch and kicking off her sandals, she laughed. Poor Mrs. Dipwell.

Her gaze fell on a basket of flowers and the laughter died. Instead of sitting directly in front of the glass fireplace doors, the silk flower arrangement sat slightly to the side. A crepe poppy lay loose on the hearth tiles.

Breathing shallowly, she strained to listen. A few crickets geared up for an evening concert. From a distance, a siren wailed.

Nerves again. She must have brushed the basket in passing this morning. She rubbed down the rise of gooseflesh on her arms. She was sick and tired of being scared by her own shadow.

She entered the kitchen and turned on the light. A soft flapping noise startled her. Newspapers on the table ruffled in a draft.

The back door stood open. A shudder rippled down her spine and her mouth watered unpleasantly. She stared out the door into the backyard and all was quiet except for birds and wind causing gladiolus spikes to whisper against the fence.

She forced herself to take a step, then another. She picked up the broom, extended it, caught the door edge with the brush end and pushed.

The door slammed. She leapt forward and turned the lock. She locked the adjacent door leading to the basement, too.

Holding the broom like a club, she tiptoed through the house. She searched the dining room, two bedrooms and bathroom and looked inside all the closets. Back in the kitchen, she lowered her gaze to her feet. Check the basement?

Oh no, she was not that brave.

Besides, how could anyone get inside with her neighbor marching around like a minuteman on patrol? She'd forgotten to lock the door this morning, that's all, and the wind had blown it open. Wind could have moved the silk flower arrangement, too. At this time of year, ferocious gusts were common.

She put the broom back in place. Head high, she plucked a wooden spoon from a jar and lifted the lid off the slow cooker. The heavenly paprika-laden scent of goulash wafted around her face. Eyes narrowed in pleasure, she inhaled deeply the savory steam.

She wondered if Rayne Coplin liked goulash. A big man like him probably enjoyed hearty meals. Her romantic musings tickled her. He probably had a wife or a dozen girlfriends. Nobody that handsome with a voice that sexy could stay single for long.

She stirred the goulash, amazed at how much it had cooked down. A spot of white caught her eye. She lowered the lid onto the slow cooker and picked up a scrap of folded paper. Hoping, praying it had blown in from outside and somehow landed on her kitchen counter, she unfolded it and read.

Looking for Mr. Simon is dangerous and stupid! You'll never see or hear from him again. Bad things happen to nosy girls! You're wasting your time and poking around will get you in trouble! Stop this foolery now before someone gets hurt!

She dropped the note and rushed to the phone.

She started to call 911 but stopped. Tell the police

someone broke into her house and left a note? She dug Rayne Coplin's business card out of her purse. Night or day, he'd said.

Rayne promised to be there in ten minutes. He arrived in eight and the sound of his steps on the wooden porch filled her with relief. He scraped his boots on the mat before entering. "Are you all right?"

The ceiling was nine feet high, but still the living room seemed too small for him. His hearty maleness left Andi breathless. "I am now."

"Somebody broke into your house?"

She urged him to follow her into the kitchen. "The back door was open."

"Is anything missing?" He looked about, his eyes sharp and inquisitive. He kept his hands on his lean hips.

"Just the opposite." She gave him the note.

He read it then lifted his gaze. "This is weird."

"Don't I know it. Would you care for a glass of wine? I could sure use one." She busied herself with the jug of wine she kept under the sink.

"Did you call the police?"

She handed him a glass of iced red wine. He gave the drink a funny look. "Ice?"

"I probably should call the police, but it isn't against the law to leave a note. Are you hungry? I was about to eat."

He looked startled. "Don't put yourself out on my account."

She sensed she'd committed a faux pas. She wondered about rules of etiquette concerning private eyes.

A pounding on the front door made her jump. Andi hurried to see who it was.

Rake in hand, Mr. Dipwell stood on the porch. He thrust his jaw pugnaciously and bunched his shoulders. "There's a strange vehicle out there." He jerked his thumb at the Jeep Cherokee parked at the curb. "Any problems, Andi?"

"I have company." She opened the screen door for him. Andi introduced the two men, then added, "Mr. Coplin is a private investigator."

Mr. Dipwell looked the bigger man up and down. "Oh, really. I hear you private eyes are pretty fast on the draw. You're going to solve that murder, eh? Good thinking, Andi. Good thinking. Bring in the big guns."

"Uh, actually—"

Mr. Dipwell placed a finger on the side of his fleshy nose. "Nothing gets past this old bird. You need any help, son, I'm right next door."

"Thank you, sir." Rayne's voice had a tight quality.

"Now I know you detectives have a reputation with the ladies." He half-turned and winked. "But you keep a lid on it with Andi here. She ain't no slinky gun moll. Watch your manners."

Andi's cheeks warmed. "Mr. Dipwell, please."

Rayne's mouth twitched and his eyes brightened.

The old man clucked his tongue. "Fast cars, fast women. What a life! Now me, forty-three years with public utilities. Had a family to consider. But now I'm a free man. Kids grown and gone. Just might consider something like spying. Hard to get into, Mr. Coplin? Need special training? I'm pretty good with a pistol." He jerked backward and whipped his hand past his hip. He held his forefinger and thumb cocked in a gun shape. "Mama won't let me keep one in the house, but I still have the touch. I was a crack shot in the army."

Sylvia yelled for her husband. He grimaced. "Gotta go. But let me tell you, son, I read everything Mickey Spillane ever wrote. You need some help, you give a holler. We'll wrap up that murder and tie it with a bow. We'll show those flatfoots how it's done."

He left and Andi closed the door. She held both hands against the wood. Repressed laughter almost strangled her. Rayne made a strange sound. Looking at his strained, choked expression undid her. She laughed so hard her eyes teared. Wiping them with the back of her hand, she said, "Oh, I'm sorry. He's a dear and he means well."

Rayne waved a hand in a helpless gesture. His face was red and he kept hitching his shoulders. "It's okay."

He had a wonderful laugh, full and rich. His smile deepened the crow's feet at the corners of his eyes and the vertical lines in his cheeks. His eyes transfixed her. They'd darkened to indigo, warm as a summer sea. Laughter felt good. Looking at him felt even better. The last traces of tension in her chest and belly eased away.

She touched her throat. He tugged at his shirt collar. A funny feeling twisted her insides and made her legs wobbly.

He looked away first. "Interesting gentleman."

"He retired not long ago." She edged past him into the kitchen. "Um, you will stay for dinner?" She pulled out a chair. "Unless you have to get home to your family?"

"Whatever you're cooking does smell pretty good. Sure, thanks." He picked up the note. "You can tell me more about Mr. Simon."

She brought out her prettiest china to set the table. "There's not a whole lot to tell." She did not have the words to explain the bond between herself and Mr. Simon. "He's the . . . he's like a father to me. Always there to listen. I can tell him anything."

"Where is your father?"

She put place mats on the table and caught a whiff of his alluring, unidentifiable scent. It raised images of early morning camp fires in a rain-washed forest. "He died when I was a baby. I never knew him. This was my grandmother's house. She was a widow, too."

His sharp-eyed attentiveness made her aware of her rumpled skirt, bare feet and messy hair.

"Grandma died when I was little, then it was just Mom and me. She was a librarian until she had the accident." She arranged silverware on the table—why hadn't she at least brushed her hair? "That was right after I graduated from college. A car accident. She had a head injury. Everyone said to put her in a nursing home, that it was too much responsibility." She lifted a shoulder. "But you know how it is when you love someone. It's hard, but it isn't that hard. You do what you have to do."

"When did she . . . ?"

She smiled to show it was okay to ask. "Die? A year ago. I didn't know what to do with myself. I painted the whole house, then I hired a carpenter and completely redid the kitchen. When I started seriously considering cleaning out the garage and attic I knew I was going crazy. So I got a job. At first it was strange living alone, but I kind of like it now." She peered at him from the corner of her eye. "Do you live alone?"

He shifted and picked up the note with both hands, staring at it. Andi wondered if she'd said something wrong. Or, as usual, talked too much. She concentrated on fixing dinner.

"Who knows you're looking for Mr. Simon?"

"No one except you." She slid rolls into the oven. "Officer Morris. And the people I work with." She shrugged. "Customers and my neighbors. I guess everybody. It's no secret I'm worried about him."

He chuckled deep in his chest. He laid the note on the table and tapped it with a finger. "This has a late-night movie ring to it. Melodrama."

Was he insinuating the note was a hoax? She replied stiffly, "I consider it a threat. I think it proves Mr. Simon is in danger. Maybe me, too."

"I'm not blowing this off, Miss Blair. But I think—"

"Please, call me Andi. More wine?"

"No thanks. Do you have a sample of Mr. Simon's handwriting?"

She started to ask why, then shot him a puzzled look. "You think he wrote it?"

He placed a finger on the word *foolery*. "Who uses that word anymore?"

It gave her something to think about while she made buttered noodles and salad and dished up the goulash. Finally she shook her head. "Mr. Simon would call and tell me he's all right. He wouldn't write a note he knows would scare me. He didn't write it. I bet he's been kidnapped."

She set a plate before him and wondered at his smile. "I didn't say anything funny."

"I doubt if Mr. Simon has been kidnapped."

His calm, reasonable tone irked her. *He* hadn't been suffering a major case of the heebie-jeebies and his best friend wasn't missing. "Mr. Simon didn't leave the note. Absolutely not."

He focused on the plate. "This smells great. Looks good, too."

She took her seat and unfolded a napkin on her lap. Part of her hoped Mr. Simon had written the note. It would mean he was safe and sound. Yet he'd never been anything other than sweet, generous and solicitous of her feelings. Imagining him penning those words was impossible. The private eye was wrong.

"You keep asking about me. But what about you, Mr. Coplin? Are you from around here?"

"Rayne," he corrected. "I grew up in Denver. Moved down here a few years ago."

"Is your family here now?"

His expression tightened and he focused on his food. He ate several bites, then smacked his lips. "This is great. How did you meet Mr. Simon?"

Andi sensed family was a delicate subject. Was he, like her, all alone in the world? "It was a few days after Mom's funeral. I looked out the front window and there was this little old man. He seemed a little lost, and sad. I asked if I could help him, and he said, 'That lawn sure is in bad shape.'" She smiled at the memory. "I try, I really do, but I have a black thumb. I hate having the ugliest yard in the neighborhood. So anyway, we started talking, then he offered to mow the grass and clip the hedges. And he did a great job."

"Did you pay him?"

"I offered, but he refused. He did eat dinner with me, though. He loves my cooking."

Rayne hoisted his fork. "I can see why."

She glanced at the window, wondering what Mr. Simon was eating for dinner, wondering where he slept. The days were warm, but this early in June some nights were cold. Small patches of snow still dusted the top of Pikes Peak. She prayed that wherever Mr. Simon was, he was warm. "We became friends—"

The lights went out.

For several disorienting seconds she was blind. Her eyes adjusted gradually. "I must have blown a fuse. I can see the streetlight working." She sighed. "Old houses. If it isn't one thing, it's another. Sit still. I know my way in the dark." She rummaged in a drawer for a flashlight.

"I didn't see a surge or a flicker. Where's your fuse box?"

"In the basement." She laughed to counter his serious, suspicious tone. She was sick and tired of being scared all the time. "We could use candles to finish dinner. But they're in the basement, too." She turned on the flashlight and played the beam across the kitchen. "I'll be back in a minute."

"Do you have extra fuses?"

She thought about it. "Extra . . . ?"

Chair legs scraped the floor. "Are you sure the box is in the basement?"

"The electrician said it's dumb to put it down there, but it's ugly and I didn't want it up here. I know where it is, but I don't know about extra fuses. It clicks on and off . . . I think."

He made a patient sound. "I'll come with you. I know a little about fuse boxes."

She started to protest, but in light of her earlier scare, company in the basement was not a bad idea. "Be careful. The stairs are narrow."

Soothed by his large presence behind her and the light touch of his hand on her back, Andi realized that he did not have to be here. When she had called him, he could have said, "Lock your doors. Bring the note by in the morning." He could have taken the note when he first arrived and left. He could have refused dinner.

Did he like her? She knew so little about how private eyes did their jobs, it was hard to tell.

She panned the light over the basement. The basement had windows, but thick bushes blocked outside light. The flashlight beam seemed puny.

"There's a lot of stuff down here," Rayne said.

Andi flicked the light over stacks of boxes, furniture and racks crammed with clothes. The only clear spaces were in front of the freezer, washer and dryer. "My great-grandfather built this house in 1892. Pack rats run in my family."

"No kidding." He sounded amused.

Metal rattled, startling her. She knocked into Rayne. "My goodness, I'm jumpy. Sorry." She swept the beam across something gleaming—and alive.

Eyes.

She screamed as a bulky shape flashed through the light. Rayne shouted. Andi had time for one thought— *There's a man in my basement*—before a heavy weight hit her and she crashed into a clothes rack.

Racks toppled like dominoes. Entangled in wool and cotton, strangled by filmy plastic bags, she struggled, but a heavy form pressed her down, trapping her. Darkness swamped her.

Heavy footsteps pounded up the stairs. The basement door slammed.

"Andi?"

She gasped for air and pushed against the weight pinning her legs. "Underneath you." Her lower lip burned and she tasted blood.

Mumbling curses, Rayne fought to get up. Metal tubing groaned and soldered joints snapped with dull clicks. Searching for a hold on something, he groped her midsection, then her breast. She slapped at him, and he caught her hand. "My feet are all tangled. Hold still. I can't see." He eased backward. Clothes hangers scraped the concrete floor. "Are you hurt?"

"He hit me in the mouth." Her lower face throbbed. She touched her tongue to her lip and winced.

"I think I did that," Rayne said apologetically. "With my elbow. Are you okay?"

Other than being trapped in a woolly pit and unable to see a single blessed thing and her lower lip doing a blown inner-tube impression, she felt peachy. It took forever to claw past the clothing, but she made it to her feet and into Rayne's arms.

He pressed her against his chest. His heart thudded and he breathed raggedly. He asked again, "Okay?" Andi worked her heart out of her throat.

The freezer hummed behind Rayne. That meant the fuse box and light switch should be directly to her left. Andi stretched out her left arm, reaching for the wall. Wary of tripping over broken racks or tangled clothes, she and Rayne inched to the left. Andi brushed the rough wall and finally found the fuse box and the ring to pull open the cover. Rayne's hands followed the progress of her hands.

"Thank God, it's a circuit breaker," he said. A loud snap cracked the darkness. The basement lights came on.

She blinked painfully. Five clothing racks, two of them mangled beyond repair, lay on the floor. It looked like the laundry day from hell. Rubbing the back of his neck, Rayne shook his head at the mess.

Realization struck Andi. "Oh," she breathed, and wobbled unsteadily. Rayne steadied her as she whispered, "He was waiting for us. He shut off the lights to make us come down here...." Her knees turned to water.

He held her again. She stared at his face, her mouth opening and closing, but she was unable to speak as fear tightened her throat and shivers at the base of her spine worked their way throughout her body until even her teeth chattered.

A stranger in her basement!

Rayne's eyes widened and filled with alarm. "Hey, it's okay. Honest, you're safe now. It's okay."

All she could manage was a high-pitched "Oh."

He shook his head and his hands clutched spasmodically against her back. He covered her mouth with a soft and tender, very distracting kiss.

Chapter Three

Rayne rattled the knob on the basement door and announced, "Locked."

Seated on a step, hugging her knees, Andi watched a black-and-white jumping spider crawl a jerky path up the wall. Light from the bare bulb hanging in the stairwell caught the spider's tiny eyes and made them glow like emeralds. It watched her.

She focused on its silky-haired body and interesting markings, but her mind lingered on kissing Rayne. It hadn't been much of a kiss; he'd been far too careful about her sore mouth. Yet his touch had snapped her out of rising panic. The way he'd slid a hand up her spine and under her hair, then lightly, ever so gently grasped the back of her neck in a gesture both tender and possessive... not much of a kiss? Quality more than made up for the lack of quantity.

She doubted if he'd meant to kiss her, though. He'd jerked away from her as if she'd electrocuted him. She hadn't helped matters by saying, "Thanks, I needed that." Smooth, she thought glumly. He still refused to look at her.

He shook the door again and thumped it with his fist. "Is there another way out of here?"

He sounded calm and unruffled. Admiration replaced the remains of her fear. They were trapped, but considering the bad things that might have happened, they were safe. "The windows are too small for either of us. There are lots of tools down here. Could we break the lock?"

"Or wait for somebody to miss us."

Andi found a hammer and a thin screwdriver. While Rayne worked, he asked, "Why a lock on the basement door?"

"To keep crazy Aunt Matilda from getting out."

He gave her a strange look and she laughed, then caught her sore face in both hands. "Bad joke. Grandma was scared of the basement. She made Mom keep it locked." She shrugged. "Grandma was kind of weird."

He tapped the screwdriver handle lightly with the hammer. "This house is solid. You said your grandfather built it?"

Apparently, no mention of the kiss was forthcoming. If he could pretend it hadn't happened, so could she. "Great-grandfather. That door is solid oak and hand planed. All the doors are. He carved the wainscoting, too. Do you think that man was a burglar?"

"Beats me." He gave the screwdriver a good whack and wood squealed in protest. "Somehow I doubt it."

"Why?"

"Law of averages."

"I don't understand." She flicked dust off her skirt. Noticing a tear in the hem, she frowned.

"Keller Poe's dying and Mr. Simon's disappearing are coincidences. There's nothing to connect your friend and a thief. But throw in a screwball note telling you not to look for Mr. Simon, and a joker in your basement, and that's way off the coincidence scale."

She mulled over his words, uncertain if she liked the direction of this conversation. "Then you think Mr. Simon did have something to do with Keller Poe?"

He grunted and his arm muscles strained his shirt. Wood cracked. "He hasn't died, at least not in El Paso County. He's not in any hospital, mental institution or detox ward. He's not in jail. I asked around at the bus station, but no one remembers seeing anyone matching his description." He looked over his shoulder. "I think he left the note. He's hiding and he doesn't want to be found. Even by you."

Andi shook her head. "Mr. Simon is very polite. Besides, he wouldn't hide from me. It makes no sense."

"It does if he saw what happened in your yard."

She hugged her knees tightly and curled her toes against the rough stone step. "You think the man in my basement is the killer?"

"He may think Mr. Simon lives here."

Her limbs went cold and her breathing roughened.

He nudged her shoulder. "I'm thinking out loud. Killers only go gunning for witnesses in the movies. Forget it. Dumb idea. The guy was probably a burglar."

Which didn't explain the note—or make her feel better. "If he's scared, that's all the more reason to find him."

"Up to you."

"What's your professional opinion?"

He took a long time to answer. "Have you seen any sign at all that the police are searching for Mr. Simon?"

"They haven't even come back to talk to me. I had to call them and ask if I could take down the yellow ribbons and the strings they left all over my yard."

"Keep looking. At his age, he's probably easily confused." He whacked the screwdriver and the jamb strip bowed. "If he did leave the note, we know he's close by. That's good. We'll find him and get this straightened out."

He took a step down and scratched the back of his head. "That's some kind of lock. I'm wrecking the door-frame."

"I prefer fixing the door to sleeping in the basement. My feet are cold."

"We need a bigger screwdriver. Something with a wide blade."

She found what he wanted. As she handed it to him his fingers brushed hers. His eyes widened, darkening, and his lips parted. She got the impression he wanted to kiss her again.

The feeling left her breathless. The stairwell felt narrower. Sound distorted; it seemed they breathed as one. Her mouth tingled with yearning, and her calf muscles twitched in anticipation of taking one more step closer to him.

He took the screwdriver and abruptly faced the door. A flush warmed Andi's face and throat. All this excitement must be making her a little crazy.

He worked the bigger screwdriver under the jamb. "I'm sorry about what happened."

The burglar? The note? Getting locked in the basement? He didn't own the blame for any of that.

He jerked a thumb over his shoulder, indicating downstairs. "Uh...I stepped out of line. I apologize. I'll keep my hands to myself. It won't happen again."

She lifted an eyebrow. She did not consider herself the type of woman with whom a man might feel free to take excessive liberties. But somehow having him apologize for a kiss, especially one so nice, and then to assure her it would never happen again, dipped into the realm of insult. She thought he was sexy and wonderful; he considered her a mistake. Terrific.

Wariness marked his sideways look. "You don't have to worry about me."

She tap-tapped her fingers against her knees. "Fine. Door open yet?"

"You looked about to faint. I—I didn't mean anything by it."

Her eyes glazed. Not a kiss, mouth-to-mouth resuscitation. She'd been out of the dating scene for a long time, but to forget the signals so completely? She slumped and sighed loudly. Nice capper for a lousy day. A burglar in the basement and a desirable man assuring her that kissing her meant nothing and he'd never do it again.

The lock gave with a metallic groan and a click. He opened the door.

Andi scrambled up the stairs. The back door stood wide open. She slammed it shut and locked it.

"Call the cops," Rayne said. Holding the screwdriver and hammer at ready, he stalked through the house and peered through doorways. Andi called the police.

After she hung up, she noticed Rayne giving her a woeful look. He rubbed his elbow. "I didn't mean to hit your mouth."

Andi touched her taut lower lip gingerly. She soothed the cut with a piece of ice wrapped in a paper towel.

The doorbell rang. Rayne murmured something about the cops being quick on this side of town. Andi answered the door and invited John Morris inside. His uniform, snappy and spit shined, eased her. His wide, thrust-forward smile struck her, as usual, as rather puppyish, but at least *he* found her attractive.

Rayne appeared to swell and his eyes narrowed to glittering slits. "Morris."

"Coplin." Morris's smile disappeared and he flexed his hands so his knuckles cracked.

Looking from man to man, Andi said, "Oh, you know each other."

Rayne turned away and thrust his hands into his back pockets. Rocking lightly on his boot heels, he stared at a framed poster of the Springs Symphony backlit by the Fourth of July fireworks display.

"You reported a prowler, Andi?" the policeman asked. "What happened to your mouth?"

"Rayne hit me." She heard how that sounded and flinched. "By accident."

"What happened?"

She told him, then produced the note warning her against finding Mr. Simon. Morris's pale eyebrows lowered into a scowl. He stuffed the note in his uniform pocket.

"Do you think Mr. Simon saw Keller Poe's killer?" Andi asked.

He glanced at the open front door and took a step closer. "I shouldn't tell you, but seeing how we're friends, I can trust you. Rumor says the coroner is ruling the death a suicide."

Rayne and Andi spoke as one. "Suicide?" Rayne added, "That's crazy. He was stabbed."

"What do you know about homicide, Coplin?" John smiled at Andi and puffed his chest. "You're not a cop. I'm the professional here."

The air crackled with hostility. Andi cleared her throat. "Uh, about the man in my basement?"

Dragging his attention away from Rayne, John pulled a slim notebook from his shirt pocket and opened it with a flourish. "Can you describe him?"

Thinking, she frowned. "It was dark. He was big. He went out the back door. Rayne?"

He shook his head.

"I'll look around." John indicated the front door with a nod. "If I were you, I'd find someplace else to stay until you get a locksmith in here. Install dead bolts."

The incongruity of a very good basement door lock and poor locks on the outside doors bemused her. Changing all the locks in the house seemed like a very good idea.

Rayne said, "I'll install new locks first thing tomorrow, Andi."

"No need to get your hands dirty," John said. "I'm not on until the afternoon. I can do it in the morning for you, Andi."

"Security is my business," Rayne countered.

"I have a one-and-a-half-horsepower drill and I can take care of her windows, too. No charge." He cocked a hip and lifted his chin as if to say, "Top that."

Andi flopped onto the couch and folded her arms over her chest. Wasn't this interesting? Nobody cared about kissing her, but mention her door locks and they squabbled like dogs over a bone. How much more could her poor ego take? "You were going to look for the burglar, John?"

While the policeman checked out back, his flashlight beam crisscrossing the yard, Andi watched him through a kitchen window.

Behind her, Rayne snorted. "Suicide. Right."

Compared to imagining a deranged killer after Mr. Simon, Andi considered a suicide ruling preferable. "The coroner must know what he's doing."

"A thief crawls into a stranger's yard and commits hari-kari? Of course. Happens every day." He snorted again. "He's trying to impress you."

She drew away at his testy tone. "You don't like Officer Morris."

"Aside from being a self-important boob and a danger to the public, he blew one of the biggest workman's comp cases I ever worked."

"He did? How?"

"I was surveilling a professional con artist who was involved in defrauding the government. I was on a hillside with a zoom lens taking pictures." He jerked a thumb toward the backyard. "Bingo brain decides I'm trespassing. Which I wasn't. Lights flashing, makes a scene, puts the cuffs on me. Of course the bad guy looks out the window, sees me, sees the camera and puts two and two together. He does a fast fade and we never see him again."

She could almost see the heat waves dancing above his head. The last vestige of her image of the ice-for-blood, hard-boiled private eye vanished. He possessed a lot of self-control, but passion burned beneath the surface.

Too bad none of it was directed toward her.

John returned. "Your gate was open. You might consider putting a padlock on it." He fixed her with a stern eye. "He might have been a burglar. Then again, a woman living alone…" He let the implication dangle. "I doubt if he'll return, but don't take the chance. There have been some problems in the area. Go stay with a friend or a relative. I'll make extra drive-bys tonight."

Icy fingers prickled up and down her spine. Staying alone held no appeal whatsoever.

He touched his pocket. "This note is probably from some kid who knows you're looking for the old man. A joke. Just in case, when you find Mr. Simon, let me know."

She saw him to the door. Beyond the porch the cool evening, punctuated by serenading crickets and heavy with the scent of flowers and lighted by soft pools from streetlights, seemed safe. Andi searched the shadows and listened to rustles and scratches and faint, stealthy thumps. The porch creaked under John's footsteps. She wondered if she would ever feel completely safe in this old house again. "Thank you, John." He swaggered down the walk.

"He is right about one thing," Rayne said. "Any bozo with a thin blade can pop those locks. You shouldn't stay here tonight."

RAYNE RAN HARD, pushing his limits. Nostrils flared, he relished the burn in his lungs and the fire in his veins. The chain-link fencing surrounding the school yard flashed silver at the corner of his vision.

He ran hard and fast for three full circuits around the empty yard. Chest heaving, he slowed to a jog. His legs tingled with exertion and his T-shirt clung damply to his chest and back. The nippy early morning air felt good against his hot face.

He jogged out of the yard, past the low, red brick elementary school and across the street toward his apartment building.

Despite the killer run, the empty ache of sexual frustration hounded him.

Why did he do this to himself?

Last night Andi had fretted and debated over which of her friends to bother at such a late hour until he finally told her to pack a bag and took her to his place—a major mistake he'd realized fully when he tiptoed through his bedroom this morning. Bathed in the pearl light of dawn, Andi lay on his bed, one smooth arm curled above her head and her face as relaxed and sweet as an angel's.

A nearly irresistible urge to kiss her and bury his face in the tawny mass of her hair had left him shaken. It still troubled him.

At his apartment door, he fingered the key hanging on the dog tag chain around his neck.

He couldn't believe he'd kissed her! But they'd both had a good scare, she'd been ready to claw through the ceiling, and impulse had gotten the better of him. It was not exactly a kiss, then, but more of a humane gesture. He was a professional and he did not, under any circumstances, mess around with a client. He'd apologized for the lapse and he could control himself. Case closed. He opened the door.

"Oh, hi," Andi said from the efficiency kitchen. "I wondered where you went. I made coffee for you. I hope you don't mind, but I found some tea for myself. You've been jogging?"

Carrying a mug, she walked around the counter. She wore a sleeveless blouse with a soft lace collar and a calf-length, gray-blue skirt. She'd pulled her damp hair back in a ponytail, but tendrils escaped to fall becomingly around her face. She looked him up and down, lingering on his bare legs, then shifted her attention to the mug. Lips pursed, she blew on the hot tea.

Rayne felt his mouth form a grin. "Help yourself."

"I'd fix breakfast, but you don't have any food. Except whatever that green stuff is in your fridge. It looks like a science project."

He raked sweaty hair off his forehead. "I don't eat here much. Can't cook."

She looked around the small apartment with its bare walls, bare floors, sparse furnishings, unpainted bookshelves and windows covered with white vinyl shades. He suspected she thought he didn't live here much, either. In contrast to the cheerful cluttered warmth of her house, the apartment looked as stark as a transient motel room.

"Thanks for letting me have your bed," she said. "I actually got a good night's sleep."

That made one of them. "No problem."

She touched the tip of her tongue to her swollen lower lip. Rayne's heart rate edged back up toward full exertion level. She smiled whimsically. "Do you give this kind of service to all your clients?"

"All in the contract," he managed to reply, and lurched toward the bedroom. "I'll take a shower. Help yourself to whatever." He kicked the bedroom door shut behind him.

Later, showered, shaved, dressed, calm and collected, he walked out of the bedroom. Andi sat at the counter reading the newspaper.

"I remembered something," she said.

He headed for the coffeepot. "What's that?" He lifted the pot, glanced at it, then did a double take. He held the pot toward the light. The brew was as opaque as ink. He suspected he risked a heart attack by drinking it but poured a cup anyway.

"I'm not sure, but I think Mr. Simon has a job."

"Why do you say that?"

She folded the paper neatly. "I remember one time he was late for lunch. We often had lunch together. On nice days we went over to Acacia Park. He said he'd been at the bank cashing his paycheck. I didn't think anything of it at the time, but if he's drawing Social Security, he wouldn't call it a paycheck, would he?"

"Can you think of anything else?" He tried the coffee and it hit his belly with a caffeine jolt. How many scoops of coffee grounds had she used?

"Is the coffee okay?"

"Perfect."

She snapped her fingers. "There is something else. He never shows up before noon. Even on Saturdays. I bet he has a part-time job."

"How's his health? Any chronic problems? A bad heart, lung disease?"

She rubbed one hand over the other. "He has arthritis, but not that bad. He's skinny. I guess you could say he looks frail. I haven't been able to fatten him up. Other than that his health is fine. He walks everywhere, and he does my yard work."

"This is good information. It'll help."

Her smile brightened the entire apartment. He forgave her completely for the lousy coffee.

He said, "Even if he's scared and hiding, he still has to live. He has habits." He paused, thinking. "Is he a sports fan?"

She shook her head.

"Does he belong to any clubs or organizations?"

"I can't think of anything. He loves books and he knows poetry. Plants. He knows all about growing things. He's very old-fashioned and not at all interested in television or music. He likes movies, but only old ones."

He wished she'd quit toying with her sore lip. Despite the swelling she had the most kissable mouth he'd ever seen—or tasted. A ghost of her fresh womanly scent lingered in his memory; the feel of her clung to his skin.

Her smile faded and a troubled expression clouded her eyes. "He's a sweet, quiet old man...inoffensive. I keep telling myself he's all right, but I'm scared. A little voice in my head keeps saying something is wrong. I'm scared he's dead."

By the time he realized he'd acted, he had closed his hand over her cool fingers and given them a reassuring squeeze. She laid her other hand atop his and the tips of her fingers traced the knobby bones of his wrist.

His throat tightened and he cleared it. He pulled his hand back. "It won't be easy finding him, but I will. Keep the faith."

"Chin up, brave face." She nodded.

He drove Andi to the bookstore where she worked. Before she got out of his Jeep, he said, "I don't want to upset you, but the man you think is following you?"

She peered suspiciously up and down the street. "What about him?"

"It might have been him in your house last night."

Her pupils dilated.

"If you see him today or think you see him, call me or Ford. Don't pass it off as nerves. And don't think it's a bother. It's not."

She blew out a long breath. "Boy, when it rains it pours."

"Who's in the store now?"

"Sharon. I'd introduce you, but she thinks I'm crazy for hiring a private eye. Excitement makes her nervous." She flashed him a brave smile and left.

He watched the swing of her skirt. Her floaty skirts and loose blouses obscured her figure except for her shapely calves and narrow waist. He imagined a full-breasted, full-hipped body, all softness and curves. She reached the door and he remembered. He called, "Andi!"

She put down her suitcase and walked back to him.

At the same time they said, "House key," and laughed.

"You know what they say about great minds." She worked a dull brass key off a ring and placed it in his palm. "I don't have any cash, but I can give you a blank check for the locks."

Sunlight sparkled on her hair, turning it to spun gold. Score one for Ford's powers of observation—she was a beautiful blonde. But he held serious doubts if he was as hard-boiled as he liked to think. "I'll tack it on your bill."

"This is kind of you. Are you sure I shouldn't call a locksmith?"

"I need to check around your property and talk to your neighbors, too." He dropped the key in his shirt pocket. "Which of your neighbors know Mr.—"

The runner materialized from nowhere. Arms pumping, feet flying, he raced down the sidewalk. Startled by his size—his chest and shoulders would put a fully geared-up NFL player to shame—and his speed, Rayne barely registered him snatching Andi's suitcase.

"Hey!" Andi shouted, "That's mine!"

The man ran faster.

Rayne slammed the transmission into gear before realizing the thief ran the wrong way down a one-way street. Andi gave chase. Rayne scrambled out of his vehicle and yelled for Andi to stop. The thief darted around the corner. Rayne caught up to Andi and snagged her shoulder, nearly jerking her off her feet. He caught her before she fell. "I'll catch him. Stay here!" She struggled, then stilled.

He raced around the corner. He stopped short and whipped his head back and forth, searching both sides of the street, but saw no one remotely resembling the thief.

Amazement left him slack jawed. That joker had to weigh at least two hundred and fifty pounds. He couldn't have run that fast.

Rayne jogged down the street, peering inside shops and behind parked cars. Morning traffic moved in fits and starts and cars jockeyed for parking spaces. Had the thief jumped into a getaway car? He found the suitcase behind a parked car. The catches were wrenched and ruined. He gathered her belongings and returned to the bookstore.

Andi stood on the sidewalk hugging her elbows. An older woman with short hair and wearing glasses had her arm around Andi's waist. A uniformed police officer looked up at Rayne's approach.

"I lost him," Rayne confessed. He held forth the ruined suitcase.

Andi frowned as she went through her rumpled clothing. "Everything is here except my toothbrush." She grimaced at a leaking bottle of shampoo. "Why didn't he take anything? Why did he break it? It wasn't locked."

The policeman looked from Andi to Rayne then back to Andi. "The description?"

Rayne said, "Tall, two hundred and fifty pounds. Dark hair." He tapped under his ear with the side of his hand. "About this long, thin on top. Tan slacks, dark shirt." He heaved in a deep breath and wiped his brow. "Runs like a damn greyhound."

Andi thrust her chin forward. "He's dirty. His arms are covered with dirt."

"I'll put it on the radio and see if I can find him." The policeman went back to his car.

Andi turned on Rayne. "Well! He certainly went to a lot of bother for nothing." She glared in the direction the thief had run.

"He was probably hoping for cash."

She pointed, her arm shaking with the force of her anger. "I don't think so. He's the man who's been following me."

Chapter Four

Rayne took the stairs two and three at a time. When he entered the office, he saw his partner with his highly polished wing tips propped on the desk. Holding the telephone handset lodged between his cheek and shoulder, Ford glanced at Rayne and touched a finger to his lips. He scribbled on a memo pad and held it up. It read, "Job for Butch—bail jumper." Rayne used both hands to close the door without a sound.

"Three televisions, Mrs. Hernandez?" Ford continued. "Now the next item in the survey. How many children under the age of eighteen live in your home? How many adults?" His tone said he was ever so grateful Mrs. Hernandez agreed to use a moment of her valuable time to help him.

Why anyone in this town bothered skipping out on a court appearance was beyond Rayne. No one could hide from Ford.

Rayne plucked a red projector pen from a jar on his desk. Standing before a dry-erase board on the wall, he thought hard...and raised an image of Andi with her large eyes sparkling in good humor. In his mind's eye he unfastened the top few buttons of her prim white blouse and tightened her skirt so it clung to her rounded backside. He added candles to the scene—no, a fire in the fireplace, burning rich mesquite—a bottle of wine, a thick velvety rug and fat cushions. Running his hand through the soft masses of her hair, testing the smoothness of her skin...

He scowled. *Come on, Coplin,* he mouthed, and glowered at the dry-erase board. *Fine, she's sexy, she's desirable*— and he would make a total ass of himself if it meant receiving one of her thousand-watt smiles. He'd already made an ass of himself.

On the board he printed "Keller—dead" and "Simon—missing." He drew a line connecting the two and atop that a question mark. He added brief comments about a man following Andi, the burglar in her basement and the snatched suitcase. Under "Simon—missing," he wrote "Don't look for me—Simon?"

Did Simon write the note? He wished he knew for certain.

Had Keller committed suicide?

He drew an arrow between the suitcase theft and the man following Andi. Intuition connected everything on the board, but whys and what-fors eluded him.

Rayne turned to a wall-mounted photomap of Colorado Springs. He located Andi's home and marked it with a red push-pin. Then he marked the bookstore where she worked. The distance between them was about one and a half miles.

The old man did not drive. He depended on his feet or buses. The last time Andi had seen him was on a Sunday, and city buses didn't run on Sundays. Ergo, he lived within walking distance of her home.

Rayne's best bet lay in finding out where Mr. Simon worked. A workplace meant employee records, including his full name, Social Security number, address and previous employers.

Hands behind his back, Rayne stared at the map.

You're a jerk, Mr. Simon, he thought. If I had her feeding me dinner and treating me like king of the world, no way would I disappear.

He focused on the downtown area between Cimarron to the south, Cache La Poudre to the north and Wahsatch to the east. An area dotted with small businesses, restaurants, senior citizen centers, the public library and residences. Who would hire a man in his seventies?

Andi had described a man with limited financial means and a shabby wardrobe. A shy man, unused to dealing with people. Was he a gardener? Janitor? Stocker in a grocery store? Craftsman? Handyman?

Andi would hire him, he decided, adopting an old man as if he were a stray cat. She was too nice for her own good. She needed somebody levelheaded to see to her best interests. Someone at whom she could direct all that generous energy.

Ford cleared his throat loudly.

"Huh?"

"You're wearing an odd expression. Problem?"

The postman walked inside, gave the mail to Ford and picked up the outgoing mail. Ford handed a slim blue envelope to Rayne.

A quick scan of the return address told him it was the monthly missive from his cousin Jackie. He knew the envelope contained a chatty letter about her family and gossip about relatives and a plea for him to come to his senses and call his parents. Good old Jackie the peacemaker.

No matter what Jackie said, he'd always be the bad guy in his parents' eyes. They'd never forgive him for blowing the whistle on his brother. Andi didn't know how lucky she was not having relatives. He tossed the letter, unopened, in a desk drawer.

Rayne brought Ford up-to-date on Andi's case, then pointed to the dry-erase board. "Any ideas?"

"One moment." He dialed a phone number. "Butch? Ford here. I think I know where your man is." He chuckled. "Of course it's only been thirty minutes. Do pardon me for taking so long."

Listening with interest, Rayne poured a cup of coffee. Butch, a regular client, called Ford whenever he had a bail jumper. Ford never disappointed him.

"I believe you'll find him at his mother's home," Ford said. "Most likely still abed. No problem whatsoever. Glad to be of service."

Ford always made it look easy. Rayne laughed. "The infamous television survey. You deserve your own Academy Award category."

"I merely tell people what they wish to hear, and they rarely disappoint me in returning the favor." Ford approached the board. Whistling softly, he studied it. "Would you care to hear my thoughts?"

Rayne sat on his chair and swung his feet atop the desk. He cradled the coffee cup in both hands. "Go for it."

"Keller Poe was an habitual thief. Thus, it is within the realm of possibilities to think he had stolen something. Perhaps something which proved a mitigating factor in his death."

"Morris said the coroner is ruling suicide."

Ford smiled. "Perhaps he chose the young lady's backyard as a possible hiding place."

"Someone chased him?"

"And it is conceivable Mr. Simon was in the vicinity."

"I'm sure of it. So he picked up whatever Keller stashed."

"That is one explanation. If so, whatever the stolen item is, its owner shows little interest in contacting the authorities, and thus is most likely not the rightful owner. Its value is also apparent enough to tempt an otherwise law-abiding elderly gentleman into coveting it for himself." Ford touched the comment about Andi's suitcase. "Something of a size to fit inside a lady's overnight case."

"Cash," Rayne offered. "Drugs. Negotiable bonds." Irritation tightened his gut. Andi loved the old guy; had he repaid her by getting greedy and stupid?

An uncomfortable sense of déjà vu washed over him. He glanced at the drawer where he'd tossed Jackie's letter. He'd tasted bitterly of this recipe for heartbreak before: take one naive person, mix with a loved one infected by incurable greed, shake well and wait for betrayal, denial and ruined lives.

"Drugs are unlikely. Mr. Simon would not only have to recognize the product, he would have to believe he could profit from it. The same could be said for negotiable bonds or other securities."

"A sackful of cash, then."

"Do you have the note?"

Rayne shook his head. "I'm certain Simon wrote it. What do you think? He hopped a flight to Mexico?"

"The wisest course of action. Yet if he left a note yesterday after having an entire week in which to flee, it means he believes flight represents a greater danger."

That puzzled Rayne. "Then we can assume," he said, imitating Ford's lofty speech, "that Mr. Simon is none too bright. Which doesn't explain why he left the note or how he knows she's looking for him."

"You have no proof he left the note."

Rayne didn't want to consider the implications if the old man hadn't written that melodramatic warning. From Simon, it had a pathetic ring; from anyone else, it was sinister.

"I suggest you consider this an intellectual exercise and continue your search. I took the liberty of making a discreet inquiry. Miss Blair's bank balance is quite healthy. It would not do to disappoint her."

"She's loaded?" Rayne smiled in surprise. Nothing about Andi said money. He ran into a lot of financial bullies, male and female, who assumed their cash bought the right to push him around. His respect for her went up another notch.

"I would use the term comfortable. With your information base so scanty, your best source will be Miss Blair. Remain in close contact and encourage her reminiscing."

Close contact. Rayne shook unseemly thoughts out of his head.

"You and Paul Sevilla worked robbery together. He's a friend, right? Think he can give us the scoop on Keller Poe?"

"It never hurts to ask."

While Ford called the detective, Rayne resumed studying the map. Should he conduct a door to door search? He enjoyed legwork, but no sense getting ridiculous about it. He searched the telephone book and found an employment agency specializing in jobs for the elderly. He also noted that Sunrise Hotel, a combination assisted-living apartment complex and community center, was only a block from Acacia Park, where Andi and Mr. Simon had enjoyed many lunch hours together.

Ford hung up the phone. "Poor Paul, I had not heard."

"What's that?" Rayne knew the detective only in passing but liked him. Unlike many in official law enforcement, Paul harbored no general ill will toward private investigators.

"Middle age and the toll of police work. His daughters have departed the nest and his wife followed suit."

Rayne couldn't think of anyone offhand—himself included—who hadn't suffered through a divorce. He clucked his tongue. "Shame."

"Such is life." Ford knew all about it; he'd endured three divorces. "However, John Morris was not entirely incorrect. The coroner ruled Keller Poe's death accidental."

"Right."

"There were no defense wounds, no signs of a struggle. Only Keller's fingerprints were on the knife. According to the authorities, he tripped and fell on the blade. A rather freakish accident, but an accident nonetheless."

Rayne pointed to the board. "Did you tell Paul about this? Simon's ripping off Keller puts a twist on things." A sickening possibility occurred to him. Did Simon help Keller have an accident?

"As an independent contractor, the coroner is a bureaucracy answerable only unto himself. His competency and reputation make overturning one of his rulings a task of Herculean proportions. One does not annoy him with unproven theories."

"What if we're right?" He hoped not.

"If so, we'll collect evidence and present it to Paul. The coroner respects evidence."

"Got it." He dropped the red pen back in the jar. "I'm going to secure Andi's house and check out her neighbors. If you get any bright ideas, call me."

ANDI INTERLOCKED the cardboard pieces of a dump display for a paperback best-seller. Fear and anger over the suitcase theft had faded, leaving her confused. Why anyone would follow her around for days in order to snatch a twenty-year-old suitcase containing a few clothes was completely beyond her comprehension.

Unless the man who snatched the suitcase had also been in her house and perhaps had murdered Keller Poe and come after her to get what he really wanted. . . .

She kept shaking those thoughts out of her head.

She set the display at the end of a shelf and loaded it with books. The hero depicted on the book cover drew her attention. The hair color was wrong and the man wore a fur pelt over his bare torso, but his strong face and proud carriage reminded her of Rayne.

She imagined Rayne in a fur pelt. Grow out his hair, go a day or two without shaving and voilà—barbarian man swinging a mighty club.

The bell over the door tinkled and Andi nearly screamed. From down the aisle Sharon turned a worried look Andi's way. She had to stop jumping every time the door opened.

The UPS man wheeled two cartons inside and set them down in front of the service counter. Andi slapped her hand atop a carton before the other salesclerk could. Debra flashed a saucy smile and said, "You're loading dumps."

Andi pointed at the filled cardboard display unit. "I'm finished. And it's my turn this week."

Andi signed for the cartons and lugged them one at a time into the back room. Sharon handled all the book ordering, so Andi never knew what a carton might contain. Opening shipments was better than Christmas.

The first carton contained paperback science fiction and fantasy novels. Andi perused cover copy as she checked the titles off on the order sheet. She inhaled the sharp, warm smell of new books. Printer's ink was the finest perfume in the world.

Funny how all the gorgeous guys on the sword-and-sorcery covers reminded her of Rayne. Wild man. She'd seen it in his eyes the first time she met him. He demonstrated control with his low, even voice and logical demeanor, but what happened when he cut loose? What punched his buttons? When was kissing him not a mistake?

"Andi?" Sharon poked her head through the doorway. Her mouth twisted somewhere between a grimace and a smirk. She rolled her eyes dramatically. "There's a lady here to see you. She says it's a private matter." She lowered her voice. "She asked for Andrea Blair."

Only telephone solicitors ever called her Andrea. "Private?"

"You can talk in here." Sharon stepped aside.

A woman crept into the back room. A floppy brimmed hat perched atop a flower-printed scarf tied under her chin. The hat and scarf completely covered her hair. Dark sunglasses concealed her eyes. She wore a cloth coat buttoned to the neck, faded pink slacks tightly fitted to her thin legs and pointy-toe, spike-heeled shoes.

An aficionado of flea markets and thrift stores, Andi recognized the disguise as a vintage early sixties outfit. An unusual ring drew Andi's attention. In the shape of a spider, the body sparkled with faceted red stones, either rubies or garnets.

The woman grasped the door with a thin-skinned, large-knuckled, very pale and trembling hand. Barely above a whisper, she asked, "Are you Andrea Blair? May we speak privately?"

"Sure."

The woman closed the door and leaned against it, hugging a patent leather purse against her breast. Andi cleared papers off a chair and offered a place to sit, but the woman acted as if she didn't notice.

Andi fought the urge to stare. Why did the woman need to hide her identity? "What can I do for you?"

"I know exactly who you are." Her voice held accusation.

Was she supposed to feel guilty about something? Andi couldn't imagine what. Or was Debra playing a joke on her? Debra had a strange sense of humor and she thought Andi hiring a private eye was hilarious. Andi adored a good joke, but this was more bizarre than funny.

"And you are...?" Andi asked.

"Tell him to leave me alone. I can't take anymore." A shudder racked her thin frame and she sagged against the door. "I've suffered enough. He just can't appear and do this to me. What does he want?"

Andi lifted her hand and the woman cringed. A bitter, metallic undercurrent wafted beneath her rose perfume—the smell of fear. This was no joke.

"No more phone calls!" the woman cried. "It's over, it's past. He's driving me mad! I can't take it. Make him leave me alone! This is all I have."

"Who? Are you sure you have—"

"Don't play games with me!" Groaning, the woman fumbled inside the purse. She shoved a thick manila envelope at Andi. Her nails were bitten below the quick, the cuticles savaged.

Andi took the envelope. "Ma'am, you're upset. Please, do sit. Would you care for a cup of tea? Let's—"

Clawing at the doorknob, she wailed, "You tell him to leave me alone or I'll kill him! I swear to God, I'll kill him." She tore open the door.

Stunned, Andi listened to the scrabbling click of the woman's heels as she scurried down the long aisle toward the front door. Feeling as if she'd stumbled onto a stage where everyone but she knew the script, she lowered her gaze to the heavy envelope.

On it was written one word: Simon.

"Ma'am?" She ran down the aisle.

"What in the world is going on?" Sharon called.

"That woman! I have to stop her." She thrust the envelope at Sharon and ran outside.

She looked up and down the sidewalk and saw the woman in the crosswalk, hunched as if fighting a gale-force wind. A minivan bore down on her. Andi's heart skipped painfully and her belly tightened. The woman jerked up her head. The minivan skidded to a stop and the driver leaned on the horn.

Andi sagged against a light pole and gasped for air.

The woman reached the sidewalk.

Cupping her hands over her mouth, Andi yelled, "Lady! Please! Wait!"

The woman broke into a tottering run. Waiting for a break in traffic or the light to change, Andi hopped from foot to foot. By the time she made it across the street, the woman had vanished. Andi asked pedestrians if they had seen a woman in a coat and hat.

A white Cadillac passed and the driver wore a big hat and scarf. Andi held out a hand, beseeching the woman to stop. Clutching both hands on the wheel, the woman gunned the engine and sped away.

Andi darted between two parked cars and stared at the license plate. "Kevin buys apples for $9.38," she said, creating the mnemonic to remember the number. Repeating "Kevin buys apples for $9.38," she hurried back to the bookstore.

Sharon, Debra and several customers met her inside the door and bombarded her with questions. Waving for silence, Andi snatched a pencil off the counter. She wrote down KBA-938.

"What was that all about?" Sharon handed over the envelope. "What is this?"

"I don't know. But I'm going to find out. We have a book about old cars, don't we? Pictures?"

She found a book about classic cars, flipped pages and found what she was looking for. She put her finger on a picture of a big car with a sleek gunboat design and tail fins. "A 1960 Cadillac. I've got to call Rayne—"

Sharon stopped her. "Andi. Back room." Her boss had never used that tone of voice before. "Debra, we'll be a few moments. You can handle the front." Sharon marched down the aisle. Andi meekly followed and did as told when Sharon ordered her to close the door behind her.

Mouth dry, Andi stared at her feet.

"Understand, I like you very much. You're a good employee. Customers like you and I enjoy working with you."

Andi tensed.

"But I have a business to run here. This store puts food on my family's table. You understand that."

"Yes, ma'am."

"This nonsense has got to stop. Right now. I hired you to wait on customers, not pester them about your missing friend. Not to play cloak-and-dagger games on my time." Her voice quavered and her hands trembled as she twisted the hem of her cotton sweater.

Sharon was scared. Deep shame coursed through Andi. "But—"

"No buts! You almost gave me a heart attack twice in one day. This is a bookstore, not Spies R Us." Her eyes shimmered behind her glasses. "What in the world is going on with you?"

"I don't know who that woman is. But she knows Mr. Simon. I can—"

"If you insist on searching for an old man you barely know, I can't stop you. But do it on your own time. As long as you're working in my store, I insist you concentrate on what I'm paying you for. I will not stand for any more of this running around, yelling and scaring people."

"Yes, ma'am." Andi pinched the bridge of her nose against the urge to cry.

The telephone rang and Sharon snatched it. "Reading Room, may I help you?" Her eyes narrowed. She thrust the handset at Andi. "It's Rayne Coplin."

Hating his lousy timing but excited about the possibility of news, she took the phone.

"I'm at your place," Rayne said. "I need you here."

"That's not a good idea right now. You see, a woman came and—"

"I think the burglar came back, but I need you to tell for sure. I already called Ford, he's on his way to pick you up. Come home right now."

After she hung up, she stood frozen by shock, her hand on the phone. Sharon's expression asked if Andi had received bad news. Andi said, "Can I have the rest of the day off? Rayne thinks my house was broken into again."

Sharon looked away.

"I'm sorry. I'll make it up to you. I promise." Her house—her house!

Sharon rubbed her eyes wearily. "Maybe you should take some time off. A few days. Heather needs the hours. Since she's on break from classes, she keeps complaining about working part-time."

"I—"

Waving a hand, her boss said, "I'm sorry for jumping down your throat. I know you're having problems, and I do understand. Or at least I'm trying to understand. So go take care of your problems. Take a few days or a week. Heather will be ecstatic."

Andi gave Sharon an impulsive hug. "I'll make it up to you. I promise."

Sharon tugged her clothes and nudged her glasses higher on her nose. "Yes, indeed. You will make it up to me. Now go on and take care of your house."

When she and Ford walked into her house, Andi realized immediately why Rayne had called. All the way home she'd imagined her home trashed and her belongings stolen, but one look dispelled that particular fear.

Yet the house felt wrong. In a sneaky, stealthy way it felt touched.

"Am I right?" Rayne swept a hand in a low, broad circle, indicating the room. "The back door was unlocked."

Andi walked slowly through the L-shaped living room, pressing her arm against the increasing ache in her belly. She crouched and felt a dimple formed by a couch leg in the thick wool rug—the couch had been moved. The fireplace doors were slightly ajar and the silk flower arrangement was out of place.

"See if anything is missing."

Grim and silent, his hands jammed in his back pockets, Rayne dogged her heels while she checked the house. In her bedroom goose bumps raised her flesh. Her jewelry box was untouched, but clothes had been moved in the closet and someone had gone through her bureau drawers and armoire. Seeing her lingerie drawer in disarray gave her a nauseating sense of violation. In the other bedroom the bedspread was askew. She lifted the dust ruffle and looked beneath the bed. A sweeping pattern in the dust showed where someone had reached under the bed and felt around.

She ended up in the kitchen. Rayne picked up a glass jar from the counter. It held change and a few dollar bills. "You weren't robbed."

"Nothing is missing that I can tell. But someone was definitely here." She rubbed her arms and wondered if she'd ever feel comfortable in her own home again.

Rayne turned to his partner. "What do you think?"

"Our ideas, apparently, have a measure of merit. This house has been searched."

Andi looked suspiciously from man to man. "What ideas?"

Rayne scratched his head, still looking at the change jar. "It's possible Keller Poe stole something and Mr. Simon picked it up. Now the owner wants it back."

The implication sank in and she bristled. "That's ridiculous! Any number of times I left him alone in here and he never stole anything. He'd never do such a thing."

"We're not calling him a thief, Miss Blair," Ford said.

She turned a glower on Rayne. "That's what you said. I'm sure you deal with all sorts of...unsavory characters, but Mr. Simon is not one of them." She sniffed and tossed her ponytail. "I bet that woman has something to do with this."

Rayne asked, "What woman?"

"The woman in the white 1960 Cadillac. KBA 938."

Rayne held up a hand. "What are you talking about?"

Andi told them about the woman in the bizarre disguise, then handed the envelope to Rayne. "She never gave me a chance to talk or ask questions. I think she was frightened, but I can't imagine why."

Ford lifted his eyebrows. "She threatened to kill Mr. Simon?"

"I don't think she meant it literally. How could she? He's a sweet little old man who wouldn't harm a fly. I've never heard him say an unkind word."

Rayne studied the padded envelope front and back. He handed it to Ford, who did the same.

Out of steam, Andi covered her eyes with a hand. "I'm so confused." The sound of tearing paper made her look. Rayne worked his thumb under the envelope flap.

She grabbed at the envelope. "You can't open that! It's personal."

He lifted it over his head and out of her reach. "Since she threatened to kill him, I doubt if he'll mind."

"That belongs to Mr. Simon." She turned to his partner. "Mr. Hayes?"

"If this mystery woman is making threats," Ford said, "I believe it is in our best interests to learn the basis of those threats."

"She was using a figure of speech."

"Right." Rayne ripped open the envelope.

"But—"

He dumped the contents on the coffee table. Thick bundles of crisp new fifty-dollar bills clunked on the tabletop.

Rayne rubbed the back of his neck. Andi smoothed hair from her face and touched her tongue to the healing cut on her lip. Ford folded his hands before him and cocked his head, one eyebrow lifted.

"This is very odd," said Andi.

Rayne and Ford nodded agreement.

She leaned over the table and searched the money pile, without touching, to see if a note of explanation had been included. "Any ideas?"

"Not really," Rayne replied. "Ford?"

"I do believe this adds a rather interesting twist. Miss Blair, please recount again exactly what the woman told you."

Rayne counted the money and Andi sat beside him, shifting her gaze between his quick fingers and the intense concentration on his face. As best she could, she reenacted the strange conversation with the woman. Ford's only comment was a soft "Hmm."

At length Rayne announced, "Twelve thousand, four hundred dollars."

Ford replaced the money in the envelope and asked for tape. Numbed by the strangeness of it all, Andi found a roll of masking tape. After he sealed the envelope, Ford asked Andi to sign it.

"Miss Blair," he said, "for security, I am going to put this in the office safe. Rayne, I'm going to immerse myself in some research concerning the late Mr. Poe." He held up the envelope. "In light of this development, I believe an angle begging exploration is whether Mr. Simon and Mr. Poe were acquainted. I smell the distinct taint of extortion in the air, and it behooves us to proceed with caution.''

Andi didn't at all like what he was saying.

As soon as Ford left, she turned on Rayne. "What exactly did he mean by that?"

Rayne urged her to sit on the couch. "We need to talk."

His face was solemn and she took neither comfort nor pleasure from the hand he placed over hers. Whatever he was about to say, she sensed she was going to hate it.

Chapter Five

Andi listened carefully to every word Rayne had to say, then stood abruptly and faced the window overlooking the alley. "Let me get this straight. You and Mr. Hayes think Keller Poe and Mr. Simon stole something from someone who killed Keller and is now chasing Mr. Simon. And that someone also thinks I'm in on it and so they're chasing me, too. That's why the man stole my suitcase."

Rayne toyed with a scrap of manila paper torn from the envelope. It made a soft, crinkling noise. "We don't have real evidence, but basically, yes."

"Uh-huh." She didn't know if he was making her mad, hurting her feelings or scaring her. She wished his tone held anything other than calm, businesslike seriousness. She wished she could read his closed expression and hooded eyes. She wished he didn't sound so darned sure of himself! "And the woman and the money?"

"I don't know, but it looks like a payoff to me. Maybe the stolen property belongs to her and she's trying to buy it back. Or it's blackmail. I think you should drop the case and let the police handle it."

Stop looking for Mr. Simon? She fussed with the curtains, arranging them so the folds hung evenly from the rod.

"Andi?"

"Hmm?"

"I'm always straight with my clients. I'm telling you how I see it."

Not look for the best friend she had in all the world? Leave a sweet, defenseless, inoffensive old man to the mercies of cops and robbers?

"Tell me what you're thinking."

She huffed in exasperation. Turning a pointed gaze on the sack from the hardware store and Rayne's box of tools sitting near the front door, she said, "I think I won't feel safe until my locks are replaced. I also think I'm hungry." She forced a smile. "I'll cook, you put in locks, and then I'll tell you what I think."

By the time Andi pulled a batch of brownies from the oven, she had reached a conclusion. Rayne and Mr. Hayes were wrong.

A power drill whirred. Rayne had installed dead bolts on her front and back doors and now put keyed locks on her windows. While he worked on the locks and she puttered in the kitchen, she'd caught a few looks he'd tossed her in passing. He'd kept his words to himself, however. No doubt, he'd been reconsidering what he'd told her and come to the same conclusion she had reached.

She made sandwiches and a salad.

She went to the bedroom door and leaned her shoulder against the frame, watching Rayne tighten a screw. Muscles flexed in fluid display under his shirt. Her gaze lowered to the fit of his jeans. He rested his weight on one leg, pulling wear-soft denim taut against his backside.

A shivery little ache knotted deep inside her. How very odd, she thought. She'd gone years barely thinking about men at all, then she met Rayne and the floodgates opened.

Every glance from his beautiful blue eyes electrified her; his low voice caressed her ears; merely looking at his broad shoulders and the chiseled strength of his neck and his corded forearms and his large hands with prominent veins and long muscular fingers fascinated her. His smile left her pleasantly weak.

The way he'd sat her down and talked straight to her about Mr. Simon said he respected her. He didn't pull punches, didn't soften his words or act as if he thought she was too dumb to get it. He took her seriously, treating her like an equal. She did not like what he had to say, but she did like him, a lot.

She drank in the way shafts of sunlight sparked reddish gold on his dark hair. He even had a sexy way of handling tools. "May I ask you a question?"

He glanced over his shoulder. "Sure."

"Are you charging me private eye rates or locksmith rates for this?"

His smile appeared a millimeter at a time. "Which is cheaper?"

"Private eye. Especially if you give me a discount for supplying lunch."

"I don't give discounts." He dug in his pocket and produced a pair of small keys. "Are you saying I'm in the wrong business?"

"Well, I think the carpenter who redid my kitchen took my money and went on a world cruise. Is that the last window?"

He worked a key in the lock, then he stepped back and saluted her with the screwdriver. "Done. Doors and windows secured.'' Sniffing, he raised his head. ''What smells so good?''

She liked his lusty appetite, too. ''Brownies. I fixed some lunch. Hope you like chicken salad.'' She inspected his handiwork and approved. She tried the key and the lock worked smoothly.

He placed tools neatly in a red metal box. Sawdust clung to his shirt and forearms. She brushed some off his sleeve and he tensed, watching her from the corner of his eye.

Awareness crackled, leaping like ball lightning. Never in her life had she wanted something as much as she craved right now the feel of his lips on hers and his hands on her body. If only—for even a brief moment—he'd hold her again the way he'd held her in the basement. Her fingers slowed against his shirt and she felt every nub and thread in the weave. His eyes were so beautiful, the irises ringed by midnight and variegated with a range of blues from silver to indigo. His pupils dilated, luminous and deep, and the heat curled through her until she couldn't bear looking at him.

Her eyelids lowered and she parted her lips to better breathe the now thick, still, silent air. Sensing rather than seeing his movement, she cocked her head slightly, and when his mouth touched hers it was as if the entire universe slipped rightly into place.

He tasted fresh and moist and his scent transported her to faraway, private places. Closing her fingers over his hard forearm, she leaned into his touch and his knuckles brushed her breast, sending shivers of aching heat to rest heavy in her belly, and she touched her tongue lightly to his and . . .

And he was gone. Metal clanked. She forced her eyes open and found him awkwardly braced against the wall, one boot atop the toolbox. Poised like a deer before a tiger, he stared at her with something akin to horror.

Fire burst on her cheeks. If he apologized—again—she would curl into a ball and die. "Uh, I'll just go put lunch on the table." She hurried out of the bedroom.

Shakily, she finished setting the table while he washed his hands in the sink. He hunched over the basin, scrubbing his hands. Thin water droplets glittered in the afternoon sunlight through the window. She felt his avoidance like a wall. What in the world was wrong here? He was an adult, she was an adult. Could it be...?

She blurted out, "Are you married?"

His face darkened; the rims of his ears turned red. "I'm divorced." He swiped his damp hands against his thighs. "I better go."

"No!" Both of them started. She realized she blocked the doorway, her arms outflung, napkins clutched in one hand and a salad server in the other. "Uh, I mean—lunch is ready and we need to talk."

His eyebrows lowered into a stormy frown and his hands curled into fists. His throat worked. He licked his lips with nervous darts of his tongue.

"About the case," Andi clarified. "Mr. Simon. We have to talk."

His features softened and his shoulders relaxed. Andi didn't know whether to feel relieved or irritated. Whichever, she knew she'd never get close enough to kiss this man again. He made her crazy!

When he sat, she said, "It's all right."

Eyeing the thick sandwiches and salad topped by her special honey-peppercorn dressing, he said cautiously, "Lunch? It looks great."

"I mean what you said about Mr. Simon. It's okay, really. I'm not upset with you."

He met her gaze and she looked away. If she could just stay away from those eyes, she'd be safe.

"You and Mr. Hayes take the facts and stick them together and force them to make sense. I admire that, probably because I'm no good at it. Sharon says I'm a sideways thinker. Instinctive-reactive." She nibbled a slice of cucumber. "I'm terrible at math, too. With numbers only one answer is possible, but I always hope for three or four anyway."

"I see." He sounded puzzled.

She added a spoonful of sugar to her iced tea. "So please don't think I'm upset by what you said about Mr. Simon. Do you like the sandwich?"

He wiped his mouth with a napkin. Before he could reply, the phone rang and she excused herself to answer it.

With distance between them, Rayne breathed a little easier and actually tasted his food. What was it about this woman that made his brain shut down? He counseled himself to be cool and mused over what she'd said.

She wasn't upset, she understood; was she dropping the case, then? He sat back on the chair and stared into the living room. She paced aimlessly as she talked, drifting in and out of his view, giving him glimpses of the soft sway of her skirt. Drop the case. Under any other circumstance the idea of quitting would have him spitting fire. In this instance all he felt was relief.

She returned to the table and settled her napkin over her lap. "Sharon's glad my house is okay, but thinks I should take some time off anyway." She speared a tomato wedge. "I didn't realize until today what an airhead I've been. It means a lot knowing you're on my side.

"Now, who do we call to find out that woman's name? KBA 938 is the license number. I bet she knows where Mr. Simon lives. Do we call the police?"

Rayne lowered his glass to the table. *"We,"* he said, dragging out the word, "don't call anybody. I mail a request to DOR and they send back an abstract."

"What's DOR? And an abstract?"

"Department of Revenue, in Denver. They send a photocopy of the registration."

"Does it take a long time?"

"Up to three weeks, but since we have an account, it usually doesn't take more than ten days. I thought—"

"It costs money?"

"Two dollars per request."

"Why are you looking at me like that?" She tapped a finger over her lower lip and chin. "Is there food on my face?"

He leaned back on the chair and slowly pulled the napkin through his fingers. He composed a new rule on the spot: make no assumptions whatsoever when dealing with Andi Blair. "I thought you wanted to drop the case."

"Why?"

"I thought we settled this. We'll turn over what we have to the police."

"Absolutely not. You said yourself you have no proof Mr. Simon did anything wrong. If you knew him the way I know him, you'd realize what you said is ridiculous."

His smile turned disbelieving.

"I don't know if that woman is a clue," Andi continued. "For all we know, she could have been paying back a loan. But since she knows me, that means she and Mr. Simon are good friends. Or maybe he works for her. She can probably—"

"Andi."

She compressed her lips and lowered her eyelashes—fetching, distracting, lushly fringed eyelashes. "I can't believe you want to quit." Her tone held accusation and disappointment.

Her words cut down his spine. "I—"

"Do you have proof Mr. Simon is a thief?" Before he could reply, she added, "Or that the man in my basement was anything other than a run-of-the-mill burglar? Or that the woman is a victim of blackmail?" She reached for the pitcher. "More iced tea?"

"I am not a quitter."

As she filled their glasses carefully, he sensed her willingness to do battle if she must.

"I said I'll find him, so I'll find him. But I have a responsibility to you, as my client, to lay out the facts as I see them."

"Fine. I appreciate that very much." Shoulders forward, hands playing restlessly around her plate, she stared at a spot in the middle of the table. "What are you going to do next?"

Finish lunch. He needed time to think. He thought he had known what stubborn meant, but this woman... Finally, he said, "I'm going to talk to your neighbors."

She gave him a brownie. "I should go with you. Some of them are quite elderly and suspicious of strangers. You might make them nervous."

Nervous? She had that backward—she made *him* nervous. The dark, fudgy brownie was still warm and nearly melted on his tongue, reminding him too much of the soft, sweet way she'd melted against him.... He cleared his throat harshly. "I don't make people nervous."

She lifted her eyebrows and smiled secretively while she cleared the table. "I know everyone on the block. It'll save time."

He stuffed the brownie in his mouth and chewed slowly, watching her scrape plates and stack dirty dishes in the sink. Handling this situation would be a whole lot easier if he wasn't so comfortable in her cluttered kitchen, and if her sun-kissed legs, with strong rounded calves and shapely ankles, didn't keep drawing his eye.

"I work alone." He made his escape with dignity. He even managed a little self-congratulation on handling his lapse in her bedroom. He hadn't actually kissed her. He'd accidentally touched her when bending over the toolbox. A silly mistake, but both of them were grown-up enough not to make a big deal of it.

He forced his concentration onto the job at hand.

Like many turn-of-the-century neighborhoods in the Springs, Mulberry Street was a hodgepodge of tiny cottages and Victorian-style homes. Large trees and thick hedges of boxwood and lilac offered concealment for anyone wishing to spy on Andi's house. Front and backyard fences ranged from low ornamental wire property markers to tall cedar privacy fences to chain link overgrown with woodbine. Red graveled alleys offered escape routes. Detached garages were set back on the alleys, but many residents parked at the curb. Several people worked on their lawns, but Rayne saw no porch-sitters or signs of anyone with a habit of watching the street. Depending on the point of view, Mulberry Street was either a surveillance dream or a nightmare.

Rayne spoke to neighbors, but other than praise for Mr. Simon's gardening advice, he learned nothing. He got the impression Mr. Simon was a man who took great pains not to draw attention to himself.

He spoke to Mrs. Dipwell last, who said, "I say good riddance."

Rayne perched uncomfortably on a wing chair in Mrs. Dipwell's front room. Her house smelled strongly of cleansers and air fresheners. Every smooth surface gleamed, and for fear of scuffing her immaculate floors, he kept his boots still and flat. "Why do you say that, ma'am?"

"Don't trust him." She nodded curtly, passing judgment. "I think he's one of those con artists like you see on TV. Sneaky. Ask him a question and there isn't nothing wrong with his ears, but he ignores you anyway. Pulls in that chin and hunches up his shoulders and won't say boo. He's hiding something."

"Why a con artist?"

Mrs. Dipwell smiled tightly. "Her grandma's money. Opal never spent a dime far as I could see." She snorted. "Shoot, I lived here six months before I even realized Opal was right next door! Millicent didn't help matters any. That's Andi's mother. Everything had to be perfect all the time. Stiff-necked widow lady, know what I mean? Had a good heart, though, and she was a good friend. She raised Andi right, but she was dead wrong about her mother. Always acting like there was nothing strange about Opal. Never did understand that, but that's how some people are."

The woman rolled her eyes and tapped her fingers on the sofa arm. "Old Mr. Simon showed up right after the funeral. Out of the blue. I bet he read Millicent's obituary and figured he'd found the perfect little pigeon to pluck. You give me one other good reason why an old man like him would run after a young girl like her."

Rayne hadn't a clue.

EVERYTHING ALWAYS TURNED out harder than it looked, Rayne mused as he shifted his gaze between his notes and the computer keyboard. Days of pounding the pavement had turned up zip, zilch, *nada*. He pursued a damned ghost.

The office door opened and Ford entered. Rayne grunted a greeting.

"I take it no results yet?" Ford asked.

"I'm starting to think Simon is a figment of Andi's imagination."

"Pity you do not search for Keller Poe. His life is a veritable treasure trove of information."

Rayne swung around on his chair to face his partner. "What did you find out?"

"As I suspected, he was on parole when he died." Ford sat and swung his feet atop his desk. "His untimely demise surprised his parole officer not a whit. According to him, Keller's days on the streets had been numbered. Rumors are circulating that Keller was involved in what he termed was a major score."

Rayne glanced at the oak-faced cabinet concealing the office safe. Twelve thousand dollars was a hefty sum, but did it qualify as a "major score"? "Any rumors about Simon?"

"Unfortunately, details are vague. I have feelers out. It would not displease me, however, if Keller's connection to Mr. Simon turns out to be coincidental after all." He acquired a grandfatherly smile. "I am growing rather fond of our Miss Blair."

You and me both, buddy, Rayne thought. He poked at his notes with a pencil. "What about our mystery lady?"

"I have given that matter serious consideration. It seems to me, though, it would be premature on our part to declare an emergency situation and involve the police.

Let us go through the proper channels as we are doing and see what turns up. Her giving the money to Miss Blair tells me she does not know Mr. Simon's whereabouts, either.''

Pounding sounded on the stairs. The office door burst open and Andi rushed inside. Alarmed by her wide eyes and flushed cheeks, Rayne jumped to his feet. ''What the—''

She slammed the door and cried, ''Where's the new police station? I drove around and around, but they moved it!''

Rayne and Ford exchanged a worried glance and approached Andi. They each took an arm. Her skin was clammy and she trembled, breathing raggedly. They led her to a chair, urging her to sit and calm down. Ford fixed her a cup of tea. Rayne crouched before her and she grabbed his hand in both of hers, clinging to him as if she were drowning.

''What happened?'' he asked.

She drew a deep breath then released it in a long shuddering exhale. ''He was on a motorcycle. At first I didn't think he was following me—''

''Back up. Where were you?''

''When I first saw him? At a Burger King restaurant. I keep thinking about her and wondering where she lives—''

''Who?''

''The woman in the Cadillac.'' She jumped up and rushed to a window. With one finger she eased aside a blind slat.

Rayne joined her, momentarily distracted by the alluring scent rising off her excitement-heated skin. He forced himself to move to another window. ''What am I looking for?''

"A big man. I think he's the one who stole my suitcase. He's on a motorcycle. There he is!" She tore away
from the window and the blinds clattered. She whispered, "Southwest corner. That's him!"

Scalp tightening, Rayne stared down. At the far end of
the block, across the street, a man stood next to a parked
motorcycle. He wore a dark short-sleeved shirt and jeans
and held a black helmet under one arm. His gaze was
fixed on the doorway to the stairs leading to the office.

Ford went to the storeroom and returned with a camera affixed with a zoom lens. He shot five pictures in
rapid succession and the auto-winder whirred. He invited Rayne to look. Rayne looked in time to see the man
turn his attention to a patrol car passing by. Through the
powerful telescopic lens he burned the man's fleshy features into his memory before the man put on the helmet
and swung onto the bike. The "dirtiness" on his arms
Andi had noticed before turned out to be copious tat-
tooing.

Rayne followed the bike with the camera but the angle
concealed the license plate. "That's a hog, maybe a '68."
The rider took a hand off the ape-hanger handlebars and
shifted gears. "Suicide stick. Got a springer front end
and a fat-bob tank. It's a hard tail." He lowered the
camera. "Can't be many bikes like that in town."

Andi stared openmouthed at him. "I don't understand a single word you said, but it's very impressive."

"Rayne is a connoisseur of wheeled conveyances,"
Ford explained, "especially those that are loud and dangerous." He winked at Andi. "Each to his own. Come,
have a cup of tea, my dear, and let us discuss this."

Rayne kept watching out the window, his ears straining for the powerful rumbling of a Harley-Davidson

motorcycle. "You were looking for the woman in the Cadillac?"

She slumped on a chair. Folding her arms tightly against her chest, she peered sideways at him. She seemed more defiant than contrite. "I want to talk to her about Mr. Simon. I've got to do something."

Ford handed her a cup of tea.

He lifted an admonishing finger. Every evening Rayne hand delivered a detailed report, outlining his investigation on her behalf. "I'm keeping you involved."

She dunked the tea bag up and down. "Well . . . I'm so worried about him. I keep having bad dreams. I dream he's dead and his ghost is haunting my house. He rattles things and tries to talk to me, but he can't." She turned mournful eyes on Rayne. "I have lived in that house all my life and never realized how noisy it is. Creaks and groans and funny little thumps. And a really creepy sound kind of like a sigh. Almost like it's breathing. I keep getting up and checking the locks."

"So you've been looking for the woman in the Cadillac."

She nodded sheepishly. "The way she was dressed and the car make me think she lives in one of the old neighborhoods on the west side." She sighed. "I've used two tanks of gas."

Sympathy replaced Rayne's annoyance. He patted her shoulder, noticing how the dark rose, sleeveless blouse she wore did nice things for her spun-honey complexion.

"I think I saw him first around noon," she said. "I stopped at the Burger King for something to eat. I thought he was watching me, but I wasn't really sure. Then a couple hours later I was over on Uintah and I saw a motorcycle behind me. I turned on Prospect." She pointed vaguely. "The Patty Jewett area seems right for an old Cadillac. And he followed me. I kept noticing how big he looked. Like the man who stole my suitcase. But he never got close enough for me to see for certain.''

She squeezed the tea bag with her fingers, watching dark liquid drip back into the cup. She dropped the bag in a wastebasket. "I knew for certain he was following me when I crossed Uintah again. I went through a yellow light just as it was turning red. He ran the red light." She sipped tea, looking from one man to the other over the rim of the cup.

Anger at the fat man prickled the nape of Rayne's neck and tightened his gut.

"You were very wise in not leading him to your home," Ford said.

She set the cup aside. "I don't feel wise, just scared. Excuse me." She walked to the bathroom and closed the door behind her.

Soft and low, Ford said, "A potentially dangerous situation. One which, considering our dearth of information, I am at a loss to explain."

Rayne patted the camera. "Turn this jerk over to the cops?"

"I am not in the habit of criticizing the police force, as you are well aware, but they are far more effective at investigating crimes after the fact rather than before. It also seems to me Miss Blair's shadow is not interested in approaching her. Which means he hopes she will lead him to something of interest."

"Mr. Simon. Or whatever it is he picked up."

"Exactly. However, human nature being what it is, her lack of progress could easily lead to frustration on her pursuer's part. Therein lies the danger."

Ford put the situation into nice words, but the possibilities flashing through Rayne's mind were solidly on the nasty side. The most prevalent image concerned the tattooed goon jumping Andi in a dark alley and choking what he wanted to know out of her. "What do you suggest?"

Ford gave the bathroom door a considering look. "I suggest you adapt your modus operandi to the particular situation. Include Miss Blair in your investigation."

"What?" His jaw dropped.

"Slay several proverbial birds with one stone's toss."

Rayne shook his head. "Let her tag along?"

"You can find Mr. Simon and ensure she is safe."

"No."

Ford cocked an eyebrow.

Rayne opened his mouth, but what was he supposed to say? He had a major case of the hots for his client? He was scared he'd lose control and do something really stupid? Already he teetered on the edge by finding lamebrain excuses to visit her house each evening when he could just as easily telephone or mail his progress reports. Then he compounded his idiocy by letting her talk him into staying for a glass of iced tea and cookies or a sandwich.

He slammed papers around on his desk. The mark of a good private eye was flexibility and adaptability, and he was good—when he wasn't wandering around bewitched and blinded by a pretty laugh or guileless, pewter-colored eyes. But Andi needed protection, and saving from herself.

Andi emerged from the bathroom. She halted in midstep and fiddled with her blouse collar. "Did I miss something?"

"Come on," Rayne said. "I'll take you home. We have a small change of plans. I'll explain on the way over."

Chapter Six

At home, Andi walked ahead of Rayne through the gate. Her head reeled with excitement over his invitation to come along tomorrow while he searched for Mr. Simon. "You can describe him better than I can," he'd said. Maybe it was no big deal to him, but it meant the world to her.

Alerted by a squeak of metal, she saw Mr. Dipwell trimming a snowball bush. He spotted her and tossed a pair of hedge clippers on the ground. Since learning her house had been broken into—twice—Mr. Dipwell had been slinking around like a shamed puppy. No matter how many times she assured him he wasn't in the least bit responsible, he blamed himself.

"Andi!" Mr. Dipwell called. "Andi! Wait!" He clutched the fence and gulped air. "Saw a man in your house!"

Andi's heart dropped into her belly and she recoiled from the house. She absolutely could not suffer again the sick, helpless feeling of knowing strangers had pawed through her belongings.

Rayne slid a comforting hand across her shoulder.

The old man fairly quivered as he gestured wildly at his narrow, two-story house. "I was upstairs and looked out the window. Saw a curtain move.'' Bouncing on the balls of his feet, he looked ready to jump over the fence. ''I called the cops and one looked around. Rattled doors and such, but didn't find nothing.''

''You're sure you saw a man?'' Rayne asked.

''Saw a curtain move.'' He waggled a hand loosely. ''Before the cop came, I sneaked over here. Figured I'd catch those no-good scoundrels in the act. I looked as best I could but couldn't see a durn thing. I've been watching ever since in case they come back. They haven't.''

Mr. Dipwell's overactive imagination must have gotten the best of him, transforming a trick of light or a draft blowing a curtain into a hulking burglar. Andi relaxed.

Rayne took her keys. ''I'll check it out.''

Mr. Dipwell hurried through his gate and around to Andi's. ''I'll go with you, Mr. Coplin. You're a big fella, but two's better than one. Got your gun?''

Andi and Rayne exchanged a glance and a smile. Rayne didn't carry a gun.

''Wait here with Andi, sir,'' Rayne said. ''That way if there's a problem…'' He nodded sagely, then entered the house.

Understanding filled the old man's eyes. He took Andi's elbow in a firm grip. His wide-legged stance and set jaw said he'd defend her to the death. Pleased he'd lost the hangdog expression and was back to his cheerfully belligerent self, Andi patted his leathery hand.

''Horace!'' his wife called from her front door. ''Will you please leave that poor girl alone!''

''It's okay,'' Andi replied. ''He may have seen something in my house.''

"He didn't see a blessed thing!" Her brow furrowed in exasperation. "Now he wants to be a private eye. Old man, I'm going to have you committed to the loony bin, I swear!"

"Don't swear, dear," he said with a snicker.

Rayne returned. He shook his head. "Nothing."

"You sure?"

"Yes, sir." His eyes sparkled. "You must have scared them off before they did any damage. Good thing you were watching, sir. I appreciate you calling the police."

The old man drew back his shoulders. He indicated his wife with a slight nod. Voice lowered, he said, "Man's got to be vigilant or the crooks will kill us all in our beds. She's just mad 'cause I bought new locks. Penny wise, pound foolish, that's her."

"I'm glad you're watching out for Andi, sir."

Mr. Dipwell swaggered back to his own yard. He gave Rayne a thumbs-up before resuming clipping the snowball bush.

Andi joined Rayne on the porch. "That was very kind of you to say that. You made him feel better."

Rayne scuffed his boot heel and lifted his gaze to the elm trees. "You're lucky to have an alert neighbor."

His niceness embarrassed him? Her heart did a slow melt. It would be so easy to fall in love with this big, contrary man. She opened the screen door. "Now what? You drove me home, but what about your car?"

"I'll walk back."

She sensed reluctance. About walking—or leaving her alone? "Do you at least want something to drink? Iced tea? Soda?" She made a gesture for him to enter the house. "I was thinking about making some chicken à la king. After you've been so kind, the least I can do is fix your dinner."

His lips parted and a hungry light filled his eyes. With the tip of a finger she touched his wrist at the cleft between strong tendons. "The very least. You've been going way above and beyond the call of duty."

He took a step backward. "I've got lots of paperwork. Calls to make. See you tomorrow."

Faint hurt spread through her. "What time?"

He reached the steps. "Eight."

"I'll be ready. Are you—" The telephone rang.

"You'd better answer it," he said, and strode down the steps and the walk.

Ford was on the line, asking for Rayne. She told him to wait and ran outside. Rayne was halfway down the block, marching like a soldier to battle. She called him and he returned at a jog.

To give him privacy on the phone she went to the kitchen. Standing before the open refrigerator door she stared blankly at the contents while cold air kissed her bare arms and face. Rayne confused the devil out of her. One minute he was stiff and formal, the next his warmth flowed over her. Then he'd shake himself and go cold again.

Still, it was nothing compared to how much she confused herself. Around him she felt as if someone had opened her skull and removed her brain, setting it aside for future use. She had more than enough problems without obsessing over a man who freaked if she barely touched him.

Trailing the long telephone cord, he entered the kitchen. "Thanks for running me down, man. See you in a short." He hung up with a flourish and hoisted the phone like a trophy. "Got a lead."

She shut the fridge but held on to the door for support. "Mr. Simon?"

"The other day I spoke to the manager of a coffee shop over on Nevada. He didn't know Mr. Simon, but one of his countermen does. He heard I was looking and called the office."

"He knows Mr. Simon?"

"Apparently Mr. Simon was a fairly regular customer."

"Does he know where he is? Has he seen him?" She had to sit down and clasp her shaking hands. "Is he okay?"

He held up a warning finger. "Don't get your hopes up. He hasn't seen Mr. Simon in several weeks. But he did say Simon mentioned someplace called Confirmation House. The impression is he works there. Maybe."

Andi racked her brain but drew a blank. "What is Confirmation House?"

"Doesn't ring any bells. Sounds like a mission or homeless shelter to me, but it's too late to call Social Services and find out. Ford can't find it in the directories. We'll have to wait until morning to run it down."

She pressed a fist to her pounding heart. "Oh, Rayne, you're wonderful! I was starting to think nobody knew Mr. Simon."

Jamming his hands in his back pockets and hanging his head, he shifted his weight from foot to foot. "I was bound to get lucky sometime."

"Don't be modest." She jumped to her feet. "This calls for a glass of wine. A celebration!"

"I should go." He inched toward the front door.

"One glass of wine," she coaxed. She chided herself for begging, but darn it, she didn't want him to leave.

Something akin to pain strained his brow and his lips parted as if words hovered there. "Maybe one. But no ice."

She urged him to sit while she poured the wine. "I'm glad you're letting me go with you tomorrow. I must have driven five hundred miles this week, but I guess there's a lot more to looking for someone than just looking." She handed him his wine. Hoisting her glass so the ice cubes tinkled, she exclaimed, "To the finest private eye in the business!"

He laughed.

She set about fixing dinner. While cubing chicken, she asked, "What happens if that man follows us tomorrow?"

He muttered something she didn't catch. The more she thought about it, the more it seemed as if Rayne had said, "Run him off the road and squash his head."

"Pardon?" she asked.

"I said, don't worry. I'll be watching."

ANDI GRABBED the telephone on the first ring. "Did you find it?"

Heavy silence answered and she opened her mouth to speak again when Rayne said, "How did you know it was me?"

She smiled sheepishly, not about to confess she'd been awake since 5:00 a.m. doing everything short of casting spells to make Rayne call with good news. She ventured, "Telepathy?"

Rayne laughed. "Right."

"So where is it?"

"What makes you think I found Confirmation House?"

She rolled her eyes. For a tough guy, he surely was a terrible tease. "You said you would."

"It's a soup kitchen in a church, about half a mile from the Reading Room."

"You're wonderful! Are you at the office? Shall I meet you? What's the address?"

"I'll pick you up in about fifteen minutes. Andi, don't get your hopes up. He probably won't be there."

Even fifteen minutes tortured her. She kept brooding about how a counterman at a coffee shop knew Mr. Simon well enough to give them a lead, when Mr. Simon was her best friend and she knew nothing. Doubts gnawed at her—was she Mr. Simon's friend?

By the time Rayne arrived and she locked her front door, the doubts had bloomed by mammoth proportions. "What if I did something to make him angry? What if he doesn't want to see me?"

Rayne nudged her elbow. "What's this?"

She looped an arm around a porch post. "He means so much to me, but what if I don't mean that much to him?" She sank to the top step and wrapped her arms around her knees.

"Andi, everything you've said—"

"We joked about him being my family. What if I put too much pressure on him and he got tired of it? What if he's avoiding me?"

"He isn't." His fingertips twitched, beckoning.

She glanced over her shoulder at the house. "This is like after Mom died and I needed tons of activity to keep from going crazy. My grandmother was pretty flaky. Maybe I inherited being neurotic from her."

He released a heavy breath and sat beside her. "You aren't neurotic."

"Mom and I were close. She was tough, but she had to be. She took care of me and her mother. Grandma was difficult, especially when she had migraines. Mom was a good mother, always concerned, always there for me." She pulled her skirt hem through her fingers. "Then I spent so many years taking care of her, and after she was gone... I latched onto Mr. Simon."

"Stand-in family."

"He might feel pressured or... frustrated. I keep thinking if he's in trouble, he'd contact me. He knows I would do anything to help. So then I think, well, either he's dead or he doesn't want my help. I don't know which is worse."

Rayne patted her arm. "Usually by the time people come to me, they expect the worst. Parents scared their kids are dealing dope. Or people who think their spouses are cheating. Employers who suspect dishonest workers. Usually, what they suspect is a lot worse than reality."

"Really?"

"Trust me." He tapped his temple with a finger. "The worst scenarios are always up here."

"What if he doesn't want to see me?"

"At least you'll know he's okay."

She eyed her yard. Without Mr. Simon's care, it had turned brown in patches and weeds invaded the flower beds. Clouds building in the northern skies said it might rain later this afternoon, but Colorado weather was unpredictable. Mr. Simon knew she'd forget to water and would let the grass burn—which at this altitude took only a few days. If he had a choice, he wouldn't let it happen.

"You really are a nice guy."

"Doing my job." He got to his feet and held out his hand. She took it. He gave her fingers a comforting squeeze before releasing her.

By the time they reached the church, the butterflies in Andi's stomach danced the tango and her palms were sweating.

What would she say if Mr. Simon was here? "Hi, been worried about you? Glad you're okay? Drop by the house if you feel like it?"

She entered the double doors of the Pikes Peak Church of Confirmation, a turn-of-the-century building made of native red sandstone with twin Gothic-styled spires and a rose-patterned, stained glass window facing due west toward the mountains. The soup kitchen called Confirmation House was in the church basement, down a long flight of concrete steps.

People crowded long tables, eating eggs and oatmeal. The majority of diners were men. Young and old, the only thing they seemed to share was an air of being lost. Andi searched grizzled, ill-washed faces for Mr. Simon. Seeing so many down-on-their-luck people in one place disconcerted her. In her silk pullover and embroidered skirt, she felt like an overdressed intruder.

They entered the kitchen. Steamy and noisy, it reminded Andi of a high school cafeteria. A few men dressed in white with paper hats worked the steam tables. Most of the workers were women, each wearing a bright yellow name tag reading Confirmation League Volunteer. One of them brusquely directed Rayne and Andi upstairs to Michelle Jackson's office.

Climbing back up the concrete steps, Andi said, "That woman was rude. She didn't even let you finish your question."

"The first thing you learn in this business is that no one has to talk to you. Lucky for me, most people will tell me anything."

"Really?"

He gave her a dry look. "You do."

Her cheeks warmed. "Well..."

"People like the sound of their own voices and strangers are safe. It's amazing what people will say, especially on the phone. There it is." He pointed at a partially open door with a brass nameplate: M. Jackson, Administrator.

Rayne knocked.

The woman behind the desk beckoned them to come in. Stacks of papers flanked her. Her coffee cup had a picture of a snarling cartoon cat with the caption, Have a Nice Day? You First.

Michelle Jackson arose and shook hands with Rayne. A tall black woman with eyes the color of copper pennies, she had a no-nonsense manner, but her eyes were kind.

"Rayne Coplin, ma'am. I'm a private investigator. We're looking for a missing person."

"We get plenty of those. Have a seat, sir. Miss. Pardon the mess, but have to keep the bureaucrats happy. How they can call it nonprofit when the paper companies are making so much money off me is a puzzle." She patted a tall stack of forms. "But before we go wasting time, have you gone through the Salvation Army?"

Andi opened her mouth to ask what she meant, but Rayne said, "We don't think the gentleman we're looking for is homeless, ma'am. But yes, I entered his name in the National register."

Andi leaned forward. "I think he has a job. A man said Mr. Simon mentioned Confirmation House."

Michelle's smile faded. Rayne sat taller and lifted his eyebrows expectantly. Fear and excitement clashed in Andi's belly. This woman did know something.

"And who might you be, miss?"

"Andi Blair. I work at the Reading Room over on Tejon. I'm Mr. Simon's friend."

The woman leaned back in her chair and her smile returned. "Miss Andi..."

Andi had to clench her fists and thighs in order to stay seated. "You do know him! Is he here? Is he all right? I'm so worried about him. Can you—"

The administrator shook her head. "Truth is, I'm worried about him, too. Man like him, well, he's different. Reliable. He's been like clockwork, not a peep of trouble."

Andi slumped on the chair.

"We haven't seen him in weeks. He just disappeared." She snapped her fingers.

Rayne said, "Ma'am, he guarded his personal life close to the vest. Did he work here?"

Michelle nodded. "Guarded. Uh-huh. He thought the world of you, Miss Blair. Would have cut off his arm rather than have you think poorly of him."

"Why would I think poorly of him? He's my best friend. Have you any idea where he went?"

"Mr. Simon wouldn't touch a meal or take a bed until he'd earned it. He impressed me, and kept on impressing me. I only have budget for three part-timers. He's one of them. Four hours a day, six days a week. I could set my watch by him."

Michelle might have offered the words as a means to soothe Andi, but they had the opposite effect. Her scalp prickled and her stomach ached. She sensed a bombshell hovering somewhere overhead.

Rayne nudged her knee and gave her a significant look she interpreted as "Be quiet." She settled back on the chair, toying with her bangle bracelets, circling them round and round her wrists until her flesh warmed from the friction.

Rayne pulled out a notebook and pencil. "It would help if you'd give us his first name and his Social Security number, ma'am."

"Simon is his first name. Everyone calls him Mr. Simon the way they call me Miss Michelle. It's Simon Foulkes, with an *e*." She tugged open a drawer and the metal desk rattled and creaked. Placing a folder on her desk, she covered it with a protective hand. "I have policies about privacy."

Rayne murmured understanding. He darted a glance at Andi. She sat rigid, leaning forward, her eyes wide and her jaw strained, as if she'd received a monumental blow. She gripped her skirt in both hands.

"Men lose their way and end up here, but most like being lost. Usually I take a phone number and if the man wants to call back, he calls."

"This situation is special." He gave Andi a reassuring smile. The look in her eyes made the hairs lift on the nape of his neck. What was wrong with her? "A man died under strange circumstances in Andi's yard. We have reason to believe Mr. Simon may have witnessed the death. When was the last time you saw him?"

Wearing a considering expression, Michelle stroked her jaw. "Two weeks ago last Monday."

At length she picked up the folder. "A man like Mr. Simon gives me hope. We keep trying, doing our best, hoping, praying." She swung her head from side to side. "But some folks? They can learn, but the learning doesn't stick." Her fingers crunched the folder. She handed it to Rayne with a quick, reluctant thrust. "You aren't the only ones looking for him."

Andi whispered, "A woman? In her fifties perhaps?"

"A pair of cons."

Blinking slowly, Andi cocked her head. "Cons? Like Newman and Redford in *The Sting?*"

Rayne studied the folder contents with a dispassionate eye, but what he read chilled him. Keller Poe made sense now. "Convicts," he said quietly. "Ex-convicts."

Andi asked, "How can you tell?"

Michelle looked to Rayne and he felt a bond of sympathy. Both of them had jobs that gave them insights into the worst aspects of humanity. Her eyes asked him how far he wished to go to protect Andi from ugly truths. His heart said go all the way; his head knew differently.

Michelle said, "Every one of those faces has a story, and after a while, well, they're easy to read. I see them all."

"Was one of them Keller Poe?"

"They didn't offer names, I didn't ask. All I know is they were up to no good."

"What did they want with Mr. Simon?" As he spoke, Rayne busied himself transcribing information from the folder into his notebook.

"Wanted to know where he was. But I have policies," Michelle explained to Andi, "If someone asks, I take names and send them to the Salvation Army. They have a national register for families trying to find lost relatives. Far as I'm concerned, folks who end up here have lost most everything anyway. No need to take away their privacy, too."

Without looking up or slowing in his note-taking, Rayne asked, "When did they come by?"

"On a Saturday, late afternoon." Her copper-penny eyes flashed. "I don't cotton to no-accounts filling up my doorway and trying to stare me down. I do the staring when it's necessary." She idly shuffled papers and toyed with loose pencils. "Mr. Simon showed up at 6:00 a.m.

Monday morning, just like always. I told him the men were looking for him. He asked who they were and what they wanted." She closed her eyes and shook her head, for a moment looking disgusted. "I was busy. I should have taken more time to talk to him, but next I looked, he was gone. Left his hat and apron and disappeared. Haven't seen him since."

"Can you describe the men?"

"One was a big fellow. Fat, but not soft." She held out an arm and stroked it with her fingertips. "Prison tattoos. Self-inflicted."

Rayne tried to catch Andi's eye, but she stared intently at Michelle.

"The other one still stank like prison. Greasy, jumpy little string bean of a man. Couldn't stand still." Her face tensed in concentration. "Had black hair. Now that I remember, his hair looked like it was painted on."

Andi lurched forward on the chair. "Keller Poe! That's him. He's the man who died in my backyard. What—" She cleared her throat. "What could those men possibly want with Mr. Simon?"

Rayne knew he had to tell her.

Michelle clucked her tongue. "He just loves you to pieces. Thinks the world of you. He said you have a pretty house and you bake—"

"Miss Jackson, please."

Rayne handed back the folder. "Thank you for your help, Miss Jackson." He gave her a business card. "If Simon contacts you or if anyone else asks you about him, please call me. Night or day."

"What aren't you telling me, Rayne? Miss Jackson?"

He closed his notebook and put it and the pencil back in his pocket.

Andi clutched his arm. "I have a right to know everything. What did those men want with Mr. Simon?"

Here he was, the bad guy again, delivering bad news. Bearing ill tidings seemed to be turning into his life's mission. He huffed. "Birds of a feather. Simon's an ex-con, too."

Andi stood and clutched her purse to her breast. Her chin quivered and moisture glazed her eyes. In a tiny voice, she asked, "Excuse me, is there a ladies' room?" Michelle directed her down the hall.

"You spoke those words in a hard way, Mr. Coplin." Michelle's tone chastised him, but her eyes held compassion. "Andi didn't have a clue, did she?"

"Neither of us did. Some things are making sense, though. The way Simon split tells me he was expecting those men. One of them is dead. The other one knows who Andi is, where she lives and where she works. Do you know why Simon went to prison? How long he was in?"

She *tsk*'d softly, shaking her head. "No to both, sir. He didn't offer, I didn't pry. As long as he kept his nose clean, it didn't matter. I know he wasn't on parole, but nothing else. My feeling is, he was in a long time. He had habits."

Prison habits, one of them being secrecy.

"But he's a good man. Whatever lesson he had to learn, he learned it. Worked for me nearly fourteen months and I never had a moment of trouble. Kept to himself, stayed clean, did his job."

Andi returned. Her eyes were bleak and sad, but dry.

Rayne hurt with her. Finding out a loved one was a crook was akin to having a pile driver ram into your belly. It left you breathless, stunned—and waiting for the next blow to fall.

He asked Michelle for permission to speak to the kitchen workers about Simon and she granted it. He invited Andi outside to talk.

Going from the coolness of the church to the bright heat outside made him a little breathless. Sunshine beat down on his head, warming his hair and the back of his shirt. Squinting up at the cloud-pocked sky, he asked, "Are you all right?"

She shook her head.

"We need to talk."

She held up a hand for him to wait. Drawing back, she straightened her spine and closed her eyes. She breathed deeply, strong, steadying breaths. "What else?"

Hurt seeped from her. Even her hair had lost some of its shine. He reached for her, pulled back his hand, then anger surged through him. Who was he trying to kid? Emotionally she'd already hooked him. Too late to play Mr. Cool and pretend her pain didn't matter.

He draped an arm around her shoulders. "Let's walk and talk. I think better on my feet."

She nodded.

"This adds a new dimension."

"I don't think I want to hear it." She matched his stride and her hip brushed his. She held his waist loosely.

He didn't want to say it. What he wanted was to take her someplace cool and quiet and let her cry on his shoulder, then talk about any or everything other than the old jailbird who'd broken her heart. "Hear me out."

She sighed.

"I suspect some digging will turn up the fact that Simon and Keller were in prison together." They reached the street corner. He tugged lightly at a strand of her hair. "Are you listening?"

"I'm listening," she said wearily.

"Miss Jackson knew he had a record when she hired him. He wouldn't have been fired if one of his buddies showed up to chat. But he ran and Keller ended up dead."

Andi faltered and he tightened his grip. "He didn't kill Keller," she insisted.

"What I think is, Keller pulled the knife to threaten Simon and he tripped. Simon and whoever that fat joker is panicked and ran. But why would Keller pull the knife?"

Her shoulder lifted in a quick shrug and her fingers tightened convulsively on his waist.

"An old debt maybe. Or Simon was holding something or was supposed to hold something. The possibilities are endless, but Simon's running is the key. Whatever connected him and Keller is something he didn't want you or Miss Jackson or the police to know about."

"You heard Miss Jackson! He's a good man. He paid for his crimes and learned his lesson."

He stroked her arm slowly, soothingly. "Listen to me. Keller was a habitual thief. He robbed jewelry stores, but who knows what new tricks he learned in prison. Bank robbery? Simon may have been his bagman."

"What's that?"

Hard sorrow in her voice made him flinch. "Someone who holds hot merchandise until it's cool enough to get rid of."

Her jaw acquired a stubborn set. "He had dinner with me on Sunday. He mowed my lawn. He hadn't committed any robberies and he wasn't scared. Everything was fine."

"I know what you're feeling."

"No, you don't!" She shoved away from him.

Yes, he did, damn it, and it hurt. Every muscle in his body quivered with ghost pains and old wounds. "Do you want to talk or argue?"

Her eyes misted and she swiped them with the back of her hand. "Talk."

He jammed his hands in his back pockets and looked up and down the street. They'd stopped in the shade of an elm tree and beyond the boundaries of coolness, the world was bright and hot.

"Simon left you the note because he knows the fat man knows who you are. He did you a favor. He offered good advice. Take it."

Her profile looked as if it were carved from stone.

"You've run up a big bill already. How much more are you going to spend to find a crook?"

"Don't call him that."

"I know he's your friend and you love him, but you need to face reality. He knew Keller, he knows the fat man is looking for him. There's a reason behind it, Andi."

"A perfectly good reason," she whispered, her lips barely moving.

"He'll lie to you. I guarantee it. One thing all criminals have in common is lying."

"No he won't."

"He already has."

Her throat worked. "He had a good reason."

For a moment his mother's face was superimposed over Andi's. Her voice came from Andi's mouth—denial, willingness to suspend disbelief and overlook any and all evidence reflecting poorly on her beloved.

"Andi, here's my professional opinion—"

"I don't want your opinion. I contracted your professional services. If you need money, I'll pay my bill up-to-date and increase the retainer. But you will keep looking."

She stalked away, her sandals slapping the sidewalk and her skirt ruffling crisply in the light breeze.

Stunned by the demonstration of steel core under a deceptively soft personality, he stared at her back. He snorted in exasperation and jogged to catch up with her.

"I don't care what he's done," Andi insisted. "I don't care why he's hiding. I don't care how much it costs. Find him."

He caught her arm and she stopped, but she refused to meet his eyes. "You don't want to believe he's done anything wrong. But you—"

"None of it matters!"

Her shout startled him. Judging by her wide eyes and parted lips, it startled her, too. Hot color bloomed on her cheeks. What was happening? He'd never argued with a client before. Needing distance to gather his composure, he stepped back.

She touched her fingers to her lips. "I didn't mean to yell. But please, find him."

"At least give yourself time to consider what you really want to do."

"I don't need to think about it because there's nothing to consider." Her eyes flashed silver. "Simon Foulkes is my grandfather."

Chapter Seven

"Are you sure?" Rayne asked. One eyebrow lifted, the other lowered as he regarded Andi with suspicion.

Andi returned his perusal. She felt strange after her outburst; it had taken her initial shock with it and left her empty and off balance. She hadn't had a fight like this since her mother was alive and she'd fought constant battles with the doctors over her care. She had not liked those fights and she didn't like this.

But darn it, Simon was her family! Why hadn't she figured this out before?

"We need to talk to the people in the kitchen," she said, and walked back to the church.

With almost detached interest Andi listened to Rayne interview the soup kitchen workers. Once assured Miss Michelle had given her permission, the volunteers spoke easily, but none had much to offer. They all liked Mr. Simon, he'd been a hard worker, he was always polite....

Her grandfather. Supposedly dead forty years, mourned by his wife and daughter to the extent that neither could bear to mention his name—liars!

The men who worked in the kitchen reacted to Rayne and his questions the way junkyard dogs reacted to rattling chain link fences, all ears and suspicion. To a man they answered his questions in mumbled monosyllables.

Had he told anyone he was her grandfather? Unfocused anger tightened her forehead and she feared if she opened her mouth and tried to speak she'd start yelling.

Seemingly unperturbed, Rayne passed out business cards. He requested a phone call if the fat man with tattoos returned or if anyone heard any rumors about Simon's location.

How could he be so cool, she wondered. Simon Foulkes was her grandfather!

After Rayne finished interviewing the soup kitchen workers, he and Andi walked down the block to a sub shop. Numbed by all that had happened, she followed where he led and sat where he told her to sit.

While he ordered lunch at the counter, she pulled a pen and an old grocery list from her purse. Bending over the blank side of the paper, she doodled notes.

Rayne waited at the counter for his order. Andi's mood disturbed him. First she'd been so combative, then she turned deathly quiet. Under that soft shell she was a tough lady, but how much could she take? He kept thinking about Mrs. Dipwell calling Simon a con artist. Con men used a person's weakness. Andi's weakness was her need for someone to love and take care of—her need for family. Why not a long-lost grandpa?

He idly tapped the tall yellow countertop and breathed the aroma of cold meats, sliced vegetables and Italian sauces. Vague anger churned his gut. He wanted to yell at someone, but the someone who would benefit had pulled a vanishing act. What the hell was the old man up to?

He carried a ham-and-cheese sub, potato chips and soft drinks to the table.

Her smile caught him off guard. "He is my grandfather." Soft, smiling words, shored by steel and total conviction. She picked up half the sandwich and bit into it with a hearty chomp.

He picked up the other half. "You don't have proof."

She played with a sheet of paper. "I made a list. There's all kinds of evidence." Her smile turned tart. She doodled little tornadoes on the paper with a purple ballpoint pen. "You've heard me talk about Mom and Grandma. And I told you about my father, too."

He nodded.

"My father died when I was only six months old, yet I know him. There are pictures of him all over the house. He was a presence, he still is. But have you ever heard me say a word about my grandfather?"

One of the first skills he'd developed as a P.I. was a knack for reading upside down. Decorated with purple flowers, animals, spirals and hearts, her list read, "Mom, Grandma, Died in the war, No pictures, Grandma's ring."

"Grandma never talked about him, ever. The few times I asked, she'd say he died and change the subject. Mom didn't talk about him, either. No arguments or anything, he just didn't exist."

Rayne held suspicious thoughts about the counterman who'd given them the juicy tidbit concerning Confirmation House. Had Simon tired of waiting for them to stumble onto the "truth" and nudged them with a phone call? Maybe the next step was a ransom demand or a plea for Andi to bail him out of trouble. He made a mental note to personally check out the counterman.

She reached across the table and tapped his hand. "Are you listening?"

"Go ahead."

"Mom and Grandma, I loved them dearly. But they had faults. Mom was...intolerant. Appearances meant everything. She'd have cut off her foot rather than let anyone think she was less than perfect. A lot of Grandma's craziness was Mom's fault. She never left the house and she was convinced people were trying to kill her. She needed professional help, but Mom refused to admit there was a problem."

Rayne knew people like Andi's mother—his mother was the same way. When his brother had gone to prison, she'd insisted, probably still insisted to this day, that he'd been framed. Keep up appearances at all costs, evidence be damned.

"Simon must have waited until Mom died, but he couldn't take the chance Mom or Grandma had turned me against him. He's afraid I'm like Mom, afraid I can't forgive him." She pursed her lips. "I was robbed."

Rayne grudgingly admitted the logic but not the conclusion. "I still advise you stop looking for him."

"Thank you, but no. We'll find him."

"He was involved with Keller Poe."

"Keller Poe died accidentally. My grandfather didn't have anything to do with it."

Her quick shift from Mr. Simon, friend, to grandfather, long-lost family, made Rayne uneasy. "The perfect little pigeon to pluck..." Mrs. Dipwell's words haunted him. He said, "As soon as he found out Keller was looking for him, he ran."

"If those men were looking for me, I'd run, too."

He knew stubborn people, but never anyone so ingenuous. Rayne laughed—it was either that or lose his temper. The dry, sour look she lowered on him made him bite down on his inner cheek. He finished his sandwich.

"I know what you're thinking," she said quietly. She wiped her hands on a paper napkin. "You think I'm ignoring the facts. But facts don't matter to me now. He may have done some bad things, but he's a good man. I won't turn my back on him."

The facts he had were circumstantial and confusing, but every instinct, inner alarm and gut feeling jangled his nerves, telling him the old man was up to no good and Andi was setting herself up for major heartbreak.

Nevertheless, he dragged out his notepad. "I've got an address. Chances of him being there are slim to none, but we can talk to the neighbors."

Her smile, shining with approval and pleasure, undid him. He drowned in the soft gray pools of her eyes. He was falling hard for this stubborn, funny, determined, bewildering woman and didn't know how to stop. "Finish your sandwich."

"You think I'm silly," she said.

"I don't."

She finished her lunch, folded her list and slid it into her purse. She slung her purse over her shoulder. "I know you're concerned, but I'm tougher than I look. I do what I have to do and I don't get all choked up about it. So let's go check his address."

Simon's address was located in a pocket of small houses and apartment buildings a few blocks off Nevada Avenue.

"This is it?" Andi studied the row of apartments stepped up a steep hill; they shared a wooden porch with a tin roof.

The roof sagged and the porch floor buckled. All six apartments needed paint, and window screens hung in rusty tatters. Two large elm trees in front were dying. Fallen branches, blown newspapers and other trash littered the yard. Tough bunches of prairie grass and weeds pocked the dirt and pushed up through cracks in the sidewalk. The place had a mean, sullen air, as if mocking the neat, doll-sized houses on either side.

Her grandfather couldn't live in a place too nasty to house a rat. As soon as she found him, he was moving in with her.

She followed Rayne to the last apartment on the east end. The door sagged on its hinges. A ghost of a number six on the wood showed where a door marker had once hung.

Rayne knocked, waited, then knocked again.

The door hinges creaked and Andi's heart leapt into her throat, but the dark, suspicious face peering out did not belong to her grandfather. An elderly man with salt-and-pepper hair and a deeply lined face looked Rayne and Andi up and down. "Whatcha want?"

"We're looking for a gentleman named Simon Foulkes. This is the address we were given."

The man shook his head and opened the door wide enough for Andi to see a one-room apartment, sparsely furnished but clean. A smell of garlic and tomato sauce wafted from a galley-sized kitchenette. A baseball game played on a television set. "I ain't Simon nobody."

Rayne asked, "Have you lived here long?"

"You a cop?"

"No, sir."

"Didn't think so. Why you looking for this Simon?"

Andi said, "He's my grandfather. He's missing. Do you know him?"

"I moved in this week. Don't know nobody." He smiled, showing gold-capped teeth, letting them know no hostility was intended. "Don't wanna know nobody. Wanna watch the game and drink my beer in peace."

Rayne cracked a smile. "Who manages these apartments?"

The man leaned his head out the doorway and looked at the rickety porch with loose boards and cracked posts. He snickered. "Manage? Yeah, that's what she does all right. Manages it real good." He laughed out loud, then wiped his mouth with the back of one hand. "Name's Hazel Gooch. Howzat for a name, eh?"

Aware of another pair of eyes, Andi looked at the adjoining apartment. A boy watched them through the window.

The old man cocked his thumb. "Got herself an office downtown. Near by the Goodwill store. Got a lot of airs, she does, but this place is cheap."

"Thank you, sir."

The old man shut the door. Andi returned the boy's smile and he ducked out of sight before popping back into view with an even bigger smile.

She stepped closer to the window. Rust and old cobwebs didn't stop the boy from flattening his nose against the screen and making a face.

"Hi, do you know Simon Foulkes?"

"Mr. Simon, yeah." He looked from one to the other. His dark eyes held the wise light of a child forced to rely too much on himself. "He's cool."

"He's my grandfather. I'm very worried about him."

The boy looked her up and down. "Your grandpa? I ain't seen you before."

"Does he have many visitors?"

"Nah, just me." He rested his arms on the windowsill and his chin on his arm. His forehead pressed the screen and a tuft of glossy black hair poked through a small tear. "He plays checkers real good. Wanna see my plant?"

Before Rayne or Andi could reply, he disappeared. In thirty seconds he returned. He cradled an old teacup with a broken handle and cracked rim containing a philodendron with four glossy leaves. "Mr. Simon showed me. See, you stick it in water and it gets hairy, then you put it in the dirt. Cool, huh? I growed it myself."

An image formed of Mr. Simon—Grandfather—patiently turning soil in her flower beds. Lifting dirt clods to his nose, inhaling the clean earth smell. Her chest ached.

"Do you know where Mr. Simon went?" Rayne asked.

"Everybody's looking for him. And boy, is old lady Gooch mad." He giggled, but his laughter held a strained note.

"Why is she mad?"

"'Cause. Mama says Mr. Simon's a deadbeat and don't pay his rent, but that ain't why she's mad." His impish eyes held a secret he was dying to tell.

Andi asked, "Do you know why?"

"The bad men." Suddenly solemn, the boy drew away from the window and held the plant to his chest. "Maybe you're bad guys, too. I'm not supposed to talk to strangers."

Rayne smiled. "I'm a private eye. Name's Coplin."

The boy's eyes grew round and his lips parted. "No joke?"

"Miss Blair hired me to find Mr. Simon. He's a missing person."

"You got a badge?"

"No."

Hopefulness colored his face. "A gun?"

"Afraid not, partner. But I have a business card." He brought out his wallet and produced a card. He used one finger to hold it against the window.

The boy breathed a soft, "Wow. Like Magnum. Cool."

"Did you see the bad men? Did they go inside Mr. Simon's apartment?"

"Yeah." He touched the card through the screen. "They broke the door."

"Do you remember what day this was?"

The boy fidgeted and played with the plant leaves. Downcast eyes said he wanted to be brave, but the bad men had scared him. "I dunno. Same day old lady Gooch came for the rent. She got mad. Says I done it, but I didn't do nothing. She was yelling at Mama and Mama yelled, too."

"What did she say you'd done, son?"

"Broke the furniture. I don't break things. Mama says I'm good and I am. I got straight A's in school."

"The bad men broke the furniture."

"I told Mama, but she says it's none of our beeswax. They was real mad at Mr. Simon." He nodded and added indignantly, "They used lots of dirty words."

"How many were there?"

"Two."

"Do you remember what they looked like?"

The boy's face tensed in concentration. "One was real fat. He broke the door. He punched it!" He made a fist and socked an imaginary foe.

"What about the other man? Do you remember what he looked like?"

"Some white guy. The other guy was real scary." He pulled a monster face and crossed his eyes. "He was a giant."

"Do you remember what they said? Did you hear them talking?"

"Lots of dirty words." He pressed his nose and lips against the screen, flattening his features. "Said killer's telling fairy tales." He looked from one to the other as if he expected them to argue about the truth of an adult doing something so ridiculous as telling fairy tales.

Andi wondered if Rayne thought the same thing she thought. Killer—Keller.

Rayne spoke to the boy a few more minutes, but he offered nothing else. They turned to leave and the boy called, "Hey, lady. When you find Mr. Simon, tell him my plant is growing real good."

Tears scratched her eyes. "Sure." Head down, she hurried to the Jeep. She stood for a moment with her eyes squeezed shut until the urge to cry passed.

Rayne touched her shoulder. "Are you all right?"

Wishing he'd hold her, she nodded. "When I was a little girl I had an imaginary Uncle Bill. Everyone else had dads and grandpas and uncles, so I made one up. I used to play checkers with him. It drove my mom crazy to find me playing both sides of the board." She laughed and shook her head. "All right, all right, so I'm sentimental. Where do we go next?"

"Let's see if anyone else is home, then we'll talk to old lady Gooch." He glanced at apartment number six. "I have a feeling she'll have some interesting comments to make."

Nobody answered their knocking at any of the other apartments, so they drove downtown and found a property management office half a block from the blue-painted Goodwill store. Hazel Gooch was in her thirties and wore a gray suit with the aplomb of a runway model. Auburn hair framed high cheekbones and perfect makeup. The woman shook hands crisply; even her smile was crisp. "What can I do for you?"

"I'm a private investigator, Miss Gooch. Is there someplace we can talk? I'd like to ask some questions about one of your tenants."

Her smile wilted and Andi could see her thinking, *I'm not getting a commission for this.* She brought up her wristwatch, letting them know her time was very valuable. "I have a few minutes, I suppose."

Rayne wore a cool, professional expression. If Hazel's increasingly put-upon demeanor offended him, he didn't let it show.

"I hope this won't take long. I'm expecting some clients."

Rayne read the address and mentioned Simon's name. Hazel's face twisted. "I hate renting to those kind of people, but what I can do? The law is on their side."

Andi bristled.

Hazel crossed her arms. "Bad enough he skipped on the rent, but he trashed the place, too. Have you any idea what a nightmare it is to be a rental agent in this town? Apartments are scarce, houses are nonexistent, then you get those kind in and they make it hard on everyone."

"Excuse me, Miss Gooch," Andi said, fighting down the urge to scream. "You're talking about my grandfather."

"Oh." Hazel perked. "Your grandfather owes me six hundred dollars." Her expectant pause made Andi wonder if she was supposed to whip out her checkbook. Andi tightened her grip on her purse and glared until Hazel turned impatiently back to Rayne.

Rayne said, "You rented apartment six to another gentleman."

"I give tenants in that area one week in arrears before I lock them out. If I don't, they walk all over me. I don't put up with it. And let's not mention the damage he did."

Another expectant pause was followed by a martyred sigh. "He completely trashed it. I had to hire a man to shovel everything out and haul it to the dump. I couldn't salvage anything."

Andi gasped. "You threw away his belongings?"

"I cleaned the apartment to make it habitable for a tenant who pays his rent. Your grandfather, you say? Is he senile?" She lifted a shoulder. "Maybe we can settle this out of court."

"What about his clothing? His books, his papers?"

"He destroyed a sofa and a mattress. He tore up floorboards and ripped outlets out of the walls."

"You didn't have any right to throw away his things!"

"He owes me six hundred dollars for damages and back rent. I'm responsible for those apartments. I'm not responsible for whatever garbage deadbeats leave laying around. Are you his guardian? Six hundred may seem like a paltry sum, but it's the principle of the thing."

Andi jumped to her feet. Trembling from head to toe, she clenched her fists. "My grandfather is not a vandal and he didn't tear up that apartment. And he's not senile!" She stalked out and slammed the door behind her.

Outside on the sidewalk, she breathed deeply to clear Hazel's cheap perfume and rotten attitude from her nostrils.

Rayne joined her within minutes. "Chill out."

"Did you hear what she said about my grandfather? I, I—oh, I could just choke her!"

Swinging his head side to side, he strolled to his Jeep.

"No wonder you aren't interested in me. I bet women like that fall all over themselves to catch your attention!"

He turned his head slowly. "What did you say?"

"I bet this whole city is one big smorgasbord for you. I'm surprised you don't carry a gun to fight them off." She snorted. "Not that you'd want to. Especially when they look like Hazel Gooch."

First one side of his mouth then the other pulled into an incredulous smile.

Hearing what she'd just said, she shifted her weight from foot to foot. A slow burn started on the crest of her cheekbones and radiated outward until even her neck and ears turned hot.

She felt stupid and unattractive, and tangled up with worry about her grandfather. Too much had happened today; she'd had too many shocks. Why did he have to stand there so gorgeous and calm with his eyes dark as midnight, reading her every miserable thought? "I don't know why I said that," she whispered.

He idly plucked invisible lint off his light denim shirt.

"I'm sorry. I didn't mean it."

Wry humor lighted his eyes as if to say, "You did, too." The heat on her face turned into a flash-fire.

"I've always admired people who can release their emotions," Rayne said. "Me, I get bellyaches. Probably end up with ulcers someday." He turned toward the Jeep. "Come on. I've got a real private eye job for you."

She placed a hand on his back and his muscles flexed. "I am sorry." He turned around and her hand grazed his ribs and ended up below his shirt pocket. She should have moved her hand, but his calmness held irresistible allure.

He put the ball of his thumb under her chin and pressed until she lifted her face. "I offer my clients one of two things. Either I save them money or I give them peace of mind. If yelling at me makes you feel better, then consider it part of the package."

"Now I feel really stupid."

"Don't."

He slid his thumb along the line of her jaw and eased his fingertips to her ear. His hand so gentle on her face untangled her emotions. When he slid his fingers over her cheek, her eyelids lowered. Why didn't he kiss her? She knew he wanted to—his want encircled her like an electric aura.

It was the strangest thing.... Here she stood on a downtown sidewalk, under the bright hot sun, with most of her brain paralyzed by the shock of learning she had a grandfather who might be in deadly peril, and yet a small part of her only cared about knowing why Rayne didn't kiss her. More than kiss her—hold her and love her and satisfy the burning curiosity and aching desire he aroused.

She whispered, "Rayne?"

He uttered a low groan almost lost in exhalation and slid his hand around her neck, under her hair, drawing her upward, meeting her halfway. He kissed her lightly, gently, giving her only enough of his smooth supple lips to make her burn for more. He drew back with a frown.

"This isn't right," he murmured, and dragged in a long, harsh breath. Giving his car keys a firm shake, he stepped aside and opened the passenger door.

For once she agreed fully with him. Kissing on the street wasn't right. That activity should take place in the privacy of her home—or even his stark apartment.

In silence, he drove them the short distance to his office.

Once there, he politely urged her to help herself to tea or coffee. Behind his desk, he listened to phone messages. Andi studied framed certificates and photographs on the walls. All the photographs were of Ford: wearing a police uniform; in groups of officials; shaking hands with the mayor; with various, stunningly attractive women. She wondered where Rayne kept his photos. She wondered when he'd get around to discussing or doing something about what he'd started outside the property management office.

He opened a door, revealing a storeroom with gray metal shelving stacked to the ceiling with cardboard boxes, telephone books and thick bundles of computer printouts. "It'll take some time to figure out how long he was in prison and for what. But we can start looking here."

"What is all this?"

"City directories, voter rolls, old phone books. He lived somewhere before he went to prison. Maybe his old neighborhood is safer than your neighborhood."

He acted as if he'd never touched her. She balked. "Did I do something wrong?"

He hauled a cardboard carton out of the storeroom. "No." He dropped it on the floor in front of the couch.

"I didn't mean to lose my temper. But that woman said the wrong things at the wrong time."

"You didn't do anything wrong." He straightened and clamped a hand on his hip. He pushed his hair off his forehead. He smiled, which confused her even more. "This is nuts."

"What?"

"Ever want something you know you can't have, something it's wrong to want?"

She thought for a moment, then shook her head. Her wants were simple. Hard work, lots of good food to cook and eat, a little fun, a family to cherish—Rayne Coplin. Nothing wrong with wanting any of those.

"I never mix business with pleasure. It's my number one rule."

Understanding dawned. "Oh."

"Rules are easy to follow when there's no reason to break them." He lowered his head and his shoulders shook with silent laughter. "I don't usually like my clients. I usually don't think about them at all. Do my job, collect my fee, go on to the next one. Do you see the problem here?"

She perched a hip on the corner of Ford's desk and twisted a paper clip out of shape in her hand. "I'm not sure." She swung her foot, watching her sandal flash under the polished cotton ruffle on her skirt.

"Damn, Andi, you're going to make me say it."

"Is that bad?"

He waggled his eyebrows. "There's a time and a place. Right now isn't it."

"I see." She lowered her eyelids and grinned. He did like her. She wasn't imagining the attraction. Her mood lightened considerably.

He held up an admonishing finger. "At the moment we have a strictly professional relationship."

The telephone rang. "Hold that thought." He answered with, "Hello, this is Coplin." His eyes narrowed. He beckoned Andi with his fingertips, then passed a finger over his mouth in a gesture for silence. He pushed the speaker button.

A raspy voice said, "So I don't wanna get Big Bird in trouble."

"I understand." Rayne pointed at a chair next to the desk.

She understood this had to do with her grandfather. Holding her breath, she crept to the desk in order to hear better.

Rayne asked, "Who is this Big Bird?"

"One of the guys. Miss Michelle finds out and she won't let him eat here no more. She don't put up with troublemakers."

"I see your problem. Is there a way I can contact Big Bird?"

"Nah, he's scared, man. Rule is, don't nobody be talking about nobody else lessen Miss Michelle says okay."

"I'm not interested in getting anyone in trouble."

"This can't get back to Miss Michelle. She'll know right off it's Big Bird."

"You have my word."

The raspy voice relaxed and lifted a little. "See Big Bird thinks those dudes are friends of old Simon. They got money or something for him, so he tells 'em Simon don't work till Monday. And says him and Simon are big friends and if they got something, he'll hold it, they can trust him." He laughed, and it turned into a cough. "Big Bird's okay, but nobody gives him nothing. He drinks."

"Uh-huh."

"And the little dude says he's got something for Simon, all right. A one-way ticket to the boneyard. Big Bird laughs like it's a big joke, but it ain't a joke and I told him so."

"Right. Go on."

Andi gripped the edge of the desk so hard her hands ached. She stared wide-eyed at the speaker phone.

"He was saying Simon's got millions and he owes him big and he's crazy if he thinks he can get away with ripping him off. Even I thought that was funny 'cause Simon ain't got fifty cents. Only the little dude got killed and now Big Bird's scared." There was a sudden pause. "Hey, I gotta go, man."

"Wait! How—" The dial tone buzzed. Muscles worked in Rayne's jaw.

Andi swallowed hard. "It can't be. The police said—"

"The police didn't care about Mr. Simon, the little old man who mows your lawn. But I'll bet they'll be real interested in Simon Foulkes, the ex-con."

"We can't call the police!" she cried. "If he thinks the police are after him, I'll never find him!"

His eyes blazed. "We've got major problems, Andi. Keller died on Monday, but if that kid is right, then two men broke into Simon's apartment on the following Wednesday. The fat man has a partner. Whatever Simon has, they're willing to kill to get it."

Chapter Eight

Andi searched a 1970 telephone directory, scanning fiercely the small grayed print. Fouche, Fouk, Foulds, Fountain—no Foulkes.

Beside her on the couch, Rayne cradled his face with both hands. "Don't blow me off. We should call the police."

He was one hundred percent correct. After she identified the Rockies cap as possibly belonging to Mr. Simon, the police had lost interest. They'd be interested when they found out about Simon Foulkes.

"The case is closed. Keller died in an accident."

"You're being stubborn."

She slammed shut the telephone book. Dust made her sneeze. "I know I'm being stubborn, but what am I supposed to do?"

"Let the cops handle it."

"Send him back to jail? No!"

Scowling and muttering, he paced, his boots heavy on the wooden floor. "Nobody says he's going back to jail."

"You think he has something to do with Keller's death."

"The real problem is there are two individuals out there who don't have a lot of respect for your property and probably not much for your person. They think you're involved."

"But if he thinks I called the cops on him, I'll never find him." She grabbed another phone book and tore through the pages to the *F*'s. "He has to know I'm on his side. There's a good explanation for all this."

He crouched and grasped her hands. "Listen to yourself. You're saying the truth out of one side of your mouth and denying it out of the other."

"He's my grandfather."

"You're better off without him."

She hung her head. "That's a rotten thing to say. It's like I'm starving and you're trying to grab food out of my mouth. He's my own flesh and blood. I have to give him every benefit of the doubt."

Sitting back on his heels, he massaged his temples as if his head ached. "I know exactly what you're going through. I lived through it. My brother Rex is a crook."

The knots in her belly jerked tighter.

"You have this romantic vision of family, but trust me, blood doesn't guarantee anything. A stranger might stab you in the back, but someone who loves you will twist the knife and dig for the spots that really hurt."

Usually she admired his blunt manner of speaking, but right now each word stung. She whispered, "What happened?"

"Rex got greedy." He jumped upright and resumed pacing, head down with his hands crammed into his back pockets. He darted hard glances her way. "Dad was a home builder and real estate developer. Rex and I worked for him until Dad had a heart attack and we took over.

"Over three million dollars in bond money disappeared. Bonds are supposed to be the safest investment available so people sank their entire life savings into them. We're talking little old ladies and parents who'd invested for their kids' college funds.''

''What did you do?''

''I went to the D.A. and snitched on my brother. What else could I do?''

He stopped at a window and stared outside. Clenching and unclenching her fingers, she longed to offer him comfort but needed comforting herself. Jumbled emotions held her still.

''I blew it. I went to Dad and Rex first. I had the phony bookkeeping, forged bank documents, falsified invoices. Two investors and another developer and three bank officials were in deep and Rex was right in the middle. But he flat out lied and Dad believed him. He kept believing him even when the prosecution team dug up more evidence and the whole thing blew up. Dad kept believing even when the jury found him guilty.'' He turned around, his shoulders stiff and his eyes flat and cold.

''Is he in prison?''

''Eighteen months and out on parole. People lost their life savings and homes, but Rex had constitutional rights.'' He looked ready to spit, as if the words choked him.

''I'm not spouting theory and I'm not talking to hear myself talk.'' His shoulders sagged and his hands dangled limply. ''Ah hell, who am I trying to kid? I care about you, Andi. I care a lot. I don't want you going through it.''

''He wouldn't hurt me.''

His tone gentled. ''Crooks don't care who they hurt. Rex didn't care about Dad's reputation. Or his bad heart. Or my parents mortgaging their home to pay for his defense. He didn't care about me. I was a damned good corporate accountant, but who's going to hire a guy who ratted on his own flesh and blood? Who wants a snitch doing his taxes? I lost every penny I owned. My wife divorced me. My family disowned me because I'm the bad guy for picking on Rex.''

The way her mother and grandmother disowned her grandfather? Hurting for him, hurting for herself, she stared at her hands.

''Greed's a disease and there's no cure.'' He lifted the phone book off her lap and tossed it on the floor. He grasped her hands and squeezed them.

''But I know my grandfather.''

''You didn't even know he's your grandfather until today. You don't know for certain who he is.''

Tears that had been hovering below the surface all day now rose, prickling and burning.

''Don't cry.'' Wide-eyed, Rayne snatched a box of tissues off Ford's desk and thrust it at her.

''What should I do? Everything looks bad, but I can't believe he's bad.''

He dropped onto the couch next to her and wrapped his arm around her shoulders. Hot tears tracked her cheeks. She tore a tissue from the box and blew her nose.

''People come in here all the time, usually women. They'll say, 'My kid or husband or boyfriend got arrested. He's innocent.' I always check it out. But every single time, when I talk to the guy, he's not innocent. No one wants to believe it. Stop crying.''

She tried, but her efforts made her cry harder. She curled her fingers in his light denim shirt. She wept for her crazy grandmother, who had preferred her husband's death over dishonor, and for her mother, who had erased her own father's memory, and for the gentle old man she'd grown to love but now had lost.

He splayed his fingers under her hair and rubbed her back. Kissing her brow, he murmured soothing noises. His lips were cool on her tear-fevered flesh. She whispered, "Please find him."

He used his thumb to wipe away tears. Inches from her face, he said, "This is a no-win situation. Give it up."

"I can't."

"Damn it, Andi, crooks belong in jail, not out on the streets where they can hurt people. I've been straight with you. I told you a lot of things I wouldn't tell anyone else."

"You care."

"A whole lot more than I should. Now stop crying."

She lifted her face to him, so close her lips almost touched his. "I have to give him a chance."

He kissed her, almost chastely, but her lips burned at his touch. She inched her hand up his chest to his neck and felt the strong corded muscle and sun-toughened skin. She kissed him, and underneath the salt of her tears she tasted the warm, outdoorsy vibrancy of him. She needed him in a way she'd never before needed anything or anyone. The thrust of his tongue and the feel of his increasingly bold hands drove away the pain.

He jerked back his head and behind the glaze of desire his eyes were startled. In a voice gone husky, he said, "Andi, we shouldn't."

"But you care."

"You're my client...." The words trailed into a low, tortured groan.

She curled her hand behind his neck and drew him unresisting, back to her. His hand slipped under her blouse, his fingers hot against her skin, and the way he buried his face against her throat with searing kisses turned dark emotion to passion, pain to pleasure, inner hurt to fire.

With quivering need, she tore at his shirt and pearl snaps popped one by one. Under her exploration of his broad chest with its thick, silky hair and supple flesh, he shivered. He laid her on the couch and she drew him down, unable to get enough of his hot, demanding mouth or the exciting sound of his roughened breathing. Eager for the touch of skin against skin they wrestled snaps and hooks and zippers, entangling themselves in denim and silk, cotton and lace.

"God, but you're beautiful," he said, his voice thick and throbbing and raw with wonder. His eyes turned black and hot and she drowned in their smoky depths. "I want it better than this. For you...."

"I want it now—you, now." Trembling began in her knees and the shudder racked her. The touch of his hand in soft, secret places sent her spiraling, mindlessly lost.

"That sound, that sound," he whispered between kissing her chin and her mouth and her cheeks and her throat, but she barely heard her own burbling cries. She arched against his clever fingers and found release. Trying as hard as she could to meld with his long, hard, hot body, she cried out. Wonderfully rough, the wild man of her dreams, he drove her deep into the soft cushions, and she caught his shoulder in her teeth and clung to him, wanting all of him. He whispered her name, hoarse and quavering, and slowly stilled.

She breathed against his neck, loving the way his scent had turned dark and erotic . . . loving him. She traced the craggy musculature of his back and drew lines with her fingernails through the light film of sweat.

He struggled until he rested his weight on his arms and looked down at her face. His eyes were heavy-lidded and dazed. "Damn, Andi," he whispered. "Are we nuts? I have my boots on."

She considered her position. Her skirt bunched around her waist and her blouse and bra tangled under her arms, freeing her breasts. All things considered, and especially considering that physically she'd never felt better, boots didn't matter.

"Is that bad?"

He pressed a soft kiss between her eyes. "It's very bad. You're too good for this, too—too beautiful. You deserve better." He made a helpless noise. His brow crinkled in worry.

She nibbled his chin. "It gets better? Then take your boots off and let's try it again."

"Be serious. I feel like a jerk. I didn't even . . ." His words trailed to a mumble and his face darkened. "What about birth control?"

Did he have to be sensible all the time? She lowered her eyelids, then raised them and sighed. "You make me crazy, but I'm not stupid. I have a slight hormonal problem so I'm on the Pill. It's okay. I want this, I want you. Don't you?"

"Too much. Since the first time I saw you. You've been driving me wild. All I can think about is you." He kissed her, hard, like a savage man unleashed. The spark rekindled, bright and burning, and she really didn't care about his boots.

His head snapped up and he said, "No."

Just that—"No"—as if he were arguing with someone Andi could not see. She tried to hold him, but he shook his head and pulled away from her until he was off the couch with his back to her. The only thing he would say was "No."

She looked down at herself, pale breasts gleaming and her legs sprawled, heavy with passion. She'd always taken pleasure in her body. It was strong and healthy and she was neither ashamed nor dismayed by her womanliness. But shame weighted her now, leaving her naked and vulnerable and angry.

He jabbed his shirttails into his jeans. His zipper rasped and his belt buckle rattled. "I've done some things in my life I'm not proud of, but I've never done them deliberately—"

"Shut up," she said.

He looked over his shoulder and his eyes held anguish, which made her feel worse. What was happening? She leapt off the couch, tugging down her bra and fumbling with the clasp. "Don't you dare apologize to me."

"But you don't understand. This isn't the way—"

She jerked down her blouse so hard that threads popped in seams. "If you want to insult me, then call me fat or say that I'm a lousy housekeeper or I'm too dumb to keep my checkbook straight. But don't you dare apologize for making love to me!" She snatched her panties off the floor. Never taking her eyes off the stiff set of his shoulders or the dark agony in his hooded eyes, she stepped into the underwear and wrestled them into place. For the first time in her life she felt ashamed of her feelings.

Unable to bear the stricken look on his face, unable to understand it, she stomped into the bathroom and slammed the door.

Rayne's jaw dropped. He was trying to be the good guy, trying to undo some of the damage. Hell, he respected her and cared more about her than he had cared about any woman. Why was she all bent out of shape? Why did she accuse him of insulting her?

A key worked in the door and Ford walked in. "Hello." He glanced at Andi's purse, stacks of phone books and boxes of records. "Still working?"

Rayne raked back his hair with both hands. He despised P.I.s who turned on the charm and played up the mystique in order to hustle female clients. He might not have much going for him, but he had his honor, his rules of conduct and his principles.

Why was he losing Andi?

"Rayne?"

Swiping the air in disgust, Rayne stalked to the coffee bar. *Calm down,* he counseled. They both needed a little while to cool off before they could talk reasonably. Despite her emotional nature, she was sensible. They'd suffered a lapse brought about by her anguish over Simon. He'd make sure it didn't happen again. He'd keep their relationship on the right track.

"Rayne?"

"What?" he snapped.

Ford sat behind his desk, slitting open envelopes. "Did I arrive at an inopportune time?"

Rayne turned on the faucet full force so it splashed the sink and spattered his shirt front with droplets. "Everything is fine. Get off my back." He jammed the coffeepot under the tap and glowered at the rising water level.

"I take it the hunt is not going well?"

The bathroom door opened and Andi peered out. Rayne's heart flip-flopped and memories blinded him. Her full breasts and hips, the indescribable softness of her skin and the sweet taste of her mouth and her unabashed, wildly passionate lovemaking. His groin tightened and his throat choked. The heady, glorious feeling of perfect rightness, perfect fit, perfect wholeness . . .

He wasn't just falling for her, he was falling in love.

"Hi, Mr. Hayes," she said in a meek little voice. High color bloomed on her cheeks. Though red-rimmed from crying, her eyes were luminous.

"Greetings, Miss Blair. Are you enjoying your sojourn into the seedy underworld of the private investigator?"

The color deepened on her face and spread to her throat. "Not really. It hasn't been a good day."

Cut to the quick, Rayne ripped off the plastic lid to the coffee can and coffee spewed forth, littering the countertop. He jammed the scoop into the can and more coffee spilled. With an oath, he swept it into the sink.

"Did the lead about Confirmation House bear fruit?" Ford asked.

Managing to get the coffee basket filled, Rayne told his partner about their efforts. He avoided the masochistic urge to watch Andi's reaction. It hurt her, he knew, but just because he broke his number one rule didn't mean he needed to start weaseling.

"Rayne thinks I should call the police."

Ford leaned back in his chair and toyed with a pencil. "What do you think, Miss Blair?"

She cast a glare at Rayne that seared through his clothing and scalded his skin. "If he wants to quit, he can, but I'm going to keep looking. My grandfather loves me and I won't desert him."

Rayne ground his teeth. Muscles jumped in his jaw. He looked to Ford, always the voice of reason, for support.

Ford pointed the pencil at Rayne. "Miss Blair is right."

Rayne started. Andi looked surprised. "I am?"

"There are puzzling aspects to this case. I made a few discreet inquiries about the late Keller Poe." He swung his chair about to face Rayne. "No recent criminal activity can be attributed to him."

"What are you saying?"

Ford indicated the red printing on the dry-erase board. "Let us say Simon, Keller, the fat man and the fourth party who vandalized the apartment committed a crime. Simon was given the ill-gotten gains and has now decided to keep them for himself. It makes sense, except that Keller began boasting of his soon-to-be acquired riches within days of his release from prison, yet nothing has occurred to say he lived up to those boasts. Or, shall we say, died for them."

Rayne shoved his hands in his pockets. "I'm not saying they robbed a bank. But what if they tangled with organized crime? Or robbed a drug dealer? What if this is some elaborate con game?"

Andi snapped, "He's not Jesse James!"

Ford lifted his gaze to the ceiling and tapped his chin with the pencil. "The name Simon Foulkes rouses within me a certain familiarity. The why eludes me at present. In the meantime, I suggest you research Simon's past. The answer may lie there."

Andi snapped her fingers. "I get it now. My grandfather was framed. The bad guys think he has the proof that can put them all away."

"This isn't a spy movie," Rayne countered. "He wasn't framed."

She lifted her chin and narrowed her eyes. "You don't have any proof he wasn't."

Ford tapped the desktop to get their attention. "Miss Blair, now that you have acquired Simon's full name and Social Security number, Hayes and Coplin Investigations has at its disposal certain resources which may be of assistance in your quest. Professionals well versed in modern electronic research."

Blinking slowly, Andi cocked her head.

Rayne translated, "Computer geeks who snoop around in databases. They're fast but expensive. An hourly rate, plus long-distance charges and access fees."

"Can they help?"

Ford said, "Simon's criminal history is public information. To obtain it, however, will require a Freedom of Information Act request sent through the postal service to the appropriate agency, then a waiting period for some minor clerk to decide if we do indeed have a right to records over which he or she holds a territorial interest, and then, perhaps, we shall receive the information. The process can take weeks."

"How can those computer people help?"

Rayne said, "Government clerks are good at fending off fishing expeditions, but fairly cooperative if we know the right questions to ask."

"Then let's do it."

Irritation prickled Rayne. Ford made a sound suggestion, but it meant tacking a hefty addition onto Andi's bill. Her scent still filled his head and the sound of her passion echoed in his mind. Taking her money seemed mercenary.

"There's another possibility." He swung around in front of Andi. She crossed her legs, folded her arms and tucked in her chin, forming a protective shield. He mourned the change from the soft, generous, yielding woman of a short while ago.

You're screwing up, a chiding voice whispered in the back of his mind. *Fix it or lose her.*

He said, "From everything I've seen, it seems likely Simon is running a con game on you."

She shook her head, her eyelids lowered and her mouth set in a firm line. Ford remained neutral.

"When your mother died, was an obituary in the paper?"

Andi replied with a sullen nod.

"From there it would be easy to find out you inherited the estate. What are you worth?"

"I don't know," she mumbled. "Two hundred thousand, give or take." She raised her head slowly and her eyes burned with dark emotion. "It isn't enough to accuse him of murder and robbery, now you think all he wants is my money?"

"I'm saying it's a possibility. Ford?"

"We should assume nothing," his partner replied in a cool voice with a hint of warning. "Research will tell us what we need to know."

Rayne understood the warning to back off. "Fine." He turned to the storeroom. "We have the directories here for starters, and the library and the newspaper."

"Let us not forget one other intriguing aspect," Ford said. "The mystery woman with her twelve thousand dollars."

Rayne hadn't forgotten and he had some ideas about the strange woman in the white Cadillac. He suspected the money in the envelope was a teaser in a con game. Or a smoke screen to distract Andi when Simon—if that was his name—made his move.

While Ford concentrated on paperwork, Rayne and Andi went through telephone directories dating back to 1964, voter registrations back to 1972 and city directories back to 1958.

Her adamant refusal to look at or speak to him distracted Rayne. At one point, he leaned over and whispered, "Please don't be mad at me."

"I am not mad," she said in a clipped, frosty, high-pitched lilt that said she was very angry, indeed. Furious, in fact. He suspected that if she had a weapon, he'd be a goner.

So he got mad, too. In glum, hostile silence they worked their way through every directory and resource in the office.

"Nothing here," he said. "Come on, sweetheart. I'll give you a ride home."

She lifted one eyebrow in a cool arch. Did he call her sweetheart? Ford's cat-ate-the-canary grin made Rayne's face grow hot.

She picked up her purse and settled it carefully over her shoulder, taking time to adjust her blouse. "I'll walk."

"And some fat joker on a motorcycle can offer you a lift."

Her pupils contracted and her throat worked. As he shifted his gaze between the two of them, Ford's smile faded. *Great,* Rayne thought. *She thinks I'm not just a jerk but a sarcastic jerk.*

He slunk out of the office.

Despite his feeble attempts to draw her into conversation, Andi refused to speak a word on the short drive to her house. She refused to acknowledge him at all. As soon as he stopped the Jeep, she hopped out and marched through the gate, slamming it with a clatter behind her.

"Ah, hell," he muttered, and tore the key out of the ignition. He caught up to her on the porch. "Andi, I'm sorry. Come on. Stop treating me like I'm a mass murderer."

She opened her door. "You have nothing to be sorry about. Good night."

He slapped his hand on the door before she could close it. She spun on her heel, her full lips hardening into a thin, furious line. "Let's talk," he said. "Please."

She stopped pressing the door and he dropped his hand. "Can I come in?" She stood her ground and he kicked lightly at the bottom of the screen door. The aluminum belled faintly. "Look, I didn't mean to hurt your feelings. But what we—in the office—"

"We had sex." Moisture filmed her eyes; her lower lip trembled. "If anyone should apologize, it's me. I mistakenly thought we were making love, but apparently it was just sex."

The voice in the back of his skull told him to shut up, cut his losses and run like hell. He drew a deep, steadying breath. "You're my client—"

"Client?"

The warning voice increased in volume, jangling his brain. "Yes, client. And there's such a thing as conflict of interest, especially when it concerns the trust between—"

She slammed the door in his face. The dead bolt shot home with a clunk.

Red haze curtained his vision and he stepped back and dropped his grip on the screen door. It swung shut with a soft wheeze of the pneumatic closer. Women! Act like a dirty, sleazy, scummy heel and they can't get enough. Try to show a little self-control and they slam the door in your face.

ANDI SPLASHED WATER on her face and eyes. Her eyelids felt lined with sandpaper. She stared at her face in the mirror. What a mess. Tangled hair, puffy red-rimmed eyes and her mouth locked into an unhappy scowl.

Just a client.

A faceless entity with a checkbook and a willingness to pay the bill.

Nothing but a client!

How could she have been so stupid? How had she mistaken his professional caring for personal caring? She'd misread the signs so completely that she hadn't just taken a wrong turn—she'd ended up in the wrong country!

Sex on a couch! Like some hoyden in a bad movie. No wonder he'd run like a rabbit. He probably thought she slept around. He was probably more embarrassed than she was. He'd warned her time after time to keep her hands to herself. Like an idiot she'd totally ignored him, blithely assuming he was interested and mistaking his niceness for affection.

She'd never be able to look him in the face again.

She slumped into the kitchen and opened the refrigerator. Rayne Coplin wasn't worth all this agony. He had plenty of faults. Tough and hard-boiled...

She heard his low, even voice saying, "Afraid not, partner, but I have a business card," and the little boy staring up at Rayne with hero worship in his eyes, saying, "Wow, like Magnum, cool."

She closed the door and scowled at the floor. That was just one of his acts, a ruse to gain useful information. The man was cynical as the dickens....

But knowing absolutely that no one had broken into her house, he'd said, "You must have scared them off.... It's a good thing you're watching out for Andi, sir." And Mr. Dipwell had puffed up like a rooster, his wounded pride restored.

How could she have been so stupid and fallen in love with him? No! Infatuation perhaps, or a crush, or her libido run amok, but not love.

Love couldn't hurt like this.

Chapter Nine

Andi tossed and turned on the bed. Sweat slicked her face and the hollow between her breasts and the small of her back. She kicked off the sheets and lay spread-eagle, but that didn't help. She was suffocating. She flipped over and turned the pillow cool side up. On her belly, she closed her eyes, her cheek pressed against the smooth, lemon-scented percale.

And envisioned Rayne. His hands, eager and expert, explored her curves; his mouth was hot against hers as they breathed each other's essences; his wry smile and gentle eyes—

Her eyelids flew open. She flipped again and stared at the ceiling, picking out shades of gray in the textured plaster.

And envisioned her grandfather, shy and gentle and infinitely patient. Grandpa, Granddaddy, Grandfather. Why had he lied to her? Why didn't he trust her?

She rolled off the bed. It was hot, too hot. That's why she couldn't sleep. Normally her bedroom, on the southeast corner, shaded by the front porch and a silver maple tree, was the coolest room in the house. She opened both windows a few inches, hoping for a cross draft.

Cool air wrapped around her bare legs but did little to ease the inner heat.

Groaning in frustration, she went to the kitchen. In the dark she found a glass and stood before the sink, drinking cool water. She stared out the window into the backyard. Very little light reached the yard except for a thin yellowish beam cast by a neighbor's back porch light filtering through the fence and tall lilac bushes.

She listened to the night: plaintive buzzing insects, and the old house shifting subtly into a more comfortable position, creaking and popping like an old woman's arthritic knees. Loneliness settled over her shoulders. Her grandfather had given her a taste of family; Rayne gave her a taste of love. Both left her hungrier, lonelier than before.

A sharp, alien noise alarmed her. Every muscle tensed, every hair on her body raised and quivering, she held her breath and turned her head slowly, seeking the source of the noise. She set down the glass and inched across the kitchen floor, avoiding the squeaky places. At the doorway, she heard it again, a noise like ripping fabric.

Heel to toe, she crept through the living room. It had to be branches scraping the roof. Wood squealed like a kitten's thin cry. She grasped the wall and peered into her bedroom.

A leg thrust through the curtain.

Andi leapt across the room, grabbed the sash and shoved down with all her might. The window crunched thickly against the leg and the intruder yowled. Something steely scraped the porch. A crash made the floor vibrate.

Then her brain caught up to her. In spite of her heart hammering in her ears and her body pulsing with adrenaline, she asked herself, quite reasonably, *What in the world am I doing?*

The intruder writhed on the porch, his leg caught at an angle that made it impossible for him to regain his footing. Andi's shoulders ached with strain and she put her entire one hundred and thirty-five pounds into holding the window down. He looked big as a bear, even as he wailed in agony.

Now what? "I've got a gun!" she yelled.

"You don't have a gun, you got my knee. Have a heart, lady. You're killing me!"

"I do too have a gun and I'm going to shoot you."

He laughed and ceased struggling. "You don't have a gun, and even if you did, we both know you ain't a shooter. So come on, be a sport. Get off my leg."

He didn't know a thing about her, she thought indignantly. "I'm calling the police."

"Fine, you do that."

His testy tone unnerved her. She couldn't call the police without leaving the window. "You're the one who broke into my house before. You were hiding in my basement."

"Yeah, so what? And let me tell you something, lady, your basement is a death trap. If the fire department ever sees that mess you'll be paying fines to doomsday. Get off my damned leg!"

He invaded her home and then dared criticize her? She flipped aside the curtain with her elbow and climbed onto the low, wide windowsill and pressed harder. He howled. She searched the street for lights coming on in neighboring houses or a passing car. This was outrageous! Wasn't there one insomniac on the block?

"Okay, okay—uncle! I give up. Damn, you're strong for a chick." He thumped the porch. "I wasn't going to hurt you. Honest. Lemme go, please."

"Ha! If you weren't going to hurt me, you could visit at a decent hour!" She pressed her nose against the glass, searching, hoping. Many of her elderly neighbors were hard of hearing, but this was getting ridiculous. "What do you want? Why are you following me?"

He laughed again, low and disgusted. "Tell you what, lady. You run over to the phone and call the cops. They'll pop me and I'll give them an earful about you and the old man and those gumshoes. So go ahead, call the cops. And I'll see you in lock-up."

Her back muscles twitched in a sharp spasm, partly from her awkward position, partly from apprehension. Why did he sound so sure of himself? "Who are you? I've done nothing wrong."

"That's what they all say."

Nervous sweat formed on her brow and trickled into her eyes. If her grandfather went back to prison, he'd die before she ever saw him again. What could he have done?

One thing she knew, she couldn't stay in this position all night. Her back cramped and her toes were going numb. "If I turn you loose, will you go away and leave me alone?"

"Yeah, yeah, no sweat. Just get off my leg. I think you broke it."

She forced her burning muscles to relax, but not too much. She stepped down to the floor and stopped pressing on the window but kept her hands ready on the sash. He twisted and turned, working his leg free. His steel-buckled boot knocked her knee, but she stood ready to slam the window, which she did as soon as his foot cleared. She turned the lock and watched his dark, bulky shape awkwardly gain his footing and hobble off the porch.

When she absorbed the sheer size of his beefy shoulders and massive arms, she swayed dizzily. Nausea stabbed her belly and filled her mouth with an acrid metallic taste. Groaning, she sank to the floor and cradled her spinning head in her hands.

"Hey, lady. *Psst!*"

She cried and lurched backward, pushing with her heels until she hit the brass bed frame.

"Calm down," he said through the window on the adjoining wall. "Think I'm stupid enough to put my head in?"

The window on that side was five feet off the ground. She stared in horror at the filmy curtain, unable to see him, half-expecting him to come crashing in a barrel roll through the glass.

"Some friendly advice, lady. You're an amateur and you ain't got what it takes to play this game. No offense intended, but you don't know what you're doing. Simon don't, either. So do us both a favor and talk sense into him. He'll get his cut, we'll get ours and everybody's happy. Right? And cut off the gumshoes, too. They're all snitches. Hang with them and you'll be crying the jailhouse blues."

Light shined through the curtain. The Dipwells! The intruder spat a filthy word. In a rush, he added, "You do what I say. Don't be stupid and no one gets hurt." Bushes rattled.

She heard a window rasp next door and a low buzz of talking, then Mrs. Dipwell's voice rising in a querulous question.

Andi scrambled to the window, slammed it shut and locked it. She rushed to the living room and snatched up the telephone, then paused, staring at the weak glow of the dial's light. The man's taunt about the police mocked her—terrified her. She could just see sweet Simon, his head hanging in shame and his frail wrists weighted by handcuffs.

She called Rayne. He answered on the second ring and sounded alert. "A man tried to break into my house," she whispered.

"Call the cops. I'll be there in ten minutes," he said, and hung up.

She refused to call the police.

Rayne arrived in six minutes and relief propelled her into his strong arms. He held her tightly, unmoving, his chin resting on the top of her head. She buried her face against his shoulder and breathed his clean forest smell until the shakiness drained from her knees and the knots loosened in her belly. By the time Andi remembered she was angry with him, she didn't want to be angry anymore.

But fright aside, she wasn't making the mistake again of thinking he cared about her personally. She pulled away from his embrace and kept her gaze averted from his.

He asked what happened and she told him. He examined the bedroom window, fingering the cut screen, mangled and ragged from the fat man's struggle. "Simon gets his cut, they get theirs. Hmm. Tell me again, exactly, what he said."

ANDI EXAMINED the small jar of instant coffee. She remembered buying it for baking purposes but could not recall how long ago that was.

She went to the living room and peered around the corner. Rayne's shirt hung neatly over a chair and his boots, with socks tucked in top, sat on the floor. He reclined on the couch, chin to chest and one foot on the floor. A pink-and-blue crocheted afghan was draped over one shoulder and his stomach.

Her throat tightened and a light shudder weakened her knees. He was so beautiful.

Even though he'd been gruff, his offer to stay last night touched her. His refraining from I-told-you-so's about her grandfather's being involved with crooks touched her even more. Poor losers were understandable, but poor winners had character flaws. Although she hadn't slept much or well, at least she hadn't been afraid of the fat man returning.

The doorbell rang and she jumped. Rayne didn't stir. She hurried to the door and peered through the glass insert.

Holding forth a pink-and-white bag, John Morris smiled. He wore a light blue sport shirt and tan slacks, and his white blond hair was combed neatly. Out of uniform he seemed younger and somehow smaller. She opened the inside door.

"Good morning, Andi." He hefted the bag. "Cops and doughnuts. My favorite cliché."

She put her hand on the the screen doorlatch but made no move to open it. "Hi, John. Gee, I wasn't expecting you." It wasn't quite seven o'clock. Did he always visit people this early?

Did he know about her grandfather's crimes?

She slipped outside, pulling the door shut behind her. She tugged the edges of her robe tighter at her throat.

"I stopped by the bookstore the other day and your boss said you'd gone on vacation. I thought you'd gone out of town. But I noticed your car out front last night when I passed by."

His words sank in and she stiffened. "Passed by?"

"Working." He indicated the street with a toss of his head. "This is my beat."

"Oh. Right." She fetched the newspaper off the lawn.

He lifted the bag. "Two cream-filled, two jellies and two chocolate-honey. Trade you for a cup of mud."

She climbed back on the porch. "I'm sorry, but this isn't a good time. I'm not even dressed."

His smile lost its cheerfulness. "Guess I should have called first. You don't look so good. Are you sick?"

"Tired." Scared half to death, worried, frazzled, stressed—multiple choice.

"Still looking for your missing person?" He moved in close, peering intently at her face. "Having any luck?"

Andi drew back. John Morris was nice enough and she appreciated his concern, but the one thing she could not stand was his disregard for personal space. She pressed the newspaper against her chest. "This really is a bad time. I'm not up to visitors."

"What about tonight? It's my day off."

"A date?" With a policeman? The kind who could put handcuffs on her grandfather and haul him off to jail?

"Yeah. Dinner?" He jammed his hands in his pockets and rested his weight on one heel. He half turned, then stopped and bent at the waist. "What happened?"

She followed his gaze and gave a start. A deep impression of a boot heel marked the wood siding below her bedroom window and scuff marks streaked the entire area. To say nothing of the screen hanging in tatters.

Rayne opened the door. Shirtless, he stood glaring at John. For a brief, mindless moment, his incredible beauty, the deep, heavy chest, sharply delineated by the curvature of his ribs and the ridge of his clavicle, struck her dumb. His sleepy eyes, now the clearest blue, glittered behind their frame of dark brows and suntanned skin. Even his stubbled cheeks and tousled hair gave him an aura of raw power. Masculinity in its prime.

John said, "Oh." His face turned crimson. "Oh." He thrust the doughnut bag at her and she took it without thinking. "My treat," he mumbled, and hopped off the porch. He strode away, never looking back.

Rayne held open the door for her. "What did Morris want?"

For fear of grabbing him and burying her face against his tan skin, she didn't dare look at him. She walked inside. "Coffee."

Following her into the kitchen, his bare feet slapping the floor, he said, "You didn't tell him about your visitor."

"What's to tell?" Wishing he'd put his shirt on, she started water heating in the kettle. She adjusted the flame. Her facial muscles twitched, foretelling another crying jag if she wasn't careful. "What are you going to do now?"

"You hired me to find Simon, I'll find him. Does Morris make a habit of dropping by for coffee?"

Was that jealousy deepening his voice? Couldn't be.

"Look at me."

She shook her head. She was a hair's breadth away from falling apart and embarrassing them both, and too weary to fight it. She put the doughnuts on a plate, stacking them in a pyramid.

"I'm a lot more inclined to trust your instinct than the word of some joker with his leg caught in a window."

She whipped her head about. Bright hope made her light-headed.

"I'll find Simon, but it's up to him to come clean." He slumped against the doorway frame, hands in his pockets and staring glumly at his feet. "If he's dirty, if he's got his hands deep in some kind of crime, I'll burn him. Do you understand?"

She was the client and he was the private eye and either her grandfather was a crook or he wasn't. Rayne offered her an opportunity to pretend none of this ever happened. But she would never see her grandfather again.

The pained furrows in Rayne's brow decided her. Maybe he only cared about her as a client, but at least he cared. If Simon Foulkes had the barest chance to redeem himself, Rayne would give it to him.

"I understand." She understood that just because he didn't feel the same way she did, he wasn't a bad person. Yesterday wasn't his fault, it was hers. His hunched shoulders and the hard lines of his face made her heart hurt.

He rolled away from the doorway. "Just so we're straight." He went to fetch his shirt.

Sighing, Andi pulled two mugs from the cupboard. She dropped a tea bag in one, and into the other she scooped several spoonfuls of instant coffee crystals. Nice and strong, the way he liked it.

Before Andi's tea finished brewing, Debra telephoned. "I hope I didn't wake you," she said. "Sorry for calling so early."

"That's okay. What's up?"

"My sister had her baby. Last night."

"Jennifer? But I thought she wasn't due for a month."

"She isn't, so everyone's surprised. A little panicky and out of sorts, too."

"Is the baby okay?"

"Small, but I think healthy. Anyway, I called Sharon and she said to ask you if you felt up to filling in for me for two days so I can go up to Fort Collins. Can you? I know you're on vacation, but—"

"No, no." Andi glanced at Rayne. Now fully dressed, he sat on the couch with the coffee cup cradled in both hands. He stared at the dark brew as if it held the secrets of the universe. Another day of playing private eye would probably push her over the edge. "I can do it."

"Are you sure? You sound really dragged out."

"A little tired." She passed a hand over her weary eyes. "Boy or girl? I want to send Jennifer a baby gift."

"Boy. I don't know his name yet. Thanks, Andi, you're a peach."

Andi hung up, then called Sharon. She told her boss she'd be in for the next two days. Rayne raised his head. When she finished, she told him about being needed at the bookstore. Part of her hoped he'd protest and insist she stick with him.

Instead, he said, "I'll drive you to and from work. Stay off the street." His sudden smile caught her off guard. "Trapped his leg in the window. You're really something."

Not much of a compliment, but her traitorous heart insisted on capturing it and holding it close.

RAYNE WALKED into the Reading Room. Not seeing Andi gave him a heart-stopping moment. He was a few minutes late and she hadn't been waiting out front for him as she had yesterday evening. Had she grown impatient and walked home? Hearing the sound of her voice from somewhere in the stacks, he relaxed.

The girl counting money at the cash register said, "I'm sorry, we're closing, sir."

"I'm here to pick up Andi."

The girl beamed. "You must be Rayne Coplin." She leaned her forearms on the counter. "I'm Heather. Nice to finally meet you." She looked him up and down. "Andi's right. You don't look like a private eye. No offense, but well, you know." She tapped the side of her head. "No hat, cigar. Trench coat? You look so...normal."

Rayne chuckled.

"Andi says you don't carry a gun or slink around in smoky cabarets, either."

"No cabarets in the Springs." Andi talked about him? The shining approval in Heather's eyes said Andi had only good things to say.

Heather's eyes lighted with curiosity. "Isn't it dangerous? I mean, don't bad guys shoot at you and stuff?"

"A man chased me with a tire iron once. Does that count?"

"Must be exciting." She sighed. "Retail is okay, but you have a great job. I'd love to get paid for being nosy."

At the moment, it was the worst job in the world. He'd had a major breakthrough in the case, but instead of pleasure or pride, he felt lousy.

Andi walked into view.

Her smile blossomed, and for one glorious moment Rayne forgot Simon. Under her welcoming smile and shining eyes, he felt ten feet tall. The world shifted off kilter and his brain blanked, leaving room for only one image: beautiful Andi in her flower-sprigged blouse and simple skirt, her hair surrounding her face like a golden cloud and her smile for him alone.

Heather sighed dreamily, loudly. Feeling suddenly naked in his thoughts, Rayne stiffened.

Andi looked away, her expression veiled. She tugged her purse strap higher on her shoulder and called, "My ride is here. See you Monday, Sharon."

Sharon's reply drifted from somewhere in the back.

Heather asked, "You're coming back to work Monday, then?" She made a disgusted noise. "Can't you take an extra week of vacation? I almost have enough for a down payment on a real car. I am so sick of driving Daddy's hunk of junk."

"Sorry."

Heather turned a whimsical grimace on Rayne. "Being a college student sucks. No respect."

Rayne and Andi laughed softly as they walked out of the bookstore. Andi looked up and down the street. Heavy evening traffic crawled in fits and starts and streetlights glowed, the filaments visible. "Where's your Jeep?"

"Down by the park. Couldn't find a parking place here." He jammed his hands in his back pockets and started walking.

Andi balked. "You found something."

"Hit the mother lode."

Her eyes dimmed. A rippling sensation made his arms itch. Her intuition was spooky. Or maybe he gave off heavier vibes than he liked to think.

She fell into step beside him. At the park, Rayne pulled out his keys but considered the wisdom of taking her home or to his office. A public location might be better for both of them. "The park looks nice. Let's talk here."

Andi stepped off the wide sidewalk and onto the gravel path. Acacia Park covered a square city block, an oasis of greenery between stone and concrete buildings. Large trees cast green-dappled shade, and flower beds bright with daisies, pansies and grape hyacinth perfumed the air.

Head down, her sandals whispering on the gravel, she walked to the middle of the park then stopped where the paths crossed and faced the old band shell.

"He's dead, isn't he?" Her eyes misted.

He grasped her upper arm. "No!"

"You can tell me." She pulled away from his grip and rubbed her arm slowly.

"As far as I know, he's alive." Once she heard what he'd learned, she might wish otherwise. "Ford's been talking to his buddies in the CSPD and over at the D.A.'s office. Even if Simon was in your yard when Keller died, the coroner will stand by his ruling."

"Serious?"

"Keller's not worth reopening a major investigation only to find out he tripped over his own feet."

"So nobody official is interested in my grandfather. Even if they know he's been in prison."

"Right."

She peeked at him from the corner of her eye. "But that's good news."

He watched a pair of magpies squabbling over scraps left by picnickers. The black-and-white birds, with their ridiculously long tails, battled with the noise and flash of professional wrestlers. "I found Big Bird. He recognized the fat man in the photos we took."

Her face paled. "How did you find Big Bird?"

"He's a skinny little bum with a neck about two feet long. Who else could he be but Big Bird?" He shook his head at the memory. "Keller and the fat man came back that Monday. Big Bird told them Simon had split. My guess is Simon was hiding out in your backyard, waiting for you to come home, when they jumped him."

"How did they know he'd be there?"

"They know you're Simon's granddaughter."

"What?"

"Big Bird swears they knew all about you."

"If I didn't know, how could they know?"

"When I was over at the newspaper office, the clerk made a comment about how I wasn't the only one interested in Simon. A few months ago another man was digging around the archives. She couldn't remember what the man looked like, so that tells me it's not the fat man. He's unforgettable."

"What do they want?"

Now for the hard part. "Does the name Hamburg mean anything to you?"

"Should it?"

He jutted his chin at the large equestrian statue of General William Jackson Palmer perched on a high base in the middle of the intersection of Platte and Nevada. "City history. Wolfgang Hamburg was a German immigrant who made a fortune in silver, molybdenum and lead, opened a few foundries and several businesses here in the Springs. A wealthy man. His wife spent most of her time traveling around the world collecting jewelry. Especially anything connected to royal families."

Like a sleepwalker, Andi moved toward a bench and dropped onto the wooden slats.

"Old Wolfgang died right after World War II. His widow spent her remaining years traveling around the country displaying her collection for charity functions. The collection was famous."

"What does this have to do with my grandfather?"

He knew she knew, so words seemed redundant. "He stole the Hamburg jewels."

Andi caught the bench with both hands and closed her eyes.

Rayne laid a hand on her shoulder and squeezed gently. "Simon was employed as the family gardener. When old Mrs. Hamburg died, he stayed on to work for her daughter. Gretchen Hamburg-Mosse died in a car accident in 1963. Apparently, Gretchen lived high on the hog and left a mountain of debt, so her daughter was going to auction off the collection. A jeweler by the name of Joseph King went to the house to appraise the jewels. The daughter left the room, and when she returned, Joseph was dead and the collection was gone."

Andi clutched the fabric of her shirt over her heart. Her knuckles turned white. "Murder?"

"Simon was convicted of manslaughter."

"He was framed," she whispered. "He's not a killer."

Unable to bear her stricken eyes and the strained set of her mouth, he dropped his gaze to his boots. "He confessed."

She snapped her head about and her mouth dropped open.

"When the cops questioned Simon, he wasn't even a suspect, but he confessed. The jewels were never recovered."

"How can that be?"

"Simon claimed he threw the jewels in the Arkansas River. Hundreds of professional and amateur treasure hunters searched the river that summer. Flyers and bulletins were sent around the world, and the insurance company offered a huge reward, but the jewels never surfaced. Take a wild guess what the fat man wants."

"You're saying my grandfather has the jewels?"

"Each time Simon went before the parole board they asked him about the jewels. Each time he denied knowing where they were. He ended up being one of the few people in recent history who ever served a full sentence.

My guess is they weren't about to let him out so he could profit from his crime. The collection is worth millions of dollars. That's a pretty good retirement fund.''

''No! He's poor. He works in a soup kitchen, for goodness' sake! He doesn't have a fortune in jewels. I'll never believe that. If he said he threw them away, then he did.''

She jumped off the bench. She paced furiously, crunching gravel and wringing her hands.

''I've got copies of everything. You can see for yourself.''

''I just . . . this is outrageous!''

Sliver by sliver, his heart shredded. He took her place on the bench and dangled his hands between his knees. For the second time in his life, doing the right thing was killing him.

''Keller and Simon were in prison together. Simon can't walk into a pawnshop or a jewelry store and plop down a brooch or necklace worth thousands. And dealing with private collectors can be dangerous. He needs somebody who knows how to fence hot jewels, like Keller. Only something went wrong.''

He rested his face on his hands. He'd never even cared about his ex-wife as much as he cared about Andi. Now he was losing her because of a crazy, thieving old man who didn't have the decency to let her know he was alive.

A light touch brushed the top of his head. Andi said, ''Oh, Rayne, don't look like that. It's not your fault.''

Astonished, he looked up. She regarded him solemnly.

''The man you're talking about is a stranger. The man I know will read six stories in a row to my neighbors' grandchildren. He'll spend an entire day dividing irises and planting new beds." Her chin quivered. "He thinks all my jokes are funny. What do we do now?"

"I don't know." He laughed dryly. "Ford doesn't know, either. Unusual for him."

"If he has the jewels, will he go back to prison?"

"If he tries to sell them."

"I can make him give back the jewels."

"If he'd told where the jewels were, he'd have been out of prison fifteen or twenty years ago. Why give them up now?"

"Because of me." She sat beside him and traced the back of his hand. "And because if the fat man gets him first, he'll lose a lot more than jewels. Maybe he intended to go partners with Keller, but he changed his mind. That's why they're chasing him."

"There are too many things that don't make sense. I think he's somewhere in the area. He had his chance to run when Keller died, but he didn't. Instead he leaves you a note. Why? And that woman. She knows who you are. Again, why? And why pay him off?"

She shook her head. "Why does it take so long to hear back from the license plate people?"

He almost heard the click, like dominoes, as pieces fell into place. It happened sometimes. In the midst of worrying about one problem, the subconscious spit out the solution to another seemingly out of the blue. "An accomplice. That explains the payoff."

"What are you talking about?"

Organizing his thoughts, he tapped his chin. "Hiding a fortune isn't easy when everybody and his brother is hot after a sizable reward. So Simon gives the jewels to somebody he thinks he can trust. 'Hold on to 'em, honey,' he says, 'and in a couple of years we'll retire to Florida.'"

"He's no Don Juan," she said stiffly.

"Thirty years ago he was a lot younger. Only instead of waiting patiently, the love of his life is busily digging out gems and melting down settings. He's locked up, she's living the good life."

"That's ridiculous."

"Possibly incorrect, but not even close to ridiculous." He stood and arched his back, not realizing until then how tense he'd been. "Simon and Keller cook up a scheme to fence the jewels, but when Simon gets out and looks up his old girlfriend, she says, 'Gee, sorry, no more jewels.' What can he do? He's an old man, too tired to fight, and besides, he has you. Case closed."

Andi looked slightly mollified and urged him to continue.

"He goes straight and hopes Keller never finds him. Only Keller does find him and he's not about to be put off by the fact that the jewels no longer exist. So Simon splits and hopes Keller goes away. But he dies. Simon's been through a murder rap before and, rather than go through it again, goes into hiding."

"Why did she give me the money?"

"I've been wondering and wondering why Simon didn't leave town—unless he was waiting for his girlfriend to come up with traveling cash. You were the go-between, Andi. He hoped you'd take the envelope home and that, being how you are, you'd never dream of opening it."

She straightened her shoulders with an indignant humph. "And I wouldn't have."

"He'd break into your house, pick up his cash and split."

Her frown drifted across her face and her brows furrowed lightly. "That kind of makes sense. But where is he now?"

"Beats me. That woman probably meant exactly what she said about killing him. It's a good guess he won't go to her."

"We still have to find her. She's the only one who can tell the fat man what really happened to the jewels."

He turned in a slow circle, his gaze lifted to the sky. "He could be in an alley, living in a cardboard box. Or up in the mountains. Or in a vacant building or under a bridge."

"If she doesn't tell the truth, the fat man will kill him."

"I'll find her. But right now, Simon is our main concern. Old friends and acquaintances are our best bet." Another mental click accompanied an image of Andi's basement, jam-packed to the ceiling with junk.

"What is it?"

"Did your mother save letters? Is it possible she wrote to him? Or he wrote to her? Maybe he mentioned old friends."

"After she got hurt, I opened all her mail. I did for years. I would have remembered a letter from . . ." Her voice trailed off and a faraway look filled her eyes. "Grandma's trunk."

"You think your grandmother wrote to him?"

She thumped her forehead with the heel of her hand. "Grandma had an old humpback trunk. It sat at the foot of her bed. Grandma never, under any circumstances, threw anything away. If he sent her letters, they'll be in that trunk."

Chapter Ten

"Andrea Blair!"

Andi and Rayne froze in their tracks and swiveled their heads toward Mrs. Dipwell. The woman marched to the ornamental wire fence between the properties.

Chin quivering and eyes moist, the woman grasped the fence and rattled it. "Young lady, this has got to stop."

Andi glanced at Rayne. He hitched his shoulders in a quick shrug. "What's that, ma'am?"

Mrs. Dipwell aimed a finger at Rayne, her entire body shaking. "All this spying! Do you know where that crazy old coot is now?"

"I haven't—"

"Shopping for a gun! He won't listen to a word I say. Not one word! *A gun!* He'll blow his fool head off. And it's all your fault! Convincing him this street has turned into a war zone."

Andi shrank back, hugging her arms close to her sides. "But, Mrs. Dipwell—"

"Bodies, prowlers, private eyes! He's up half the night convinced he's seeing criminals behind every tree." Her voice caught and a single tear slid over her cheek. "All this nonsense is giving him heart palpitations. If I lose him it'll be on your head!" She turned on her heel and marched back to her house. She slammed the door so hard the echo cracked off the trees.

"Damn," Rayne breathed.

Shaking her head, Andi climbed on her porch and opened the door. "Poor thing. He's driving her crazy."

"She doesn't have to take it out on you."

His indignation amused her. "I can see you didn't grow up in a neighborhood where everyone watched your every move." She unlocked the front door and laughed. "I never got away with anything."

"Where I grew up, adults didn't talk to adults that way."

"You don't understand. He is driving her crazy. On the very first day after he retired, he reorganized her kitchen. He had a scientific method, he said. She's still trying to find some of her pots and pans." She prayed Horace Dipwell didn't try to bring a gun into his house—his wife might very well shoot him with it.

"Even so..."

"And then there was the motorcycle. He took it apart down to the nuts and bolts. It cost fifteen hundred dollars and now it's in boxes in his garage."

Rayne lifted his eyebrows. "What kind of motorcycle?"

She looked at him askance. "The point is, she only yelled at me because he won't listen." She rolled her eyes. "A gun."

She pointed at the kitchen. "There's soda in the fridge. Help yourself while I change my clothes." She gave his jeans and sport shirt an up-and-down look. "It's pretty dirty in the attic. Dusty."

"No problem. I wash."

He wandered into the kitchen and opened the refrigerator. A piece of beef was marinating in a bowl and a fruit salad pressed spots of red, yellow and green against the translucent sides of a plastic dish. His stomach growled, but at the thought of the fast food he'd probably grab later, he grimaced.

He missed the comforts of home. His apartment didn't qualify as a home; it was only a place to sleep, shower and store his belongings.

He pulled a soda from the fridge and popped the tab.

Dressed in a T-shirt and cutoffs, Andi entered the kitchen. Soft cotton clung to her breasts and emphasized her narrow waist. He prayed she never felt the urge to diet away all those glorious curves.

He watched her fill a glass with ice, then water. As much as he desired her body, he desired her comfort, her sense of homeyness and belonging. He wanted those bright smiles beaming approval at him, and high emotion drawing him close to her soul. She loved unabashedly, without passing judgment, without fear.

"What are we looking for exactly?" he asked.

She looked toward the ceiling. "An old trunk. I hope it's up there, because if it's not, then it's in the garage. I really don't want to dig around in there."

She didn't sound as if she wanted to dig anyplace. Admiration for her courage swelled inside his chest. Every time they turned over a new rock, they found fresh slime smearing Simon. Still she kept going and remained hopeful. He didn't believe in fairy tales or happy endings, but he wanted one for her.

"How do you get to the attic?" He envisioned a narrow trapdoor in a closet ceiling.

"The stairs." Andi opened the double doors of a tall pantry cabinet. She pulled the shelves, laden with canned goods, forward and folded them back, then slid a wide panel aside, revealing a set of steep wooden stairs.

His jaw dropped and he clamped his hands on his hips. "A hidden passageway?"

She laughed. "It's not hidden." She indicated the back door, basement door, two big windows over the sink and wide doorway separating the kitchen from the living room. "I have no wall space in this kitchen. In fact, a wall used to be open to the dining room, but I covered it. I had no room for a pantry. So the carpenter replaced the swinging door with a sliding door and built in these cabinets. See. They fold completely out of the way." She worked the shelves back and forth on smooth, silent hinges. "Pretty clever, huh?"

"I see how he got away with charging you so much." He peered up the stairs. He could smell the hot stuffiness from down here.

"Hope you're ready for this." She hesitated, drawing back from the stairwell, her eyes wide and thoughtful.

He waited patiently. More admirable than her determined courage was her lack of anger. When he'd begun finding evidence about his brother's theft, he'd been furious. Anger had made it possible to continue digging; anger had given him the courage to testify for the prosecution. Anger had also turned his family against him and driven him from their midst. He'd stayed angry for years, and that had resulted in nothing but regret.

She stiffened her shoulders and went upstairs. He followed, making an effort not to notice the taut roundness of her buttocks and graceful hips. "There's only one light," she said. "Watch your step."

Stifling heat made him breathe hard and sweat slicked his face. But discomfort couldn't begin to compete with his astonishment.

Lighted by a single bare bulb, the attic looked like a central collection point for a flea market. Furniture, boxes, crates and odds and ends crammed the area from floor to rafters, except for a narrow pathway down the center.

She pointed to a door. "Would you believe that used to be my bedroom? It has two dormer windows. A vent in the floor lets in heat and it's nice in the winter. But I about smothered in the summertime. I camped out in the backyard a lot."

Dust tickled his nose and he sneezed. He stared at a wasp-waisted dressmaker's dummy. "You must have a fortune in antiques up here."

She lifted a shoulder. "I keep meaning to clear it out, but...well, I don't mind hard work, but this would mean a career change."

She pointed out a sepia-toned portrait in an oval frame hanging from a rafter. It showed a stern-faced woman and an even sterner-looking man. "My great-grand-parents. He owned an ironworks, but the freeway runs through where it used to be. Grandma was born and died in this house. Mom, too. There's a lot of history up here." Grimacing, she rubbed her nose. "Dust, too. *Ptooh!*"

He swiped at the back of his neck and brought his hand away damp. Sweat trickled off his forehead. As his eyes adjusted to the gloomy, shadowed corners, he realized he was in the midst of something akin to an archaeological dig. Hundred-year-old furniture and trunks were on the bottom layer, then wooden crates and storage lockers, and finally modern cardboard boxes, all of it overlaid with enough dust to grow a garden.

"How do you find anything?"

She grinned sheepishly. "I don't. This is just a place to stick stuff. I hardly ever come up here. Did I tell you pack rats run in my family?"

"Why this amazes me, I don't know. I've seen your basement."

"You ought to see the garage. I don't remember anyone ever parking a car in there."

Rayne rolled his eyes. "There are a lot of trunks up here. Which one are we looking for?"

"A humpback trunk." She stood on tiptoe to peer over the stacks. "It seemed huge when I was kid, but it's probably about this tall." She held her hand at mid-thigh. "I seem to recall that it's red. But it might be brown."

Rayne tackled the clutter on the left side of the path. He moved boxes full of Christmas ornaments, plastic flowers, sewing patterns, old magazines and blue-tinged canning jars with zinc lids. He peeked under white sheets draped over furniture.

"Hey!" Andi held up a paint can. "I remember this. Mom and I painted the living room. It's supposed to be beige, but it looked like the skin of something that lives in a cave. Creepy. Mom finally put up wallpaper." She swished the can close to her ear. "Sounds like it's all dried up."

He uncovered a silvery cylinder and frowned for a moment until he realized he was looking at what had to be the world's oldest vacuum cleaner.

He climbed over an old couch. "I think I found it." He moved boxes out of the way and ran his hand over the high mound of a trunk lid. Half an inch of dust covered the wine-red leather. Andi made her noisy way to his side and perched on her hands and knees atop a gateleg table.

"Good work, detective! That's it. I wonder how Mom got it up here?"

"Better question, how do we get it down? I'm suffocating." He wiped sweat out of his eyes.

"It's only about a hundred and twenty degrees." She brushed damp curls off her face and left smudges on her cheeks. "If we can get it on this table, we can—aah!" The table leaf collapsed under her.

Rayne shot out an arm and shifted under her weight, catching her. He hauled her in a tangle of long arms and legs to sit atop the old trunk. She clung to him, heat causing waves of her heady woman-scent to reach him. His throat closed and he buried his face in her soft hair.

Her hands pressed his chest. "Uh, thanks." She squirmed, but damn it, he did not want to let her go. Quick arousal fuzzed his brain—pleas for her to love him caught in his throat.

He had no choice, however, since she was playing by his rules. He cleared his throat and said gruffly, "All right?"

"I'm fine." Dark rose suffused her cheeks. She worked her careful way to the floor on the opposite side of the trunk. "Straight up and over, okay?"

He held his doubts. "I'll get it. Don't hurt yourself."

She looked at him askance and grasped a leather handle. "On the count of three?"

Together they wrestled the clumsy trunk onto the table. Clouds of dust filled Rayne's eyes with grit. He sneezed several times in succession, then patted the lid of the trunk. "I think I know where Simon is."

She laughed. "It's not that heavy."

Once they had the trunk in the clear and could maneuver, they got it downstairs with no problems. The kitchen felt icy in comparison to the attic. Rayne flopped on a chair and fanned his face with his hand.

Andi filled two tall glasses with water and handed him one. "I sure hope there's something good in there."

A cobweb clung to her bare thigh and he brushed it away. She glanced at him, gorgeous despite a dirty face and dirtier hands. The importance of why he insisted on sticking to his no-involvement-with-clients rule eluded him. He wanted her right now, in the kitchen.

She sidestepped out of reach.

He indicated the trunk with his water glass. "Padlock. Any idea where the key is?"

Her gaze became distant and she chewed her lower lip. A lip he'd very much like to kiss right now. She hurried out of the kitchen, returning moments later bearing a faded cigar box. She opened the lid and revealed a jumble of keys.

There had to be a hundred keys in the box, ranging from tiny piggy bank keys to long skeleton keys. "You can't make anything easy."

"Mom always said if it's easy, it isn't worth it."

They tried key after key. The padlock was brass and ornate, probably valuable. Still, when none of the keys fitted, Rayne was ready to break it.

"Can you pick it?"

"Sorry, left my burglar tools at home." He lifted the lock and turned it toward the light in an attempt to see the tumblers inside.

"You own burglar tools?"

"That was a joke." He tugged the lock and the hasp rattled against the dried-out, leather-covered wood. "Get a claw hammer." When she gave him a hammer, he eased the claw between the hasp and the trunk and rocked it slowly, trying to keep damage to a minimum. With squeaky groans, the brads popped free.

"Come on, Grandma, show me something good," she breathed as she lifted the lid.

A large brown spider scurried over the rim. Rayne shouted, and jumped. He raised his boot to stomp it.

"Don't!" Andi held her hand over the spider. "It's only a wolf spider. It won't hurt you."

"Smash it, and then it won't hurt anybody."

"Don't be silly." She cupped one hand and goosed the spider with a finger. It crawled onto her palm and crouched there.

His skin crawled. "It'll bite."

Smiling, she carried it to the back door and put it outside. "Rayne Coplin, you're a million times bigger than that poor little spider. Besides, don't you know spiders are lucky?"

Smashed spiders maybe, he thought as he settled uneasily on a chair. He leaned over to peer inside the trunk.

A moiré-lined tray was filled with trinkets and small jewelry boxes. Andi picked up a mirror in a silver frame. "Pretty. I never knew she had this." She opened a velvet-covered box and showed him the ring inside. "I bet this is Grandma's wedding ring. Mom never took hers off, but Grandma never wore hers."

He studied the old-fashioned cut of a two to three-carat diamond surrounded by smaller diamonds set in white gold. "Nice rock. Bet it's worth something."

She snapped the lid shut with a click. "Sentimental value only." She riffled through the trinkets, then lifted the tray out of the trunk.

The trunk was full of loose papers, albums and scrapbooks. Andi sat back on her haunches. Her eyes clouded. "I'll start dinner first. I'm starving."

She went to the sink and began washing her hands. "Mom and Grandma were unfair. I can accept them being upset by him going to prison. But they erased him. They never gave me the chance to make up my own mind.'' She looked over her shoulder at the trunk. ''It's still unfair. If there's anything in there, then it's all their side of the story. What about his?''

''He had his chance.''

She rested against the sink, one slim, bare foot cocked behind the other and her head back, her hair trailing in ripples of flax and gold to her waist. ''And think how many problems I wouldn't have now if he had told me his side.'' She turned slowly and picked up a towel. She wiped her hands in an idle motion. ''Everybody assumed they knew how I'd feel. If he'd said, 'I'm your grandpa and I was in prison,' what did he think I'd do? Tell him I never wanted to see him again? Is that what kind of impression I give?''

Inner discomfort tweaked Rayne and he shifted on the chair. Her words roused unpleasant memories of the last time he'd spoken to his mother. She'd asked, ''Why are you doing this to Rex?'' And he'd said, ''If you don't know, I can't explain it.'' He wondered what might have happened if he had explained it, or at least tried.

She waved the towel at him. ''*You* don't act like I'm too dumb or too wimpy to hear what you have to say. You're straight with me and I don't fall apart.'' She lifted a shoulder. ''Maybe I do get excited, but I get over it.''

She eyed the trunk. ''Dinner can wait.'' She scooped out a handful of papers and tried to give them to him. He made her check first for spiders. Her narrowed eyes and tight grin called him a big baby, but he didn't care. He loathed spiders. She pulled out a photo album and sat on the floor with the album opened on her lap.

He sorted through ancient receipts, newspaper clippings, coupons, song lyrics and old letters in yellowed envelopes. He checked envelopes for return addresses and postmarks from Canon City, where Simon had been imprisoned.

"Look at this." Andi brushed her fingers against grayed areas on the black pages where photographs had been removed. "That's Grandma, there's Mom. The baby is me. This is my dad. I don't know who these people are. But some pictures have been removed."

He sorted more papers and found an official document. He read it quickly and rubbed his thumb over the notary seal. Then he gave it to Andi.

As she read, her face grew wistful. "Divorced. That must have been the ultimate humiliation for Grandma." She laughed dryly. "Divorce was a dirtier word than . . . any four-letter word."

"Divorced in 1956," he mused aloud. "He must have been going bad long before he ripped off the jewels."

Her eyes sparked. "That's unfair."

"What?"

"Divorce doesn't make him bad. You're divorced."

He drew his head aside and narrowed his eyes. "Different circumstances."

"You don't know my grandparents' circumstances. Maybe she went bad first. Why did your wife leave you?"

He started to say because of Rex, but looking back, he realized that wasn't so. "We married too young. I was twenty, she was nineteen, and the only thing we really wanted was to get out of the college dorms."

She leaned forward, and her eyes were soft with curiosity. "Do you miss her?"

"We weren't going in the same direction." As he spoke the words, he finally heard the truth in them. He hadn't lost his wife because of Rex; he'd lost her long before Rex stole his first dollar. Rex had been a handy excuse for both of them. He studied Andi, knowing what had been missing from his marriage. He'd placed his ideals above his ex-wife. She hadn't meant enough to him to make compromises. But Andi shook the very foundations of his soul, made him question his personal truths.

"Old history." He lifted a shoulder. "Unlike this—" he patted the papers "—not even interesting history."

"Has she remarried?"

He nodded.

"Did your family really disown you?"

"Enough about me. We've got work to do."

She fumbled with a photo album. "Sorry."

Hearing how sharply he'd spoken, he winced. *Quit being a jerk, Coplin.* "Yeah, they disowned me. Or I disowned them. It's hard to remember exactly anymore."

"Your parents are alive?"

"And my brother and sister."

She rubbed the divorce decree between her fingers and thumb. "Don't you miss them?"

He started to say no, but she'd hear the lie. "Yeah, sometimes. But too many things can't be unsaid, too many hurts can't be healed."

"You should at least call your mother."

"She isn't calling me."

She set the album aside and reached for more papers. "Maybe she's scared. Like you are."

He opened his mouth to protest, but she'd hear that lie, too.

"You should call her. It's a lot better than this. Lies, secrets, lost grandpas. Such a waste. You can't love somebody without getting mad at them at least sometimes, but you get over it. You do love your family, don't you?"

"It's complicated."

"Either you do or you don't. There's nothing complicated about it."

"I know how they feel about me."

"Sure you do." She cast him a disgusted look.

For more than an hour they went through the trunk. He found a newspaper clipping dated May 6, 1963. The headline read Gardener Nabbed In Jewel Heist.

Andi stiffened. "You found something."

"Your grandmother followed the story." He gave her the clipping. "I have a copy of this article."

Color drained from Andi's face and her eyes shimmered.

"Hey, I told you about this. Don't cry."

She swiped at her eyes. "I won't. But seeing it in print... It's so hard to think of him killing anyone. If only you knew how gentle he is. Patient and sweetnatured, never an unkind word about anybody." She put the clipping aside.

Rayne found another clipping. The headline stated Judge Henry Throws The Book. Not remembering this article from his research, he read quickly. "This is strange."

"What is it?"

"An article about the trial. The nontrial actually. No trial by jury, just a hearing before a judge."

"Why would they do that to him?"

"He did it to himself. He waived his right and pleaded guilty." Puzzled by the stupidity of Simon's attorneys, he lifted his upper lip in a scowl. "No witnesses, no jewels, no evidence. Why didn't his attorney advise a jury trial?"

"Because he confessed?"

"A confession is only as good as the evidence to back it up. Any half-decent attorney can sidestep a confession."

"Maybe he was so ashamed of what he'd done, he couldn't face a jury."

"That would be a historical first. Quote," he said, and began to read.

"'Judge Barry Henry admonished the defendant, saying, "You are mistaken in your notion that a show of repentance grants you the leniency of this court. Your crime is most foul, the ultimate betrayal against your employer. The state of Colorado will not allow you to profit from your crimes.' End quote."

"But he didn't profit."

"We won't know for sure if he did or not until we find him." Nagged by a feeling that he'd missed something, he studied the clipping again. He'd dug up dozens of articles from the newspaper and library, learning plenty about Simon and his crimes. But something was missing; something important. Finally he set the clipping aside. It would come to him eventually.

Andi reached into the trunk for more papers. "If he did have the jewels, he could have removed the gems and melted the settings the way you said that woman did. He didn't need Keller—" Andi jerked her hand out of the trunk as if something had bitten her.

Rayne jumped on the seat. "Spiders?"

"No." She swallowed hard.

He looked inside. Nestled in the bottom of the trunk was a leather-bound case, about fourteen inches wide and twenty-four inches long. Emblazoned on the top, in gold leaf, was a large, ornate *H*.

Chapter Eleven

Rayne lifted the case out of the trunk and set it on the table. His jaw worked and he flexed his fingers over the fine dark leather like a pianist preparing to play. He lifted the lid.

Andi jammed her hands under her armpits. Around her the kitchen grayed, fading out of focus—except for the bracelet Rayne draped over his hand. Sharp and clear, the sight hurt her eyes. Each slight turn of his wrist caused the diamonds to flash and sparkle with fiery white light. The setting was shaped like a vine, and dark blue sapphires, cut into tiny flowers, bloomed amid thousands of brilliant stones.

"Those are not the Hamburg jewels," she said.

He laid the bracelet inside a slim, velvet-lined box. Similar boxes of all shapes and sizes nestled like puzzle pieces inside the monogrammed leather case. He opened a square box, revealing a large circle brooch made of gold and inlaid with carved bloodred stones.

Andi clenched her fists. "Those absolutely cannot be the Hamburg jewels. They can't be!"

Another velvet box held a choker necklace made of four strands of pearls linked by green gems. "I saw a book at the library. It has pictures of the collection."

Rayne rubbed a pearl, his finger trembling slightly. "I recognize this. And the brooch, too. It's Celtic, over a thousand years old."

Panic attacked Andi from all sides until every breath hurt and she thought her heart might explode. Up until Rayne had opened the case, the jewel theft and murder had been theory, her grandfather's role open to conjecture. She could find an explanation, reasonable or otherwise, for everything. But not now. Not for this.

He put the pearls back in their box, rearranged the velvet cases to their original fit, then closed the case. He slumped on the chair and let his arms dangle. "Call the cops. Ask for robbery."

She leapt across piles of albums and papers and caught his shirtfront in both fists. "Grandma's not a thief!" She shook him, needing to knock sense into him. He caught her wrists.

"Calm down."

"No! No." Sagging, she turned him loose. He eased his grip and slid his hands to her hands and entwined his fingers with hers.

"When did your grandmother die?"

"1976," she whispered.

"Are you sure?"

"Of course I'm sure."

"You didn't know your grandfather was alive."

"She died in her sleep in this house. I went to her funeral."

"Don't get mad. In light of this development, these are reasonable questions. You've never looked inside this trunk."

"I was ten years old when she died. I remember the trunk in her room, but . . . no, I'd forgotten about it until today." She laughed, but her laughter caught in a sob. "Those are not the Hamburg jewels. They can't be."

"Only an expert can tell for sure, but we'll let the police dig up the expert." He stood and pulled her hands against his chest. As he studied her face, his eyes were kind but troubled. "This is good, Andi. We turn over the jewels and by tomorrow it'll be all over the news. The fat man and his buddies will know the jig's up and Simon will know it's safe to come out of hiding. Then you can deal with him."

"Mom must have known about this. She had to." She rested her forehead against his chest and squeezed his fingers with all her strength. "They were crooks," she said, her voice squeaky. "For all I know they were robbing banks or trains!"

"Sweetheart, calm down."

"I always thought Grandma's money came from her inheritance from her parents, but now I don't know."

"You're being melodramatic. Cut it out."

"If the police come, then we have to explain where the jewels came from. Then reporters will find out. I can just see the headlines!" She gave her head a violent shake. "We have to think of something else."

"You sat here in this kitchen, this very day, lecturing me about lies and taking the good with the bad. Now's your chance to put your words into action."

"But Grandma? Mom?" She pulled away from him and opened the refrigerator. She grabbed bowls and plopped them on the counter. "There has to be a good explanation for this. There has to be. Grandma was crazy as a bedbug, but she wasn't a thief. And Mom was a librarian, for goodness' sake!" She snatched a butcher knife out of a wooden holder.

"You're going to hurt yourself waving that knife around like that." He flopped on a chair, crossed his arms and scowled at the leather case. It gleamed richly under the kitchen lights. The gold *H* seemed to wink.

She removed the beef from its pepper-and-wine marinade and started to slice it. The familiar work soothed her a little. Rayne's silent strong presence soothed her even more. *Think,* she ordered herself. She flipped on the broiler oven. Rational explanations eluded her.

Arranging the meat on a broiler pan, she said, "I know! We'll wrap up the case in brown paper like a regular old package and sneak it over to the Hamburg house. We'll ring the doorbell then run. That way they get the—"

"We can't give the jewels to the Hamburgs."

"Why not?"

He sighed patiently. "An insurance company paid off the family for the loss. They've got first dibs on recovering their money."

"Oh." She mulled over his words. "Fine, we'll wrap it up in brown paper like a regular old package and pretend we're a delivery company and—"

"All right!" He threw up his hands and turned a martyred expression toward the heavens.

"Really?"

"It doesn't matter how we turn them in as long as we do it." He looked disgusted—with himself or her, she couldn't tell. "But you're right. Smearing your grandmother and mother when they can't defend themselves is, well, it's...unsporting."

She wiped her hands on a towel.

"It'll take some doing. But you'd better prepare yourself for some heat. The press has to find out so we can get the fat man off Simon's back. This will be major news and some swiftie will dig up the connection between you and Simon. Count on it.''

''Just as long as nobody knows the jewels came out of my grandmother's trunk.'' She moved beside him and eased the hair off his brow. She wanted so much to plop onto his lap and kiss him and hug him—and tell him she loved him. She settled for ''You have such a good heart.''

He snorted and slapped a hand atop the case. ''And a soft head.''

Andi finished fixing dinner. While they ate broiled beef in tortillas with rice and a fresh fruit salad, they read old letters. Rayne recorded every name and address they found. Andi searched for clues as to why her grandmother had hidden a fortune in jewels in her keepsake trunk.

At intervals, Rayne tried to call Ford. ''Must be on a date,'' he kept saying. ''Ford refuses to take calls when he's with a woman. Says it's impolite.''

They moved into the living room, and each sat on an end of the couch, surrounded by piles of fragile old papers.

Andi began to suspect Grandma had always been emotionally fragile. In letters, friends asked veiled questions about her ''little depressions.'' After the robbery in 1963, the letters dwindled in number, until by 1964 there was no personal correspondence at all.

Andi understood some of her grandmother's many quirks now, like her refusal to answer the phone. Or how a stranger on the sidewalk in front of the house would drive her to her room with a migraine. And her habit of suddenly setting aside her crocheting and creeping to the window and peering outside made sense now, in light of years spent waiting for the cops to show up and arrest her.

She also understood why Simon and Opal had divorced. Grandma's friends had held the conviction that Simon married her only for her money, that he was a scoundrel and wastrel and, worst of all, a common laborer lacking ambition. Andi could only speculate about the pressures put on her grandmother from friends and family while her marriage was intact.

"Listen to this." When Rayne looked up, she read, "'All of us are pleased that you have found means to finally rid yourself and dear Millicent of that man. I will not belabor what for you must indeed be painful beyond measure.'" Andi frowned in bemusement. "It's dated a month after the robbery. I'm sure she's talking about my grandfather."

"Means to rid herself of that man?"

"As if she's responsible for sending him to—" Hearing where her words led, she snapped her mouth shut.

Rayne finished for her. "Sending him to prison." His eyes widened. "What if she committed the robbery and—"

"I refuse to even discuss anything so outrageous as my grandmother framing him."

He opened his mouth as if to argue, then grinned and shook his head. "Whatever you say."

She tossed aside the puzzling letter. "I thought I had a perfectly normal family. Sure fooled me."

He chuckled. "Keep reading. If we're lucky, someone might have an idea about where Simon would hide out."

"My eyes are killing me." She leaned her head against the back of the couch and closed her eyes to rest for a minute....

A muffled sound startled Andi and her eyelids flew open. Befuddled, she studied the light in the room. Lamps were on, but most of the light came from outside. She hadn't merely dozed, she'd slept through the night.

She grew aware that the hard object pressing her cheek was Rayne's belt buckle. He draped one heavy hand over her back. She was curled on her side between his legs, and one hand grasped his thigh. The other, crushed under her body, and her feet, jammed against the unyielding couch arm, were soundly numbed. She couldn't feel her toes at all.

Eyes closed, chin to chest, one arm dangling off the couch, Rayne slept. She listened to him breathe. How had she ended up like this?

"Rayne?" He snorted softly but didn't open his eyes. She said, more loudly, "Rayne? I'm stuck." His eyelids flickered and he scowled. "I can't move."

He lazily caressed her back and a twitch of a smile teased his lips. Nice... His hand explored her shoulder blades and moved higher, until his fingers slid gently under the neck of her T-shirt. Suddenly her cramped legs and numb arm didn't matter. "Rayne?"

He squeezed his eyelids, then looked at her. Now his changeable eyes were like mountain pools, still and deep and darkest blue. "Must've nodded off," he muttered. He winced and turned his face away from the sunshine streaming in golden banners through the lacy curtains.

"I can't move. Let me up."

He struggled against the pull of sleep. His lopsided grin made him look very young. "You're pretty in the morning," he said, tickling the back of her neck.

She clamped down on the rising pleasure. He was half-asleep—she was only a client—he didn't mean anything by it. "Let me up."

It took several clumsy maneuvers for both of them to untangle themselves off the hard-cushioned camelback couch. Joints popped and they grimaced and rubbed pinpricking numbness from their arms and legs.

"Waking up with you in my arms is nice, but this couch is a killer."

The sleepy comment, spoken idly as if to himself, caused a hopeful catch in Andi's throat. Did he want to awaken with her in his arms? As quickly as hope rose, she knew she had to quit wishing and pretending he cared about her in that way. Her crazy impulsiveness had already created enough grief between them.

Wincing at each tingling step, she hobbled to the bathroom. When she returned, Rayne sat hunched over with his elbows on his knees, resting his head on his hands. She asked if he was okay.

"Just reminiscing about the all-nighters I used to pull in college. I'm getting old." He stood and stretched, reaching for the ceiling and arching his back.

Andi forced herself not to stare. "I'll make you some coffee. Is it too early to call Mr. Hayes?"

He looked at his watch. "Serves him right if I wake him up."

She paused in the kitchen doorway and frowned. "Wait a minute. Now I'm confused again. If the woman in the Cadillac isn't my grandfather's accomplice, why did she try to give him money?"

"I don't know, sweetheart." He flopped a hand in her direction. "Let's do what we can with what we know and worry about the other stuff later."

She grinned. He really needed some coffee.

She started water boiling and leafed through a cookbook for a coffee cake recipe. He wandered into the kitchen. He carried the telephone, trailing the long cord. He stopped short, staring at the table.

Wondering what he saw that made his mouth hang open and turned his brow thunderous, she followed his gaze. It took a few seconds to realize it wasn't what he saw, it was what he didn't see.

The jewel case was gone.

"Hold on a minute, Ford," he said, and pressed the handset against his chest. "Did you put it back in the trunk?"

Her heart began beating in triple-time. She thrust open the trunk lid. A sheet of paper, folded in half, fluttered to the floor.

Her scalp tightened and breathing grew painful as she picked it up and opened it. The scratchy scrawled words made her light-headed. She sat on the floor with a thump.

"I've got a problem here," Rayne said into the phone. "I'll call you back in a minute."

Andi raised a pained gaze to Rayne. "Omigosh."

He crouched and took the paper.

My dearest Andi, You will never understand because I cannot explain. Know only that these things are cursed and must never be found. I am so sorry. Please, I beg you with all my heart, stop searching for me. Mr. Simon.

He dropped onto a chair, gaping at the note. "You did lock the back door last night. Right?"

"I never unlocked it." She pushed off the floor and grabbed the knob. It turned easily. Her knees went weak and she staggered. The spider. She'd opened the door to release the spider. "Omigosh."

Rayne scrambled to his feet and whirled in a tight circle. He slammed both fists on the kitchen counter.

Crockery rattled. Through his teeth, each word clipped, he said, "That crazy old son of a bitch ripped us off."

"I'm sorry. I, I—" Her eyes burned and her throat tightened.

Rayne's shoulders slumped and he pulled her against his chest, stroking her hair. "It's okay, it's not your fault. Don't start crying."

Fighting tears, she snuffled. "How did he know? What do we do?"

He snatched up the telephone again. As he punched in the numbers, he bounced on the balls of his feet. "Ford! Man, we have a major problem here. Get over here now. Andi's house. You aren't going to believe this."

Andi didn't believe it. How could she have been so stupid not to check the doors? How could her grandfather do this to her?

When Ford arrived, Rayne patted her shoulder and told her to shower and dress. He'd explain to his partner what had happened. By the time she finished dressing, the men sat in the kitchen, each with a cup of coffee. A cup of steaming tea waited for her. Rayne no longer looked angry.

Unable to look either man in the eye, she sat on a step stool and stared at the note.

"Ford thinks your house is bugged," Rayne said. "It's the only way he could've known we found the jewels."

"Like with microphones?" She looked about.

"Too late to worry about it. He has what he wants. We'll sweep the place later and see what we can find." He rubbed his temples with his fingertips. "Simon scammed you but good. He's no more sweet little old man than I am. This is what he wanted all along."

"We must call the police," Ford said.

"What can we tell them? He stole the jewels he stole thirty years ago? Jewels I found hidden in my grandmother's trunk?" She lowered a withering gaze on Rayne. "He did not scam me. There is more to it than this." She slapped the note. "The jewels are cursed. He's protecting me."

Rayne leaned back on the chair and folded his arms over his chest. "I told you, man."

"Unearthing old scandals makes for pleasurable reading in the tabloids, but it's never pleasant when it concerns one's own family. However, the police are equipped to apprehend the culprit where we are not."

She knew Ford was right. She looked at the trunk. "How could he do this to me?"

"Greed," Rayne said quietly.

"I will contact my friend Paul Sevilla. He will find a way to handle this delicately."

"If he doesn't try to sell the jewels, he won't go back to prison, right?" Storms of emotion made sitting still impossible, and she fidgeted on the stool. "He already served his sentence for the robbery. And if he didn't know where Grandma hid the jewels, then he was telling the truth . . . technically. And—isn't there some way we can stop him?"

"Andi—"

"We have names from Grandma's letters. Someone has to know where he is."

Ford said, "He's committed a burglary, my dear."

She clamped her arms over her chest and hunched against her knees. "It's my house, so it's only a burglary if I say it is."

Rayne slapped the tabletop. "Don't do this."

Uneasy under his blazing eyes, Andi straightened her back.

He snatched up the note and waved it under her nose. "It's plain as day what's happening here. He knew the jewels were somewhere in this house. He used you to find them."

She pushed away from the table, left the kitchen and flopped onto the couch. Hugging herself, rocking on the cushions, she fought tears of frustration. A chair scraped the kitchen floor. She squeezed her eyes shut.

"I know you're upset," Rayne said gently.

She pinched the bridge of her nose to stop the tears. "I'm not upset, I'm furious. I feel so stupid! They all lied to me. All of them. This whole house is a lie!" From the corner of her eye she saw Ford with the telephone. "Is he calling the police?"

He sat beside her. "It's the only way to put a stop to this."

She rubbed her burning eyes. "He's going back to prison. He'll die in there. He was my friend, how could he do this to me?"

"He didn't do it to you. He did it for himself."

Ford finished on the telephone. Holding the note, he said, "Paul will be by shortly. He understands your desire for discretion."

"Thank you." Andi plucked at her skirt.

Looking between Andi and the note, Ford cocked his head and frowned. "While you were otherwise occupied, Rayne took the liberty of showing me your attic, my dear. I hope you do not mind. I admit to a small measure of skepticism about the jewels remaining undiscovered for so many years. A look at your attic erased my skepticism."

Andi couldn't hold back a sheepish smile.

"The more I consider this matter, the more I realize there are some rather puzzling aspects to it. If I understand correctly, your grandmother lived her entire life within these walls?''

"Yes."

"And we can assume she lived here during her married life, as well?"

"Yes."

"Which leads me to think Simon is well aware of your family's proclivities toward retaining possessions. He was also aware, despite the clever carpentry over the attic door, of the existence of the stairs leading to the many treasures above."

Unsure where this was heading, she nodded. "Of course he knew. In fact, I met Mr. Simon before I had the kitchen redone. He helped me clear out cabinets and put up the new wallpaper." She looked at Rayne; he peered suspiciously at his partner. "What are you saying, Mr. Hayes?"

"When the necessity of searching the past for clues to the present grew apparent to you, your grandmother's trunk came to mind. Why would Simon not have the same thought? He was, after all, married to her for some years and had some understanding of her thought processes and habits."

Rayne shook a finger at his partner. "I see where this is leading."

Andi asked, "Where?"

"You gave Simon many opportunities to search the house. But he didn't." Ford waved the note slowly back and forth. "Perhaps his story about discarding the jewels was not so much a lie as a misconception. Perhaps he requested your grandmother to dispose of them."

She shot an accusing glare at Rayne. "Then he wasn't scamming me!"

"Wait a minute," Rayne blustered. "What about Keller and the fat man?"

Ford settled on a chair and rested a foot on his knee. "Prison communities foster active imaginations but offer little outlet for imaginative energies. It is my understanding that gossip-mongering and repeating rumors are favored pastimes. No one in the law enforcement community believed Simon actually threw the jewels in the river. Why should Keller Poe?"

"Why did Simon run?" Rayne asked. "Why not pull out his empty pockets and tell Keller he was full of it?"

Ford swung his gaze to Andi. "Because Simon had something to lose."

"Me," she said, smiling in wonder. "He thought if he hid, they'd give up and go away. And then he'd never have to tell me who he was or what he'd done."

Rayne clamped his arms over his chest and jutted his jaw stubbornly.

"I suspect your discovering the jewels surprised Simon as much as it surprised you. Which leads me to believe that whatever urge drove him to attempt destroying the collection thirty years ago remains with him to this day."

"Aw, come on, Ford, there are holes in that theory big enough to drive my Jeep through. This stinks of a con game and you know it."

Andi scowled. "I am getting sick and tired of you being so cynical all the time."

Rayne tightened his lips and his eyes blazed. Tendons strained as his long fingers squeezed his biceps.

"We're not talking about some faceless monster. He's my grandfather and I love him and he's all I have in the world, and you're so set on throwing him back into prison that you don't even care how I feel!"

"I'm looking at the facts," he said through his teeth.

Ford made a soothing noise, but Andi leapt to her feet and whirled on Rayne. She shook a finger at his face. "Just because you're so self-righteous and—and too chicken to care about your family doesn't mean I have to stop caring about mine!"

"I am not chicken!"

"You won't even call your own mother!" She stomped into the kitchen and pulled a mixing bowl from a cabinet.

Behind her, Rayne's boots shook the floor. "We're not talking about me. We're talking about you and it's about time you started using your head."

She slammed flour, brown sugar and baking powder on the counter. "Now I'm stupid? Thank you." She turned on the oven then began jamming brown sugar into a measuring cup.

He huffed and caught her shoulder. She twisted away, but he closed in, backing her into a corner. He clamped his hands on the countertop on either side of her. "Hasn't he done enough damage to your life—your house messed up, strange men threatening you, all the money you're spending. Look at you, you're exhausted."

"I'm just a client. What do you care?"

"Rayne," Ford said from the doorway. "There is an easy way to test my theory."

Rayne and Andi turned on Ford. He leaned a shoulder against the doorframe, his posture jaunty and his expression amused. As one, Rayne and Andi asked, "How?" They glanced warily at each other.

"Miss Blair, on your first visit to our office you made a passing comment about believing someone had invaded your home."

"The fat man...."

"Before then. And have you not complained about odd noises? Misplaced items?" He swept his hand toward the pantry double doors. "If I am correct, then there is only one way Simon could have known you found the jewels."

Andi stared at the ceiling. Her lungs compressed. "He's in my attic?"

"I believe that would be past tense, my dear."

She tore open the pantry and swung back the shelves.

"That's the screwiest thing I ever heard," Rayne said, but when she ran up the attic stairs, he followed hot on her heels.

At the door to her childhood bedroom, she paused, her hand on the knob. She glanced at Rayne and he lifted his shoulders in a quick shrug. She jerked open the door.

A wave of heat took her breath away. The dormer windows faced east and the full force of the morning sun turned the closed room into an oven. One look around showed the truth of Ford's words.

The narrow iron-frame bed was no longer piled with boxes and junk. Dirty dishes and two glass gallon jugs, one full of water and the other half-full, sat on the floor. A book of poetry, dust-free and with a place held by a tasseled bookmark, sat on a box. Unwashed body odor gave the overheated room a zoo stink.

She picked up a small plastic bowl and turned it in her hands, recognizing it as one for which she'd found a lid the other day but had been unable to find the bowl. She sagged against the doorjamb and covered her eyes with a hand. "He was right here under our noses. Above our noses! How could I be so stupid?"

Mouth agape, Rayne stepped into the small, cluttered room. "I'll be damned. Mr. Dipwell was right. He did see a man in your house."

A car door slammed out front. Andi looked out the window and recognized Sergeant Paul Sevilla. The sight of him roused unpleasant memories of Keller Poe's sightless eyes. A nasty taste filled her mouth—had her grandfather killed Keller Poe? He'd confessed once. Would he do so again? "He's here. What do we do?"

Ford said, "We speak the truth, my dear."

They went downstairs. Andi offered to make coffee. Rayne urged her into the living room and told her he'd make the coffee.

Wearing a dry, I've-heard-it-all expression, Sergeant Sevilla sat on the easy chair. Where his jacket pulled back, Andi could see a spiral-bound notebook in his shirt pocket. His leaving it in his pocket made him seem less official and eased her nervousness somewhat.

She started at the beginning, with her grandfather's disappearance. Ford and Rayne filled in a few details, but she covered most of it. Sevilla showed no reaction until she reached the part about Grandma's trunk and the jewels. He lifted his eyebrows and tapped his thumb against his coffee cup.

"And now they're gone again." She gave the policeman the note. "He's been hiding in my attic."

Sevilla's thumb tap-tap-tapped against the ceramic mug. His dark eyes glittered. "Ford, all that snooping around about Poe, and you didn't say a word about the Hamburg jewel robbery."

"The jewels are a most recent development in our investigation." Ford, all bland innocence, sipped coffee.

Sevilla snorted. "You talk more and say less than anybody in the world." His gaze roamed the room. "You have a lot of old stuff in this house." He stared at her silver and stone necklace. "Are you sure those were the Hamburg jewels?"

She lifted a shoulder.

Rayne said, "We're sure."

"Why didn't you call me last night?" the detective asked. "You have a history of break-ins. You know those jewels are valuable."

Rayne started to answer, but Andi placed her hand against his chest and shook her head. "It's all my fault. I don't want everyone in the world knowing my grandparents are thieves. I wanted to find a way to give the jewels back anonymously." She sighed. "Guess I messed that up."

Ford disagreed. "What is gained by sullying the name of a woman long dead and unable to defend her reputation? It is my hope that on the lady's behalf we arrive at a solution to this problem in a manner designed to save her embarrassment."

"I don't know if I can do that."

"Driven by will and ingenuity, all things are possible."

"You're talking about a cover-up. How many people know what you just told me?"

"All of it?" Andi shook her head. "We only found the jewels last night." She buried her face in her hands. "I know I should have called the police! I'm so sorry."

"It is my belief, Paul," Ford said, "that Simon spoke a peculiar truth. Perhaps some deep-seated delusion causes him to believe the jewels are indeed cursed. Or if not delusion, then obsession. Whatever his motivation, it's conceivable that he intends to dispose of them."

The detective tapped both thumbs against his coffee cup. "Neither of you brain boys has any idea where Simon is now. Or where he might go."

"We have a list of names," Andi offered. "People my grandparents knew."

Paul leaned forward abruptly and put down the coffee cup. "Miss Blair, do you intend to file a burglary complaint against Simon Foulkes?" His brusque words rang with accusation.

"Ease up, man." An undercurrent of threat laced Rayne's voice. His shoulders stiffened. "She's not the bad guy."

"I'm getting mixed messages here." Sevilla locked a narrow-eyed gaze on Ford. "Friendship is one thing, but I'm getting the idea you're wanting something shady."

Ford waved his hands gracefully in small arcs. "Now, Paul, we have known each other many years. You're aware of the value I place upon my reputation. I but seek your advice in the handling of this most unusual and potentially explosive situation."

"Talk English."

"Two gentlemen of dubious character are in pursuit of Simon. Now that he has been flushed from concealment and has in his possession the Hamburg jewel collection, the danger to him is great and grave. Rayne and I will devote our undivided energy toward finding Simon, but his possession of the jewels falls into an area considerably gray. Already Simon has served an inordinately lengthy incarceration."

The detective stared at him pointedly. "You don't want the old geezer going back to the joint."

Andi brightened. "Is that possible? I know he's confused, and he's done something wrong, but—"

"It's up to the district attorney."

"Suppose he has the jewels," Andi asked, "but doesn't try to sell them?"

"The D.A. will take that into consideration." Sevilla stroked his jaw. "Understand, I won't let you pull anything."

Ford grinned. "You know me better than that."

The detective snorted. "I'll do what I can do. In exchange, you let me know the minute you find Simon or the jewels. If you want cooperation from the D.A.—and me—you got to cooperate first."

"Understandable."

"Rayne, Ford tells me you keep good case notes. I want copies. Don't give me any crap about confidentiality."

Ford nodded. "You'll have copies by this afternoon."

Andi remained seated until after the detective left her house. His comment about her grandfather's fate being up to the district attorney kept running through her mind. After all the lies, the sneaking around and restealing the jewels, did he stand a chance? Hope proved as elusive as Simon.

Chapter Twelve

Rayne told Andi to stay home and keep the doors locked while he and Ford ran down leads. He suggested she contact the people who'd written letters to her grandmother.

All morning she tried. She called directory assistance for countless small towns in southeastern Colorado, Kansas, Nebraska and Texas, but the women who'd once corresponded with Opal Foulkes had either died, moved or married and changed names. The passage of thirty years defeated her.

Disgusted with her failure, needing desperately to do something, she drove to the library. In the local history section, she found several books containing information about the Hamburg family. One, a biography of Wolfgang Hamburg, had pages of color photographs depicting the fabulous jewels.

Her grandfather was sunk.

She checked out the books and went outside to her car. From where she stood, Colorado Springs seemed huge—its wide streets and sidewalks stretched forever. The tall Antler's hotel, a grand dowager, towered over downtown, and the office buildings shadowed the streets with polarized windows like dark, anonymous eyes. Who cared about one frightened, confused old man?

Who would help him?

She pulled into traffic but drove slowly, ignoring glares from drivers who speeded up to whip around her. She studied the face of every man she saw on the street.

She cruised up and down streets from Platte to Fountain and back again. On Nevada, waiting for a traffic light, she saw an elderly man garbed in a sweater and jacket despite the heat. Head down, stooped, he shuffled across the street. *Not my grandfather,* she thought sadly. The light changed and she took her foot off the brake, then noticed where the old man was headed. A pawnshop. On its window, in big yellow letters, it stated We Buy Gold, Silver, Watches. A car blared its horn behind her. She found a parking place, twisted on the seat and watched the old man enter the pawnshop.

Would he?

Pawning even one piece of jewelry would get her grandfather enough cash for a bus ticket out of Colorado Springs. Which meant he would go back to prison.

Unless Andi stopped him.

She grabbed the book about Wolfgang Hamburg and hurried into the shop. She eyed the merchandise for sale. The place was well lighted and cleaner than she'd expected, but it unnerved her to see so many rifles affixed to wall racks and handguns in cases.

"May I help you, miss?" A woman behind a glass display case smiled.

"I'm not sure." She clutched the book to her breast. "I have a problem."

The woman kept smiling and it occurred to Andi that the clerk probably dealt with all sorts of people with problems. Andi opened the book to the photographs and looked about to make sure no one was eavesdropping. "My grandfather might have sold some jewelry. Or he may try."

The woman arched a suspicious eyebrow. "We don't deal in stolen goods."

"Oh, no! That's not what I meant. I mean—oh, it's very complicated. Here, look at these."

The woman ran her finger over the pages. "Am I on 'Candid Camera'?" She fluffed her hair and peered at corners.

"He's a dear, sweet little old man, but he's frightened. All I'm asking is if he comes in and tries to sell any jewelry, you call me."

"Sorry. If I suspect stolen goods, I call the cops. That's how I stay in business."

"Please? I'll give you my number." She pawed through her purse for a pen. "My grandfather is very confused. He's in his seventies, about my height, but frail with gray hair and blue eyes." She wrote her name and number on the back of the shop's business card. She handed it to the woman. "Please?"

The woman backed away, unsmiling, taut with hostility. Andi prayed her grandfather didn't try to sell anything in this store.

Wondering what Rayne would think about her activities, but somehow doubting he'd approve, she visited every pawnshop she could find in the downtown area. Everyone she spoke to reacted much the way the first woman had, and her voice grew hoarse from pleading her case. Her only consolation was that no one acted as if her grandfather had already sold anything.

She remembered an antique store not four blocks from her home. Antique dealers probably paid cash, too.

As soon as she showed the owner the photographs, the man lost all color in his face and whispered, "Good God, the Hamburg collection. Are you for real?"

"You know about this?"

"My dear woman," he said stiffly, "any person who knows even a jot about collectible jewelry understands the importance of this collection. The theft and disappearance of this remains one of the great mysteries of the century!"

"So you'd recognize it if he tried to sell you something?"

He leaned an arm on the counter. "Have you any idea what this collection is worth?"

Andi ventured, "A lot?"

He put a finger on a photograph of a necklace. "Created for a Russian crown princess." He moved his finger to the picture of the Celtic brooch. "Reputed to have held closed the cloak of King Arthur, or the king upon whom the legend is based."

"Really?"

"We're talking millions." His eyes lighted up greedily. "Part of me is convinced you're pulling my leg, but part of me is going crazy thinking up a way to get my hands on some of this. On the off chance your grandfather does have these jewels, and if he tries to sell them anywhere in the state of Colorado..." He shook his head. "He's a dead duck."

Andi swallowed hard.

"That collection is so hot it'll start forest fires. There isn't a reputable dealer in town who wouldn't call the cops as soon as they got a whiff of this. And there are some people not so reputable. Catch my drift?" He eyed the photographs with longing. "I can't help you. Sorry."

Thoroughly disheartened, she left the store. Passing cars had their lights on and the streetlight glowed pink yellow. It appalled her to see how far the sun had dipped toward the mountains. She slid onto the seat and accidentally knocked the library book against the steering wheel. It flew onto the gravel parking lot, landing open with the pages down. She groaned in dismay, picked up the book and checked it for damage. A picture caught her eye.

In a stark black-and-white photograph, Gretchen's daughter, Marilyn Hamburg-Mosse, posed like a movie star with her head high and her long neck extended. She clutched one shoulder. The caption said she was sixteen, but in a draped white gown and with her pale blond hair swept high, she looked much older.

What drew Andi's attention was the large ring Marilyn wore. Andi peered closer and closer until her nose nearly touched the page.

She knuckled her fatigue-sore eyes, then looked again. No doubt about it. The ring in the picture was identical to the red-jeweled, spider-shaped ring worn by the strange woman driving the Cadillac.

Understanding hit with such force she sat frozen, wide-eyed and openmouthed.

For whatever reason, her grandfather had stolen the jewels and given them to her grandmother to hide. But he got caught, and he couldn't squeal on his ex-wife, so he confessed and went to prison. He must have contacted Marilyn to apologize, but she'd assumed a murderer was after her. So this whole thing was a huge misunderstanding. He wasn't trying to sell them; he was trying to give them back to her!

Invigorated, she drove home and rushed inside. She snatched up the phone, dialed Rayne's office and reached an answering machine. She tried his home number and reached another answering machine. Frustrated, she carried the phone into the kitchen and found the phone book. She searched for Ford's home number but couldn't find a listing.

From the corner of her eye she caught a movement. Every hair on her body stood erect and her heart skipped a painful beat.

The fat man grinned at her.

Arms crossed over his bullish chest, he filled the kitchen and squeezed out all the air. He was taller than Rayne and at least seventy pounds heavier. His arms looked as big around as her legs, their size accentuated by crude tattoos—black snakes, crosses, skulls, thunderbolts and patterns formed by dots.

"Okay," he said in a patient tone. "You got your decent dead bolts. But since you got a window in the door, leaving the key in the lock is dumb. I understand you worry about fires and stuff, but you gotta use your head."

He broke into her house to lecture her about proper security? She licked her lips. "What do you want?"

He swung his heavy, bullet-shaped head. "I been watching you hit pawnshops all day." He snorted a soft laugh. "Amateurs! What did they give you? A penny on the dollar?"

He thought she'd been pawning the jewels? She swayed dizzily and caught the kitchen counter for support.

He placed a hand over his heart. "Don't be looking like I'm some kind of Jack the Ripper. I ain't gonna hurt you."

"Then leave."

His smile made his eyes disappear in crinkles of flesh. "Gimme the rest of the goodies, then I split. No problemo."

"I don't have anything." He blocked the way to the living room, but if she could reach the back door... "I swear, I don't."

He had the biggest hands she'd ever seen, with thick, muscular fingers and palms the size of bread plates. An image of those hands around her throat, snapping vertebrae like dry wood, made her choke.

"All right, lady, let's work a deal to make both of us happy. To hell with Simon and the gumshoes." He waggled his eyebrows as if he honestly believed she'd play along. "How much did you hock?"

The attic. Get him up to the attic and he'd think she was trapped, but if she could get to her old bedroom, she could lock the door, get out the window, scream her head off and alert the neighbors. Or jump off the roof.

"I didn't pawn anything."

He scowled, making it look as if thinking hurt.

"Honest. I have no idea what you're talking about," she said. Her cheeks burned. Good grief, couldn't she even lie to a crook without feeling guilty?

"Liar, liar, pants on fire." He *tsk*'d and wagged an admonishing finger. "I'm telling you this for your own good. This ain't your game. Not all the players are nice guys like me. Some of 'em would slit your throat just for the hell of it. And trust me, there ain't no such thing as beginner's luck. Even if some sharpie don't rip you off, the cops will tag you." He looked about the kitchen. "You wouldn't like prison."

The telephone rang. Andi eyed it, wanting to grab it and scream bloody murder so badly her mouth watered.

"That might be Rayne. If I don't answer, he'll know something is wrong."

He pulled a short black object from his back pocket and whopped it against his palm. It made a solid thunk. "This is a lead sap, lady. If I pop your elbow you'll be crying the blues the next couple of months."

The incessant ringing jangled her nerves, but when it stopped, the silence choked her.

She stared at the sap. About eight inches long, it didn't look big enough for the heavy thuds it made against the fat man's hand. "Dump your purse," he said.

She squeaked, "Purse?"

He took a step closer. She snatched her purse off the table and upended it. Wallet, papers, comb, cosmetics and gum spilled in a messy pile. Shifting his gaze between her and her belongings, he pawed through it. He emptied her wallet and glowered at the few dollar bills it contained.

"I told you, I didn't sell anything. I don't have anything."

"Yeah, like no sense." He took another step and she could smell gasoline and sweat. "But I'm a nice guy. So one more chance before I get mad and start breaking things. Like your arm maybe."

"All right, all right! You want the jewels."

He licked his lips hungrily. "Bingo."

"They're hidden in the attic, but I'll have to show you where they are."

"STILL NO ANSWER?" Ford asked. He craned his neck over the steering wheel and stared ahead at the traffic crawling south along I-25.

Befuddled, Rayne stared at the cellular telephone. "I don't like this. I told Andi to stay put today."

Rayne slumped on the luxurious Mercedes seat. He hated Denver and he especially hated Denver traffic. They'd been creeping along at less than twenty miles per hour for at least twenty minutes and still no sign of what caused the backup. He tried calling Andi again. No answer.

"I feel as if I am in a cage with a tiger." Ford smirked. "Aren't hungry, are you?"

"There must be an accident ahead. Get off the freeway."

"Surely you cannot be in that great a hurry to share our bad news with Miss Blair?"

Bad news was an understatement. This entire affair was merrily snowballing into the case from hell. Paul had run the Cadillac plate through the police computer and turned up one Marilyn Hamburg-Mosse. From there Rayne and Ford had gone to the American-Southwest insurance company headquarters in Denver, and all the puzzle pieces had slipped neatly into place.

The insurance company suspected Joseph King, the murdered jeweler, had discovered the collection was overinsured. Marilyn couldn't sell the jewels for enough money to pay off her massive debts. The insurance investigators speculated Marilyn had arranged for Simon to kill Joseph and take the jewels. With Joseph King out of the way and the jewels missing, the company had no choice except to pay off the insured value of one and a half million dollars.

When Simon confessed, the police had closed the case, but the insurance investigators kept digging. They were so convinced it was a case of fraud, they'd influenced Judge Henry to give Simon the maximum sentence in the hopes he'd crack and implicate Marilyn.

Marilyn... Rayne opened a folder to a photo the investigator at American-Southwest had given him. At age eighteen she'd been beautiful.

Simon had lived in a cottage behind the Hamburg mansion. According to the neighbors and servants, whenever Marilyn's mother left town, Simon had moved in with Marilyn. Everyone the investigators had spoken to claimed Simon and Marilyn were very close. Lovers. No wonder he'd taken the heat for her.

No wonder he wanted vengeance now.

Rayne and Ford suspected the twelve grand had been only one payoff among many. Simon had probably begun blackmailing Marilyn as soon as he was released from prison. Marilyn fought back by hiring Keller and the fat man. If not for Keller's freak accident, Andi would have found Simon's body in her backyard.

Rayne closed the folder. "Do you honestly think, after his run-in with Keller and the fat man, Simon is stupid enough to go to Marilyn in person?"

"I believe he will telephone her. In which case we may need to enjoin our voices with Paul's in order to find a judge who will authorize a wiretap. Patience. I'm certain Miss Blair is in no more of a hurry to hear what we have discovered than you are willing to give her the bad news."

Rayne checked his watch and growled. He shook his head in disgust at himself, this case and Simon. He was sick to death of hitting Andi with bad news every time she turned around. "It's nearly seven o'clock. At this rate it'll be nine or even ten before I can get to Andi's." Rayne stabbed the air with a finger. "Why can't these bozos drive like human beings?"

Ford grinned. "You're in love with her."

Rayne's back twitched. "She's my client."

"Client." Ford rolled the word off his tongue. "Might I inquire as to when you began spending nights with your clients? Or engaging them in shouting matches?" He cast Rayne a long, lingering look. "Calling them sweetheart?"

Rayne stared out the window at the cars creeping alongside them. An icy draft from the air conditioner brushed his chin and he adjusted the flow.

Ford laughed. "In all the years of our acquaintance I have observed your carefully constructed armor shielding you from emotional involvement. But she has found the chink."

Dismissing the too-close-for-comfort words with a shrug and a shake of his head, Rayne said, "How I feel about her makes no difference." He laughed dryly. "You know what's going to happen as well as I do. Simon's going back to prison and Andi will look for someone to blame. Guess who?"

Ford's smile faded. "Your willingness to underestimate her so thoroughly astonishes me. It rather disappoints me, too."

Ford so rarely criticized anyone, his words packed a double whammy. Rayne winced. "You think I'm wrong?"

"I also hold the opinion that you are an utter idiot."

Rayne bristled and clenched his fists. "Now—"

"Not to mention a coward." Ford arched his brows in careful disdain and blazing challenge. His dark eyes glittered with the passing lights. "The true difference betwixt us is that I am self-aware and you are not." He held up a hand to halt Rayne's rising protests. "Your brother's thievery was not your fault. You did the right thing. That you suffered for your deeds doesn't make what you did wrong. Nor does it make you undeserving of another's regard. Or a woman's love."

Rayne fiddled with the radio, searching for a traffic report. "Your card says private eye, not shrink, old man. I don't need lectures."

"But you do need Andi Blair."

Unable to force out a denial, he tried Andi's number again—still no answer. No matter what Ford said, before this was over, Andi would end up hating his guts.

LISTENING to the telephone ring, praying Rayne would take the hint and hurry to her house, Andi slowly climbed the attic stairs. She was too aware of the fat man's heavy tread behind her, and of his massive hands and that lead sap guaranteed to make her sing the blues.

"Be careful," she said. "The light is bad." *Three more steps, then run like crazy.* Her breathing roughened. Two more steps. One.

She caught the railing and launched herself down the narrow aisle. The door looked a million miles away. Gasping sobs, she stretched her arms before her, reaching for the door, praying she got inside the room before he caught—

White pain exploded in her head. He'd caught her hair! Her head snapped backward but her feet kept running, slipped and flew into the air. She struck the fat man and they both went down. She screamed; he grunted. She scrambled to her feet. Kicking and screaming, she leapt in a wild belly flop atop stacked boxes. Glass shattered and boxes toppled. Massive hands grabbed her ankle. She slipped and knocked her face against a box. The shocking pain spurred her into furious kicking and clawing. She connected with his belly and he staggered, losing his grip.

A stack of boxes collapsed, sending her tumbling in a cloud of dust to the floor. She landed on her shoulder between a tall stack of wooden chairs and a trunk. She squirmed on her belly and touched something cold and hard. The old paint can. She grabbed it by the thin wire handle and fought in the narrow space to turn over. The fat man yowled and lurched over boxes, crushing them under his oppressive weight. Andi screamed and swung the can of paint. It hit the top of his head with a solid thud that rattled her to her shoulder.

In the dim, gloomy, dusty light she saw the whites of his eyes. He looked shocked. She heard another thud. Air rushed from his mouth in a wispy sigh and he slumped, one hand dangling so it brushed her foot.

She struggled to her feet.

In the aisle, holding a spiral-carved bedpost, Simon Foulkes stood. Andi blinked slowly, wondering if she saw an apparition, her grandfather's ghost.

She dropped the can with a clatter, then lowered her gaze to the fat man's hanging head. Blood gleamed wetly on his hair. "Oh, no. I think we killed him."

Chapter Thirteen

Relief and shock made Andi tremble, causing the task of tying up the fat man to be a difficult one. His size alone was cumbersome. Fully conscious and on his feet, he was huge; unconscious and limp, he made Andi feel as though she was wrestling a whale.

Andi tied the last knot with a jerk. Trussed like a turkey, the fat man nestled between boxes on his side. He breathed regularly and his pulse was good. Andi checked his eyes, and as far as she could tell, his pupils looked normal.

She stood, using both hands to wipe sweat off her face, and stared at her grandfather. He looked horrible, worse than any attic ghost she could ever conjure. His cheeks were drawn and gaunt. His beard was patchy, iron gray streaked with pure white, and his complexion had a yellow cast. Even in the shadowy light, she could see his filthiness.

Andi picked her way over the clutter to the aisle. She was torn between wanting to gather him into her arms in a great hug and throwing up her hands in disgust. Limp and sore, she sat on a trunk and glumly eyed her grandfather. "I can't leave him up here forever." She narrowed her eyes. "Will you please explain to me what in the world is going on?"

He looked at the stairs and the floor and the ceiling. "I'm a bad man. Worse than that, I'm a stupid old fool." He peeked from under bushy, unkempt brows. Humble as a shamed dog, he shuffled to another trunk and sat carefully.

She blew out a long breath. "Bet you thought it was pretty funny hiding from us. How could you do this to me?"

"I didn't mean to." His gaze flicked at her as if he expected her to yell at him or hit him, before he focused on his hands.

Grimacing, she rubbed the back of her smarting head. She felt the bruises forming on her arms and legs. "It's bad enough you stole the jewels the first time. But it's worse to steal them again. Where are they?" She looked around the attic with dismay. He could have hidden them anywhere.

She drew a deep breath and felt cold despite the stultifying heat. He was so small and frail-looking. His bad color made him seem near death. "What am I supposed to do? You lied to me, you betrayed me. I thought you loved me."

"I do."

She shook her head. "If this was anyplace else, I would believe you. But in my attic, where you hid the jewels, hid yourself from me? I know you knew how worried I've been." She buried her face in her hands. She didn't want to cry, she was tired of crying. She pressed the heels of her hands against her eyes until she regained control.

"I'm sorry I lied to you. I thought it best."

"You're my grandfather."

"I promised Opal." He spoke barely above a mumble.

Exhaustion weighted her shoulders and made every movement drag. "Where are the jewels? I no longer care how this turns out, I just want it to end." She glanced back at the fat man and hoped bopping him on the head hadn't done any permanent damage.

Her grandfather's rheumy eyes grew moist and his lower lip trembled. "No."

"When I get my hands on them, I'm turning in the jewels. You'll have to figure out what to do with yourself."

"Andi, honey, you can't."

"Give me one good reason!" she yelled. "Tell me something that isn't a lie."

He cringed. "They're fakes."

Her jaw dropped. "Stop lying to me. I can only help you if you tell the truth."

"Look in your garbage can under the sink. I sneaked a few pieces in there while you were out today." He nodded. "That's what they are, honey. Garbage." His lips trembled in a faint smile. "If we put out a few pieces at a time for the garbage men to take away—"

Andi pushed off the trunk and raced downstairs. She snatched her garbage can from under the sink and dumped the contents on the floor. She rummaged through paper towels, chicken bones, meat wrappers and bottles and found a newspaper-wrapped bundle. She unfolded it, revealing the pearl choker, a boxy brooch and a ruby bracelet.

From the base of the stairs, her grandfather peered around the pantry shelves. "Good fakes, but fakes nonetheless. Paste and glass and gilt, nothing more. They must be destroyed."

She tried to make him look at her. His sheer misery floored her, muddled her thoughts. She should be good and furious, but how could she vent her anger on a man who looked so sad? "Fakes. Did Marilyn Hamburg-Mosse know they were fakes?"

He looked ready to weep. "You have to keep her out of this. She's innocent, I swear."

The sweet sincerity she'd always cherished appeared in his eyes. She shifted her stunned gaze to the choker; the pearls gleamed like tiny perfect moons. Fakes? She shoved the jewels in her skirt pocket and began cleaning garbage off the floor. "She did know. Now I'm really confused. Why did you go to prison for stealing fakes?"

He sank to a step, his thin shoulders slumped and his hands dangling loosely over his knees. Andi's anger crumpled, leaving her sore and empty and so very weary of it all. "When you showed up after Mom died, I needed you then. Your friendship meant so much to me. Now you've stolen that, too. How can I ever trust you again?" She threw the remaining debris in the garbage can. "You sure don't trust me."

"After your mother died, I just wanted to see you. I didn't even mean to talk to you."

She inhaled deeply and forced herself to her feet. "I can't take anymore. No more lies, no more worry. Rayne is right. Crooks never change, they never care. I'm sorry, I can't. This is too much." She turned to the sink and ran water to wash her hands.

"Andi, please."

She shook her head. "It has to end." She longed for Rayne right now. His cool head, his soothing voice, his touch, his smell. She needed him so badly she hurt. Where was he? What would he do?

She knew exactly what he would do. Call the police, tell the truth and take the consequences.

"If you call the police, you'll destroy Marilyn," Simon pleaded. "Please don't."

Her bewilderment deepened. "Then she knows they're fakes?" It took several seconds before the implication sank in. "You went to prison and she got rich on the insurance?"

His mouth dropped open and for a moment his eyes burned with a fire she'd never expected from him.

"She gave me twelve thousand dollars for you. Why?"

"Twelve thousand?" His squeaky voice held genuine confusion. His entire body shook in negative reply.

She slapped the edge of the sink. "I can't take this. I'm so sorry. I love you so much and I care so much about you, but I am not living like this the rest of my life! Stolen jewels, men in my attic. I am going out of my mind." Ignoring his protests, she picked up the phone. "I'm calling the police."

"No! You can't, honey."

She held a finger poised over the nine button. "Give me one good reason."

He looked up the stairwell with fearful eyes. "Because I think David's partner is a cop."

"Who?"

He pointed toward the attic. "Keller Poe was a snitch. He worked on and off for the police for many years. All he knew were cops and robbers."

"You don't know the other man is a policeman, though."

"Keller knew about Opal and this house. He boasted that I'd never be able to hide because his partner had police connections."

She hung up the telephone. She had to sit down. She pressed a fist to her aching chest.

Eyes downcast, he crept to the other chair and eased onto the seat.

"Why did Grandma have the jewels? Please answer me. Don't you see I want to believe you?" She waited in silence so thick she could hear their breathing.

At length he said, "I told her what happened and she agreed to help. I was supposed to come back for them, but then . . ." His voice trailed away and he shrugged. "I promised her it was the very last favor I would ever ask. I promised if she helped me, I'd never bother her or Millicent again."

"And she agreed to that?"

"I tried to be a good father to Millicent, but I was never good enough. She despised me." He lifted his head and light glinted off his thick eyeglasses.

"Did Grandma know you killed Joseph King?"

He resumed studying his hands. "I didn't kill him."

Andi chewed that one over. "Marilyn killed him."

"It was an accident! He was trying to steal the jewels. He knocked her down. He hurt her!"

Andi caressed the telephone. Rayne had to hear this. Ignoring her grandfather's woeful protests, she dialed the office again and again reached a recording. She hung up with a bang. "How was it an accident?"

He worked the pads of his fingers under his glasses. "For years he'd been helping Gretchen break out the stones and melt down the settings to pay for her travels and clothing and cars. He'd been replacing the pieces with fakes he manufactured."

He held out a beseeching hand. "Vanity. Gretchen's life had been one of endless vanity. She could not abide losing the famous Hamburg jewels, so she replaced them with glass and glitter . . . and lies."

Andi brought the pieces out of her pocket. The gems gleamed with depths of rich color. They looked and felt so real.

"He told Marilyn he would save her from financial ruin by destroying the fakes. Because they were insured for a great deal of money and she could pay her debts, he told her to say they were stolen. He would take a percentage, of course."

"He said this while you were there?"

He hunched his neck, turtlelike. "I was nobody, only the gardener. Marilyn was going to let him do it. She panicked. She was but a child and didn't know what else to do, and that greedy monster would have owned her. He would not have stopped with a mere percentage. He would have spent the rest of his life blackmailing her. Do you see what I'm saying?"

It sounded like a soap opera—crazy enough to be believable.

"We fought over the jewel case. All of a sudden, Marilyn came running out of the bedroom with a gun. She tried to shoot him, but the gun wouldn't fire. I don't think it was loaded." He finally looked at her, his eyes morose. "Marilyn pushed him down the stairs."

The last sentence emerged in a rush and Andi heard how much it cost him to say it.

"Why didn't you call the police?"

He showed her the palms of his filthy hands. "We panicked. I had beaten him severely, so no one would believe it was an accident. I couldn't subject Marilyn to the publicity—the papers had already been unkind. The things they said about Gretchen . . . the scandal. I couldn't."

"So you made it look like a robbery."

"The police came with their questions. They weren't after me, they were after Marilyn. I suppose Joseph's words planted a seed in her mind. She saw a way out."

"She blamed you?"

"No. But she did call the insurance company. Since she had done that, no one would ever believe it was an accident. So I confessed. My bruised knuckles proved I had beaten him. I told them everything they wanted to hear. I had to. They would have put her in prison. She wouldn't have survived."

"If you'd told the truth—"

"You don't understand. She was impoverished. She needed the money. If I had produced the fakes, she would have been ruined."

"This is unbelievable," she whispered. "I still can't believe you got Grandma involved! Why did she ever agree to this? She was a little nutty, but she wasn't dishonest."

"It was only supposed to be for a few days, but by the time I was arrested, it was too late." His eyes drifted guiltily. "And I didn't exactly tell her the truth. If I told what really happened and why, well . . . I couldn't."

Andi bristled. "What did you tell Grandma?"

He sighed. "I told her Marilyn's creditors were trying to take the collection and so they needed to be hidden for a few days."

Dumbfounded, Andi stared hard at him, imagining the scenario when Grandma opened the newspaper and saw she'd been duped. Grandma, a woman who'd feared scandal and impropriety and the censure of strangers more than death itself. She must have been horrified to learn she was an unwitting accomplice to murder and robbery. "Guilt drove Grandma mad."

He blinked owlishly, his eyes swimming behind the thick lenses.

"You didn't know." She raked back her hair with both hands. "Are you hungry?" If she didn't feed him, she feared she might kill him.

He gave a meek little nod.

She handed over the jewelry. "You go upstairs and put these back in the boxes and then you bring the case back down here."

"But—"

"No buts. I'm at the end of my rope! If we're going to get you out of this, you're going to cooperate."

He climbed the attic stairs.

Rayne and Mr. Hayes could figure out a way to clear up this mess. She called the office and reached the recording. "Where are you?" she said. "You won't believe it, but I have my grandfather and the jewels . . . sort of. I don't care what time it is, please come to my house. And don't call the police! I'll explain when you get here." She tried his apartment, reached another machine and left the same message. At a loss, she went to the refrigerator.

Simon inched down the stairs. He set the leather case on the table. The gold *H* gleamed. "If these are ever found, everyone will know what Marilyn did."

Andi couldn't bear to look at him. "Is that man okay?"

"His name is David. He's coming to. I don't think he's badly hurt." His forehead wrinkled in a puzzled frown. "He's healthy enough to make impressive threats."

She rolled her eyes. "We can't leave him up there. I have to call the police sooner or later." She rested her forehead against the cool metal door of the fridge and sighed. "Oh, Grandfather! Why? You could have come to me. I would have helped you."

"I am a weak man. Weak and frightened and not at all wise. I ruined my marriage to Opal. She was a good woman. She had strange ideas, but she was good. I turned Millicent against me. I broke too many promises and let her down too many times. Protecting Marilyn is the only good thing I've ever done."

His self-delusion and justification boggled her mind. What was she supposed to say? You're wrong, you're a fool? After so many wasted years in prison, didn't he know that by now? "Did you kill Keller Poe?"

"No."

"How did he know about the jewels?"

"He didn't." He sat at the table with his arms folded. Andi set a ham-and-cheese sandwich before him and he murmured a humble thank-you.

"Over the years, hundreds of men approached me with schemes and wild plans to sell the collection and make us rich. I managed to convince them I had destroyed the jewels and eventually they believed me."

She made a sandwich for herself and brought out left-over salads. "But not Keller Poe."

"He was . . . an odd young man. I could not dissuade him, I could not discourage him." He gave her a quick smile. "I could not bore him with silence. He knew fences, he knew brokers and private collectors who didn't care where their prizes came from. I wasn't to do anything until he got out. We were going to be rich." He ate a few bites in thoughtful silence.

"I began hearing rumors. Keller was looking for me, telling everyone he was going to be rich. I thought I was safe, honey. I was only an old man who washed dishes."

"But he found you."

"I feared for you, for Marilyn." He hunched his head against his shoulders. "I feared for me."

"Why didn't you come to me?"

"What was I supposed to say?"

It occurred to her that he felt unloved and worthless. No one had ever cared about him. His own wife and daughter had despised him and bargained with the devil in order to rid him from their lives. Why expect him to believe his granddaughter cared?

"I called Marilyn to warn her. If something happened to me, I'm certain the newspaper reporters would dredge up the past. I told her dangerous men were looking for me. I asked her for help."

"You scared her half to death!"

"I did?" Bewilderment swam in the age-clouded depths of his eyes. His bewilderment deepened as she told him about Marilyn's strange visit and the twelve thousand dollars. "Help me destroy the jewels," he said.

"I will not. Do you intend to hide in my attic the rest of your life?"

He wriggled on the chair and rolled his eyes as if he seriously considered it.

She ate without tasting the food. "I love you. You're my grandfather. I'll always stand by you."

His eyes grew moist.

"But you're too old to be a fugitive, and I'm no good at keeping secrets."

"This will destroy Marilyn."

"You love her? You honestly and truly love her that much?"

He hung his head.

"But she doesn't love you. She let you take the blame. She let you rot in prison. She'll let you go back to prison."

"Joseph tried to steal her inheritance. She was impoverished through no fault of her own." He clutched her hand. "I am but a weak and foolish old man. I keep trying and trying to do the right thing and everything goes wrong. I destroy all I touch."

Aching for him, she murmured soothingly.

"Give me one more chance, Andi."

"I can't."

"What's past is past. No justice is served by Marilyn's suffering." He shoved the jewel case a few inches farther away from him. "Help me destroy these . . . things. We'll bury them in the mountains, throw them off a bridge. I don't care as long as they are never found. Then take me to Pueblo. I'll get on a bus and go away. No one will ever see or hear from me again. I'll never harm anything again."

"*I* would never see you again."

"It's the only way."

She stood abruptly. "I want you to go take a shower. A nice long shower. I'll find you some clean clothes. Do what I say. We'll both feel better and it'll give me some time to think."

"Yes, dear," he said in a meek little voice.

With her hand between his shoulder blades, she walked him to the bathroom. She gave him clean towels and an old plaid robe. She pulled the door shut, then stood clutching her elbows. Eyes closed, she asked, What would Rayne do?

She saw him standing so tall and sure of himself, unafraid of hard choices. The answer was as evident as if written on a fifty-foot-tall billboard. Call the cops, turn in her grandfather and the jewels and get that awful David person out of her attic.

Her belly ached.

Back in the kitchen she eyed the jewel case. The strangest thing was, she understood. His actions were crazy and misguided and bordered on ridiculous, but he loved Marilyn and that she honestly understood. She lifted the lid. Her lips curled in a wry smile.

Water banged in the pipes. Good old grandfather.

Andi closed the lid and choked down the lump in her throat. She knew exactly what she had to do. For a moment Rayne's disapproving scowl swam before her vision. He wasn't going to like this one little bit.

RAYNE RANG Andi's doorbell. Cramming his hands in his back pockets, he rocked on his heels. He rang the bell again. At length, the door opened a crack and Andi peered out. He tugged on the screen door, but it was locked. "Let me in."

"No."

His scalp prickled.

"Not tonight," she said. "I have a terrible headache and I just want to be alone."

Apprehension slithered through him. "I know it's late, but we had to go to Denver. We got caught in traffic—"

"If you'd pick up your phone messages occasionally, we wouldn't have to have these stupid conversations."

Her words held the force of a slap. "Now hold on a—"

"Just because we did it once doesn't mean we have to do it again. Don't get any ideas about being my back-door lover."

His mouth dropped open.

"Good night." She closed the door and the dead bolt clunked.

Stunned, he gaped at the door. Did it once? Backdoor lover? What kind of crazy talk was that? Is that what she thought? That he'd come over for a quickie? What the hell was wrong with her?

He turned on his heel and stalked off the porch and down the walk. He slammed through the gate. He'd broken every rule for her and look where it had gotten him. To hell with her! He didn't need her. He jumped into the Jeep and started the engine with a roar.

He drove halfway down the block and from the corner of his eye saw a large white car he didn't recognize as belonging in the neighborhood. He drove to the end of the block before realizing it was a 1960 Cadillac. He stomped on the brakes.

Jamming the transmission into reverse, he backed up until his headlights shined on the license plate. KBA 938—Marilyn?

Hanging over the steering wheel, he stared at the license plate. How did Andi know about Marilyn?

It didn't matter. Marilyn knew about Andi. His mouth filled with the acrid taste of iron.

He drove around the block, parked and jogged down the alley to Andi's house. Rather than risk the noisy gate, he hoisted himself up and over the fence and dropped into her backyard. He waited a moment, listening, then crept to a kitchen window. He grasped the wide ledge and pulled himself up until he could peer through the gap in the curtains.

He saw two plates on the table and two water glasses. His shoulders began to burn and his fingers became numb, but he kept staring, wondering who'd been eating dinner with Andi. Marilyn? Even in the most oddball circles, blackmailees on a rampage made poor dinner guests.

Slowly it dawned on him what else sat on the table. A large, leather bound case he knew had a gold leaf *H* emblazoned on the top.

Andi entered the kitchen. She glanced over her shoulder and her lips moved, but the window was shut and he couldn't hear what she said. She picked up the case and carried it to the living room.

Rayne lost his grip and dropped to the ground.

Indecision held him frozen in a crouch under the window. Andi had the jewels. What the hell was she doing with the jewels?

The first answer knifed across his heart. She'd played him and Ford like a pair of violins, using them to test the waters, using them to...

Images of Andi cut through the black thoughts. Andi laughing, loving, warm and generous and earthy. Andi who was honest, Andi who...

Backdoor lover! Use the backdoor, idiot.

He sneaked up on the porch, wincing at each squeak and creak. Glass crunched under his boot and he froze. He carefully felt the window in the door and sliced his finger on jagged glass. He jammed his finger in his mouth and peered closely at the broken pane. The doorknob turned easily.

He envisioned Simon making a call to Marilyn, setting up a meeting, and both of them converging on Andi. So which one, Simon or Marilyn, busted in through the back door and ordered Andi to send her caller away?

He eased open the door and slipped inside. In a crouch he froze, holding his breath, his ears straining. He heard Andi, her tone pleading and reasonable and frightened. Placing his boots carefully, he crept through the kitchen. The pantry doors stood open, the shelves pulled back and the staircase revealed. What had Andi been doing in the attic?

A man stepped into Rayne's view. A red plaid robe swathed him and his bony legs were as frail as withered sticks. His hair gleamed wetly. Simon. Simon had been hiding in the attic—Simon with the jewels—Simon out for Marilyn's blood and not caring who got hurt.

The old man held out his hands. "I never meant for it to happen this way. I never wanted to hurt anyone." He slipped a hand into the robe pocket.

He's got a weapon! Rayne thought, and he lunged into the living room, aiming to catch Simon's stringy arms.

An explosion deafened him. He hit the floor.

Chapter Fourteen

Andi crouched next to Rayne and yelled at Marilyn, "Are you crazy?"

The woman moaned and her hands shook so badly it was a miracle she could hold the gun. A thin wisp of blue smoke curled from the barrel.

Rayne slowly got to his feet. Eyes wide, he brushed the hair off his forehead then stared at his palm as if fearing what he might see. He pounded on his left ear with the heel of his hand and shook his head. "You tried to shoot me." His eyes glittered dangerously.

Andi hugged him tightly and closed her eyes. Her ears still rang from the pistol's sharp report. "Oh, Rayne, why didn't you come in quietly? You charged in here like a bull!"

"I thought Simon had the gun."

"Why in the world would you think that?"

"He was going for his pocket."

She pushed far enough away to see his face. "How could you think my grandfather would have a gun?"

Marilyn screamed, "Shut up!"

Andi and Rayne started and clutched each other. "Marilyn, put away the gun before someone gets hurt,"

Andi said. "You don't want to hurt anybody. I know you don't."

"It's over, it's supposed to be over," Marilyn whispered. Tears tracked her gaunt cheeks.

Simon said, "It is over, honey. Put down the gun."

She swung her entire body and pointed the small black pistol at him. "All these years I've been waiting for you. Every time the phone rings, every time someone comes to the door, I think it's you. I have nightmares about you every single night! I gave you all the money I have. Why can't you leave me alone!"

Simon stretched out a hand, palm up, to her. "I didn't mean to frighten you."

Rayne squeezed Andi and peered questioningly into her eyes. She glanced at the wall and the sight of a bullet hole in the plaster made her shiver. Marilyn had missed Rayne's head by less than an inch.

"The lies have to stop." Andi rested her cheek against Rayne's shoulder. "Thirty years is long enough."

"What are you talking about?" Rayne asked.

"Didn't you get my message? I tried to find you and Mr. Hayes, but all I got were answering machines."

"You called me?" He ran his hands up her back.

She glared at her grandfather. "The jewel collection is phony."

Rayne looked from her to the jewel case. "Phony?"

"Marilyn's mother sold the real jewels and Joseph King replaced them with reproductions. He was going to stage a robbery so Marilyn could collect the insurance money."

"You told!" Marilyn tightened her grip on the pistol. "You were never supposed to tell!"

"I made him tell, Marilyn."

Simon's rheumy eyes misted and his lower lip sagged.

"Oh, Grandfather. Every time you had a chance to tell the truth, you told a lie instead. Now everything is all tangled up in a horrible mess. Good intentions don't count!"

Andi looked at Marilyn and her heart ached. The beautiful maiden of long ago was gone. In her place stood a thin, stringy, guilt-ravaged woman with tormented eyes and fingernails chewed below the quick.

"You lied to protect Marilyn, then you kept telling lies to protect Mom and Grandma, then more lies. Look what you've done to Marilyn." Andi patted Rayne's chest, assuring herself he was okay. His heart still thudded. "You're right, Rayne. He'll never change. Marilyn, that's why I called you. The only way this will end is for you to tell the truth, because he's not going to."

Marilyn gestured wildly with the gun. "On the couch, both of you! I'll shoot! I swear to God, I'll shoot."

Rayne and Andi looked at the bullet hole. They moved to the couch. Marilyn grabbed up the jewel case and shifted her grip on the gun. "You can't prove anything. It's your word against mine, and I'm a Hamburg and no one will believe you!"

Andi leaned past Rayne to see her grandfather. He clamped one arm tightly across his chest and covered his mouth and chin with the other hand.

"You're not getting away with your revenge, old man," Marilyn whispered.

Andi laughed. "Look in the case, Marilyn. He was trying to throw the jewels away. I found them in my garbage can. He still refuses to cooperate. Look in the case."

Marilyn dropped the case on a coffee table and fumbled open the lid. The case was full of old paperback books.

Andi rested her chin on a hand and sighed. "I'll find them. It might take months to figure out where he stashed them, but I'll find them. Don't you see, Marilyn, he'd rather have you shoot him than let you get in trouble."

Marilyn closed the lid. Her mouth hung slack and she moved as if great fatigue dragged her limbs. The gun slipped from her fingers, bounced on the rug and landed under the coffee table. Andi felt Rayne tense to grab it, but she stopped him with gentle pressure, pleading with her eyes for him to wait. She arose and reached for Marilyn.

The woman's knees wobbled and Andi caught her before she collapsed. "All those years," Andi said. "It's been horrible for you, hasn't it?"

Marilyn wept. "You don't know."

"Waiting, wondering, unable to share your guilty secrets."

"Why?" Marilyn asked Simon.

Staring at his hands, Simon said, "You were the most wonderful little girl. Do you remember the flowers we planted? You loved hollyhocks and gladiolus and bearded iris. Blue and purple were your favorites."

Marilyn's tears soaked Andi's blouse.

"Do you remember the grotto in the scrub oaks where we made feeders for the birds and squirrels?"

Marilyn snuffled against Andi's shoulder. "You carved me a squirrel caller. I still have it."

"Do you remember Brownie?" He chuckled deep in his chest and for a moment his eyes were young, his smile rich.

A wan smile tugged Marilyn's mouth. "He was the most awful old pony. He stole laundry off the lines and chewed it like a goat. The housekeeper hated him so much."

"You made him wear straw hats and put ribbons in his tail."

Marilyn closed her eyes. "You were always there for me. All the other servants went away. Mama always went away, but not you." A shudder racked her bony frame and Andi patted her back. "I have nightmares about what happened. I can't walk down those stairs without seeing Joseph. I kept waiting for you to tell."

Andi smoothed strands of gray yellow hair off Marilyn's damp face. She studied the square cut of Marilyn's brow and nearly perfect circle of her chinbone. A crazy idea began leaping and waving for attention. She helped Marilyn onto a chair and studied her grandfather. She leafed through the book about Wolfgang Hamburg and found the portrait of Marilyn at age sixteen.

"What is it?" Rayne asked.

"Just a minute." Staring at the photograph, she went to her bedroom and picked up a photograph of her mother. Millicent at age twenty-two, newly graduated from college. She looked from one to the other and couldn't help a laugh.

Back in the living room she placed the book and framed photograph on Simon's lap. He blanched. Andi folded her arms. "Boy, you really know how to keep a secret. But don't you think it's time you told her?" She looked to Rayne. "I guess parents will do anything for their children. Even if it is crazy and misguided. Right, Grandfather? Marilyn's your daughter."

Marilyn gasped. "I'm your daughter? No. My father is dead. He died before I was born."

"Tell the truth, Grandfather," Andi urged. "She's suffered enough. You've hurt her too badly with your lies."

"Gretchen was—it was wartime," Simon said. "We made a mistake. Her parents shipped her off to New York and made up the story about her marrying the oil baron or whatever he was supposed to be, and then him dying. Gretchen promised me a job for life if I never told anyone. I was married and needed the money, so it wasn't as if I could argue. Andi, honey, I'm sorry. I loved your mother and your grandmother, but I wasn't good enough, I wasn't smart enough or rich enough. Marilyn and I, we had each other. A pair of mutts nobody else wanted."

"You're my father?"

He grinned sheepishly. "I couldn't be your daddy, honey. All I could be was your friend."

Rayne stood. "You've spent thirty years trying to protect your kid? Because of a box full of junk jewelry?" Pacing, brow furrowed, he muttered to himself. He stopped and whipped about to face Marilyn. "What did you do with the insurance money?"

She cringed. "I paid debts."

"Is there any left?"

She shook her head. "I've—I've been unwell. I've never had a job."

He rolled his eyes. "Factor in interest and spite, you'll never be able to pay back the insurance company. If they find out they paid off for junk, they'll be screaming for blood. Unless . . . how much is your house worth, Marilyn? A good-faith effort might soothe tempers."

Andi parted her lips. Was he actually seeking a solution, looking for a way to get them out of this? Whatever happened to his adage, "Crooks belong in jail!" Aloud, she said, "No."

"No what?"

"Every single problem began with a lie. And it always had a really good reason. There's no such thing as a good lie."

"I'm not talking about lies. They've got to come clean." He scowled at the bullet hole in the wall.

Andi exchanged a hopeful glance with Simon. Rayne curled an arm around her shoulders and squeezed.

Marilyn sat trembling, rubbing her hand over the photograph of Millicent Blair.

Andi remembered. "Oh, Rayne, I forgot. David is in the attic."

"Who's David?"

"The fat man. He's tied up."

Rayne stepped away from her and swiped his brow. "I suppose you have a good reason."

She told him what had happened, starting with David surprising her in the house and her attempt to escape through the attic. She ended with, "And Grandfather saved me. We knocked him out."

"And you didn't call the police." He sounded more resigned than surprised.

"Grandfather says David's partner is a policeman and that they don't know the jewels are phony."

Rayne turned on Simon. "A cop? Are you sure?"

"When Keller found me he knew things he could not have known unless a source connected with law enforcement told him. He knew I once lived in this house. He knew Andi is my granddaughter. Even the newspapers back in '63 did not print anything about my marriage to Opal."

Rayne whistled low and long. "That's what I missed."

Heavy pounding sounded on the back door. All four of them jumped. A man shouted, "Open up! Police!"

Andi clutched Rayne's arm. "I didn't call the police. Did you?"

John Morris, weapon drawn, burst through the door and landed in a shooter's crouch. "Everybody freeze!"

Thick, uneasy silence filled the house. Andi darted a glance at the jewel case. Rayne stood stone-still. Simon's face turned gray. Marilyn slumped in a near swoon on the chair. Blood rushed in Andi's ears as she stared at the scowling police officer.

John slowly straightened. "What's going on here, Andi? I've got a complaint from a woman about a man with a gun. Says he's in your yard. Your back door's busted." Raising the weapon to shoulder level, he marched toward the living room. Something dark flashed above his pale head. He grunted and his eyes rolled up in their sockets.

Andi and Rayne each took a step closer toward the kitchen. Andi whispered, "John?"

A massive shape emerged from the attic doorway. David snaked out a beefy hand and caught the revolver. John hit the floor with a thud.

David stepped over the unconscious policeman and pointed the revolver at Rayne's chest.

Andi's knees wobbled and she caught the fireplace mantel for support. David's previous good humor had disappeared. His small eyes were red-rimmed. Both wrists had rope burns. Blood caked at his hairline.

Hands in the air, shielding Andi with his body, Rayne backed up.

"Like the man said, don't nobody move." He threw a disdainful glance at John. "That is one stupid cop. What are they teaching them these days at the academy?" He backed Rayne and Andi into the living room. Seeing Simon and Marilyn, he lifted his eyebrows. "Simon, I swear, you're nothing but a walking accident. First Keller, then conking me." He lifted his upper lip in a snarl.

Andi caught Rayne's furtive glances toward the coffee table. Marilyn's gun was barely visible.

"Everybody on the couch."

Simon scooted over to make room and Andi, Rayne and Marilyn squeezed together between the high, upholstered sofa arms.

David planted a massive hand atop the jewel case, covering the gold *H*. "Have to hand it to you, Coplin. For a dumb gumshoe, you done good." He picked up the phone and used his thumb to punch in a number.

He listened, then said, "Don't give me any crap about taking so long! I got a headache the size of the moon!" He trained the gun on Rayne. "But I got the goods."

Andi's belly turned to stone. If he lifted the lid on that jewel case and found the books...

"Yeah, there's witnesses!" He glared at Andi. "Don't you worry about witnesses. I'm ready to take care of them just fine. No more mister nice guy. I've breathed so much dust I'll probably get pneumonia." He shot Andi a withering look. "Crap! She's had them all along? After seeing the attic, I believe it."

Rayne gave Andi a wondering look and she sank lower on the couch.

"All right, all right. Fifteen minutes tops." He hung up, then gestured with the gun.

"Lady, find me a roll of good, strong tape. Stuff for wrapping packages. And get the cop's handcuffs off his belt. Try anything stupid and I'll give pretty boy here a third eye."

Andi forced her body to comply. "I didn't mean to hit you, but you scared me."

"Ha! I was being nice and you had to get stupid." He huffed indignantly and gingerly fingered the back of his head. "No more nice—"

A man bellowed, "Freeze, scumbag!"

David whirled. Rayne dived for the coffee table, hitting it with his shoulder and toppling it on its side. Rolling, he scooped up Marilyn's gun. Andi raced for her bedroom door. She whipped around the door frame and pressed her back against the wall. Eyes squeezed shut, she tensed for the sound of gunfire.

Rayne shouted, "Drop it!"

"Drop it or I play plastic surgeon with my twelve-gauge!"

Andi opened her eyes. *Mr. Dipwell?* She knew then what had brought John Morris to her house. Mrs. Dipwell had called the police on her own husband! She peeked through the doorway.

Holding a shotgun in a commando grip, her neighbor stalked toward David. His upper lip lifted in a snarl and he hunched his shoulders. On one knee, Rayne held the small pistol in both hands, training it on David's bullish chest. David leaned to the side and dropped the revolver.

"Kick it away from you," Rayne said. David did so and it skittered toward the front door. "Secure that, Andi."

"Talk about a good night's work. Yes, sir! Got ourselves a crook." Mr. Dipwell hooted gleefully. "Mama says I'm crazy, but when I saw that bad boy peeking in your windows and sneaking around your porch, Andi, I knew that something was going down. Yep, thought everything was okay when the cop broke in, but then I see this yahoo bust him and knew I had to do my civic duty!

We got him, didn't we, Mr. Coplin?'' He looked David up and down. "You looked smaller outside."

Andi reluctantly, gingerly picked up the revolver. Its weight astounded her and she swallowed hard against the metallic taste in her mouth. She'd never touched a gun before in her life.

"Hey, lady," David said, grinning nervously. "Mind keeping your fingers away from the trigger?" He raised his hands higher. "No offense, Coplin my man, but she's about to shoot somebody in the foot."

Afraid to take her eyes off David, Andi pressed her back against the front door. The doorbell rang. She jumped, screamed and lost her grip on the gun. It hit the floor with a thud.

With frightening speed, David lunged at Mr. Dipwell. He shot out a hand and grabbed the gun, and with his other hand straight-armed into the old man's face. Mr. Dipwell's feet flew into the air and he crashed through the dining room doorway.

David ducked behind the wall, swinging the shotgun toward Rayne. Andi tried to scream, tried to move, but all she could do was watch the rising tendons in the back of David's hand, the great knobs of his wrist, the thick finger squeezing the trigger. The thought flashed that she'd never told Rayne she loved him.

Click.

Andi wondered what happened to the boom. Didn't shotguns boom?

Face pale under his tan, Rayne raised the pistol. "Gee, no more bullets."

David threw the shotgun. Rayne ducked, but the spinning firearm clipped his shoulder and knocked him to one knee. The shotgun struck the window drapes. Glass shattered.

Scrambling for the revolver, Andi kicked it with her toe, sending it skittering across the polished hardwood floor into the bedroom.

David grabbed the jewel case. Rayne dived across the fallen coffee table. He caught a foot and David roared, hopping, making the house shake. He struck an over-laden bookcase and it toppled. Rayne dug both hands into the man's pant leg and scrabbled for footing. Swinging the jewel case at Rayne's head, missing Rayne by a whisper, David hopped backward, struck the fire-place and fell. He hit the floor flat on his belly and air rushed from his lungs in a great whoosh.

Andi snatched up the revolver.

Mr. Dipwell staggered out of the dining room. Carry-ing a large, wicker basket, he warbled a rebel yell and slammed it atop David's head. Rayne scrambled to his feet and dropped with his knees square in the middle of David's back. The fat man made choking sounds and his toes drummed the floor.

Andi rushed forward with the revolver. Rayne threw up his arms and shouted, then snatched the gun out of her hands.

Realizing she'd been pointing it at his head, she flinched. "Sorry."

Mr. Dipwell sagged against the wall and smiled weakly. "Good night's work, eh, Mr. Coplin?" He slid down the wall until he sat on the floor. His face had gone gray. Andi rushed to his side.

Rayne yanked one of David's arms so the big man's hand squeezed between his shoulder blades. David grunted inside his wicker helmet.

A man's shape appeared in the back doorway. Andi gasped. Rayne jerked up the gun.

Ford Hayes raised his hands and said, "Knock, knock."

Rayne growled an ugly word and drew a ragged breath. "See if Morris is still breathing and get his handcuffs."

Rayne handcuffed David, and Ford checked the unconscious police officer. Andi crouched next to her neighbor. His breathing was labored and his color was sallow. She suspected his old ribs had taken a good pounding.

"Caught the bad guy," he murmured.

"You are so wonderful, Mr. Dipwell. You're a hero."

"Got 'em good," he whispered.

She lifted her gaze to Rayne and reaction caught up to her, making her eyes glaze and her limbs tremble. She'd come so close to losing him and he was so brave and she loved him so much. "I'll call an ambulance," she said.

Rayne shouted, "Don't touch that phone!"

Chapter Fifteen

The next hour passed in a blur of flashing red and blue lights, squawking police radios, paramedics tending Mr. Dipwell and John and a tearful Sylvia Dipwell hovering over her husband, alternating between threatening to have him committed to a psychiatric ward and apologizing profusely for calling the police on him. He kept mumbling, "It's not like the gun was loaded or anything."

Ambulances carried the injured men away. It took three police officers to drag David out of the house. He roared his innocence and yelled at the top of his lungs that Andi and Simon were the real crooks and the cops were crazy for not arresting everyone in the house.

Andi huddled with her arms around Simon and Marilyn, dreading the inevitable moment of truth.

A police officer gathered the lead sap, shotgun and the pistol. He sniffed the pistol and said, "This has been fired."

Simon and Marilyn went rigid. Andi's throat closed. She stared at the handcuffs on the officer's belt and in her mind heard them clacking on Marilyn's frail wrists.

Rayne stepped forward, his hands on his hips. When he looked over his shoulder at Andi, his eyes were dark and unreadable. He shifted his gaze to Marilyn. *Crooks belong in jail,* Andi thought. Crooks like Marilyn who pushed men down stairs and let innocent men go to prison and kept tragic secrets that drove her to the brink of madness. Her chin quivered.

"Accidental discharge," Rayne said. He pointed at the wall where the bullet had cracked the plaster. "No harm done." Briefly his eyes met Andi's, and she read what lay in them then. Compassion. In that moment she knew, no matter what happened, she'd never stop loving him.

Finally only one police detective remained. Detective Williamson studied her notebook. "You say there's a cop involved in this?"

Rayne eyed his partner. "I think it's Paul Sevilla."

For once Ford was not smiling. "Please elaborate."

Rayne jerked a thumb at Simon. "He says Keller said a cop is involved. Plus Keller knew Andi was Simon's granddaughter and that Simon once lived here. That information wasn't in any of the newspapers, but his marriage to Opal is noted in the police files. When David made his call he acted surprised to hear the jewels had been here all along. Paul's the only person we told."

Hands behind his back, Ford faced the broken living room window. His head moved slowly from side to side. He fingered the torn drapery.

Ford turned around. "Paul has been under a lot of stress lately. His wife left him." He smiled, but his eyes were grave. "Everyone is aware of what a devil Paul is about research. A rumor about Simon and the jewels may have intrigued him in the beginning, then became more and more plausible as time went on. I fear this is conceivable."

Williamson made a hissing noise.

"One way to find out." Rayne picked up the telephone and extended it to Ford.

Ford pressed the auto-redial button and held the phone to his ear. He tugged his lapel straight and smoothed back his hair with the flat of his hand. "Hello? Ah, Paul, how are you? There is someone here who needs to speak to you..."

CASE CLOSED. Simon was no longer missing. It was over for Rayne, but with his belly aching and a cloud of foreboding hanging over his head, he followed the events of the next few days. He spoke to Andi only once. On the telephone, sounding anxious and distracted, she said, "The police want to know if I'm going to press charges against my grandfather or Marilyn. It's awful. Trespassing, burglary—kidnapping! I'm not. Are you?"

He kept envisioning Simon, shriveled and humble but his eyes glowing as he explained to Marilyn, his daughter, why he loved her and why he'd gone to hell for her. Somewhere along the line Rayne had lost his zealotry; he'd gained an understanding of why people could do the wrong things for the right reasons. He told her simply, "No."

The district attorney still had the option of pressing charges on behalf of the state, but until he made his decision, they could only wait and see.

So Rayne waited, giving her time to straighten out the problems she'd inherited with her new family. Only time would tell if there was anything between Andi and himself worth salvaging. Ford kept urging him to contact Andi. Rayne kept saying, "Her call. Her move."

He and Ford gave depositions against Paul Sevilla, but the evidence against the detective was weak and circumstantial. David talked freely. According to him, when

Keller was released from prison he'd hung out in bars, boasting about his major score, and Paul had grown interested. Research had shown him Keller's boasts weren't idle, so he'd hired David as his muscle man to keep Keller on track and find Simon. Ford doubted if the D.A. could ever accumulate enough hard evidence against Paul for an arrest and trial, but he did think the police department would force the detective to resign.

"Pity," Ford had said, "how so few of us are constitutionally equipped to withstand the stress of greed."

On a Wednesday morning, the district attorney, Garret North, summoned Rayne and Ford to appear. "Bring your complete files and case notes," he said.

Rayne and Ford waited in the hallway while the D.A. read the file on what had started as a simple missing persons case.

When the gentle slap of sandals on tile made Rayne turn and see Andi, his heart lodged in his throat. She herded Simon and Marilyn before her. Both wore the faces of prisoners riding the tumbril to the guillotine. Radiant in a cream-colored peasant blouse and a tiered-ruffle skirt, Andi smiled at him. Fear strained her eyes and mouth. Her fingers played nervously over her purse, but she smiled.

He asked, "How's it going?"

"Confusing. But you know it's not hard to confuse me." She eyed the D.A.'s office door and her throat worked. "Did you hear about the jewels?" She stepped close and lowered her voice. "It hasn't hit the papers yet, but when it does, oh, boy."

Her perfume distracted him and he shoved his hands in his pockets, fighting the urge to grab her and bury his face in her hair. "What's up?"

She whispered, "They're real. Joseph King lied. They're worth over five million dollars, maybe more."

His mouth dropped open.

She eyed the door again. "Mr. North said a representative from the insurance company will be here. Is that why you and Mr. Hayes are here?"

"Final showdown. Nervous?"

Her beautiful eyes shimmered. "Rayne, I—"

The door opened. The district attorney wanted to see them all now. Andi gave Rayne's arm a little pat, then urged her grandfather and aunt into the office.

Rayne sat stiffly on a tweed-covered chair in Garret North's office. The El Paso County district attorney barely said ten words while first Marilyn, then Simon, then Andi told their stories.

Pride welled inside Rayne. He knew full well the only thing Andi wanted to do was gather her newfound family and shield them from the world. But she'd meant it when she said that the lies would end. When Simon spoke, each time he veered from the truth, she'd murmur, "Grandfather…" and put him back on track. When it was her turn to speak, her low voice was strong and sure. No excuses, no justifying. Nothing but the truth.

Finally the D.A. leaned forward and swung his shaggy head to face the man seated closest to the desk. "Mr. Bancroft, I do believe the next move belongs to American-Southwest."

The insurance company representative cleared his throat. "I would like to call the office, please."

North pointed at a doorway. "Help yourself." He waited until Bancroft had closed the door to the anteroom, then looked from Marilyn to Simon. He opened his mouth, closed it, frowned, then chuckled. "Neither of you ever entertained the remotest possibility that Joseph King lied? You never once thought about checking his story? You never had the jewels examined by an expert?''

Marilyn shrugged. Simon hunched within himself.

North rubbed his eyes with his fingers. "Of course not."

Ford leaned close to Rayne and whispered, "It's almost a pity Andi discovered the jewels when she did. Our little town could have boasted the world's richest landfill."

Rayne crammed a fist against his mouth to stop a laugh.

Bancroft returned. He pulled a long, multipage form out of his briefcase and laid it on North's desk. "The office has decided, on the condition Miss Hamburg-Mosse signs a quit claim relinquishing all proceeds and profits from the sale of the collection, we will drop all charges."

Andi reached across Simon and patted Marilyn's hand. "Sign it, Aunt Marilyn. Then it'll be all over."

Marilyn whispered, "I'll sign."

Bancroft looked both pleased and relieved. Why not, Rayne thought. The insurance company stood to triple or even quadruple the money they had paid to Marilyn thirty years ago. Not a bad investment—especially without an accompanying court battle to eat up any profits.

Marilyn signed. Bancroft shook hands all around and left the office.

Andi asked, "Can we go now, sir?"

North opened a folder. "Not quite yet." He fixed a hard glare on Ford and Rayne. "Have you heard anything you wish to contradict, embellish or refute?"

Ford said, "Not I."

Rayne shook his head.

North nodded curtly. "Thank you, gentlemen. Now get out."

Ford rose and shook hands with the D.A. "It has been a pleasure, Garret. As always."

"Don't press your luck, Ford. I still haven't changed my mind about private eyes."

Rayne gave Andi a lingering look before he followed his partner out of the office.

In the wide hallway, he leaned a shoulder against the wall and crammed his hands in his pockets. "Think he'll press charges against Simon or Marilyn?"

"You sound worried." Ford lifted an eyebrow. "Prosecution seems pointless. I'm fairly certain the statute of limitations has expired concerning any crimes committed thirty years ago. Neither you nor Miss Blair saw fit to file a complaint. I cannot see where it benefits the state for the D.A. to file charges."

Unable to stand the suspense, Rayne said, "I'm dying." He went in search of a water fountain or a soft drink machine. Ford called to him, but Rayne waved to let him know he'd be back in a moment.

After he'd cooled his parched throat and regained his composure, he returned. The door stood open, but the office was empty. Even Ford had deserted him. He wondered if he'd ever get used to winning and losing at the same time.

THE OFFICE DOOR OPENED and Rayne looked up from the file cabinet drawer. Upon entering and seeing him, Ford looked startled.

Rayne was dying to know what had happened, but he couldn't bear to hear why Andi had left the courthouse without so much as saying goodbye.

Andi peered around the door and his heart nearly stopped. She eyed Ford strangely. "You said he had an emergency. Is everything all right?"

"My apologies," Ford said. "It seems I misunderstood."

Rayne closed the drawer. "It doesn't matter. Is everything okay?"

"It's over," she said. Her beautiful eyes misted. "Mr. North isn't going to press charges. He's not going to do anything."

Weak with relief, Rayne groped for his chair and sat.

"He did suggest Aunt Marilyn see a psychologist. I don't think he meant it as a suggestion, I think it's an order. But it'll be good for her. It'll help. And he made me promise to keep an eye on the two of them to make sure they stay out of trouble. But that's no problem at all."

"So what's next?"

"We need to sell Aunt Marilyn's house, for one thing. She's been living like a hermit and it's in terrible shape. It won't be easy. A twenty-three-room fixer-upper is kind of a white elephant." She shuddered delicately. "And Grandfather is uncomfortable in my house. I think there are too many bad memories for him." She gave Rayne a searching look. "Or maybe he feels he interferes. I'm hoping to find a nice little place for him and Aunt Marilyn."

"Sounds like you'll be busy."

Her glorious smile lost wattage. She opened her purse and dug around inside. "I need to pay my bill."

Rayne patted his desktop. "Got it ready for you."

She perched on the chair next to his desk. "Did you ever call your mother?"

"No." He pulled the itemized bill from the case folder and handed it over.

Nose wrinkling, she studied his figures. "Guess you're too busy to call."

He winced at the gentle rebuke. Had she been expecting a call from him?

While writing out the check, she said softly, for his ears only, "Or you're too chicken."

"Hold on a minute—"

"You can't sit around and wait forever. All that preaching to me about the worst scenarios being in my head and then you spend all your time worrying and thinking the worst. If you care about someone, why tiptoe around trying to figure out if it's right or wrong? Sometimes things are right for no good reason at all. Things like family and good friends and, and—" Her voice caught.

She tore out the check and slapped it in front of him. "Case closed. Thank you. Mr. Hayes, thank you. I'll never be able to repay you two for giving me back my family." In a swirl of ruffles and with her bracelets clinking, she walked out.

Dumbfounded by her outburst, Rayne sat behind his desk with his mouth hanging open. She hadn't been talking about his mother.

"Question," Ford said. "Will Rayne allow the lady to have the last word?"

Rayne sprang out of his chair and launched himself across the room. He jerked open the door. "Andi!"

Halfway down the staircase, she stopped and turned. "Yes?"

He hurried to one step below her, putting them eye to eye. "I'm sorry. I never meant to hurt you. I was trying to do the right thing, be a good guy."

Her eyelashes lowered. "You are a good guy, but why didn't you call me?"

For one of the few times in his life what he wanted—*really* wanted—sprang full-blown and crystal clear in his mind. He wanted her, forever. Those soft, sparkling eyes locked with his, her low voice always in his ears. He wanted a family. A houseful of children and a dog and even her crazy grandfather and aunt.

"You had your hands full with Marilyn and Simon. I thought you needed some time." Excuses weak as water. "I love you, Andi." Saying his thoughts aloud shocked him, but they were the right words.

Her eyelids lifted and her eyes were soft and tender, like her smile. "You have a funny way of showing it."

He slid his arms around her waist, canted his head and kissed her properly, deeply, mindlessly. Warm and passionate, it was a perfect melding of soft lips and firm, questing tongues. And when they parted for air, he didn't have the slightest urge to apologize for anything. "How's that?"

She kissed the tip of his nose. "A good start." She draped her arms around his neck. "I love you, Rayne." Her smile blossomed and she hugged him tightly. "I do love you. And do you know what? We finally agree about something."

Reluctantly, he eased her back. "We're going to do this right this time. Dinner. Seven-thirty. I'll bring flowers."

She chuckled deep in her throat. "Yes."

"Yes what?"

She lifted her shoulders in a quick shrug. "To anything else you might suggest." She kissed him again, heart, body and soul. This time when they parted, her expression was solemn. She toyed with his collar and the short hair at the nape of his neck. "I loved you even before I found my grandfather and my aunt. Even if the worst had happened, I'd still love you. You're a good man, Rayne Coplin. I knew it the first time we met.''

With some surprise but no reservations, he believed her. Yet with belief came a measure of shame. He saw himself from the outside looking in, and instead of a logical, hard thinker with a solid grasp on how the world worked, he saw a cynic. He didn't like what he saw; now was time for a change.

She loved him anyway?

"You took a big chance on me," he said.

"Love is worth it. You're worth it."

He chuckled. "I suppose you're a package deal. You, the house, your crazy relatives."

She looked away, her brow wrinkled in thought. She nodded. "Yes. But don't worry, you'll like it. I promise."

He believed that, too. So he kissed her again, reminded her about their dinner date and saw her on her way. Floating on her heady perfume, he went back to the office.

Ford asked, "Well?"

Rayne dropped onto his chair and kicked off with his heels, making the chair spin. He clamped his hands on the desk, bringing his chair to an abrupt halt, and grinned.

"All is well, I take it."

"Only to satisfy your beady little matchmaking heart . . . yes, Ford, I'm going to marry her."

"Soon?"

"Eventually. Happy?"

"Indeed. So what is next on your agenda?"

He pulled open a desk drawer and stared at the scattered letters from his cousin Jackie. What was the worst that could happen? She'd tell him to go to hell? Or maybe, just maybe Andi might be right and he had wasted years in lonely denial, because maybe his mother loved him, too?

"I have an important call to make," he said, and pulled the telephone near.

Intrigue

*It looks like a charming old building near the
Baltimore waterfront, but inside lurks
danger, mystery...and romance.*

**A brand new three-monthly
mini-series by bestselling
author Rebecca York.
Starts in September 1994 with**

Life Line

A SENSATIONAL NEW LOOK

To keep pace with this thrilling series of suspense, adventure and passion, we are introducing new covers in July.

So look out for the bright new fuschia-pink covers.

From: July 1994   Price: £1.95

A SPECIAL NEW LOOK

Silhouette are pleased to present a new look for the
Special Editions you know and love. We will continue to
bring you six realistic, emotional stories by favourite
Silhouette authors every month, and hope you'll agree
that the new design really does make the novels look
even more special!

From: July 1994   Price: £1.95

HE WHO DARES

Starting in July, every month in **Silhouette Sensation**, one fabulous, irresistible man will be featured as *He Who Dares*. When Silhouette Sensation's best writers go all-out to create exciting, extraordinary men, it's no wonder if women everywhere start falling in love. Just take a look at what—and who!—we have in store during the next few months.

In July:
MACKENZIE'S MISSION by Linda Howard

In August:
QUINN EISLEY'S WAR by Patricia Gardner Evans

In September:
BLACK TREE MOON by Kathleen Eagle

In October:
CHEROKEE THUNDER by Rachel Lee

He Who Dares. You won't want to miss a single one, but watch out—these men are dangerous!

▼ SILHOUETTE

Sensation

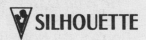

NORA ROBERTS

SWEET REVENGE

Adrianne's glittering lifestyle was the perfect foil for her extraordinary talents — no one knew her as *The Shadow*, the most notorious jewel thief of the decade. She had a secret ambition to carry out the ultimate heist — one that would even an old and bitter score. But she would need all her stealth and cunning to pull it off, with Philip Chamberlain, Interpol's toughest and smartest cop, hot on her trail. His only mistake was to fall under Adrianne's seductive spell.

AVAILABLE NOW   **PRICE £4.99**

WORLDWIDE